# The Specialist

# The Specialist



Gordon Aalborg

Five Star • Waterville, Maine

This novel is a work of fiction. Names, characters, places and incidents are either the product of the author's imagination, or, if real, used fictitiously.



First Edition
First Printing: December 2004

Published in 2004 in conjunction with Tekno Books and Ed Gorman.

Set in 11 pt. Plantin by Christina S. Huff.

Printed in the United States on permanent paper.

**Library of Congress Cataloging-in-Publication Data**

Aalborg, Gordon.
The Specialist/Gordon Aalborg.
p. cm.
ISBN 1-59414-261-0 (hc : alk. paper)
1. Women cyclists—Crimes against—Fiction. 2. Vancouver Island (B.C.)—Fiction. 3. Serial murders—Fiction. 4. Sisters—Fiction. 5. Mystery fiction. I. Title.
PR9619.2.A622S63 2004
813′.6 22 2004056366

This is entirely for Deni, who believed.

# ACKNOWLEDGEMENTS

1. Rick Coles is an active caver on Vancouver Island. He is a past president of the Vancouver Island Cave Exploration Group and the British Columbia Speleological Foundation, and South Coast coordinator for British Columbia Cave Rescue. His thirty-plus years of caving experience and the advice he provided were invaluable in setting this book.
2. Grant Vowles is a Tasmanian policeman and an old friend. He knows from experience that "country cops" are a breed apart—born, not made—and nearly on the endangered species list in our increasingly urbanized society.

My thanks to both Rick and Grant, and my assurance that any errors are mine—I had the best of advice.

# ONE

## Tasmania

## [Where there be devils]

The bicycle was the penultimate temptation. It was European, a top-of-the-line touring bike, sleek, exquisitely designed and engineered. The rich crimson of fresh blood, and not a single scratch to mar the finish. Even the saddle leather was pristine, although sensitive nostrils could, perhaps, detect a subtly blended odor of saddle leather and . . . femininity?

The specialist's fingers roamed along the lines of the bicycle with a lover's touch, caressing, flickering, almost as if such a touch could rouse a tactile response from the machine. Temptation surged with all the urgency that a new lover can create, almost explosive in its intensity at one point, before being throttled down, choked off by the coldness of logic.

"Careless," the specialist whispered. Still tempted, still rapt in the sensuality of the machine, but yielding to the power of the mind, the strength of the intellect over the ferocity of emotion.

Still, there was time. Fingers continued to caress, eyes following with a languorous gentleness overlaid with intensity. Nimble fingers plucked at a pedal, ears pricked to the whisper of perfection as the rear wheel spun in a smooth, effortless blur of crimson spokes.

"Careless," the specialist whispered again, and this time the whisper was almost a moan, vibrant with sexual tension as if the bicycle could react to such, could somehow respond, somehow ease the frustration that ebbed and flowed like a great, inner tide.

"No."

And again . . . "No!" Stronger this time as intellect began to win.

"NOOOOO!"

And the frustration took the voice up almost an octave even as one hand released the sleek bicycle frame and grabbed at the handle of the well-padded vise as if to try and crush the ultra-light tubing in a single wrenching yank.

Breath almost sobbing, now, but controlled—always controlled—the specialist forced the hands to become steady; eyes closed with mental efforts aimed at stillness. Slowly the breathing steadied, the sensitive fingers relaxed from an almost claw-like cramping.

"Careless. It would be just toooo careless," the specialist whispered, and reached out to pick up first the auto-darkening welding mask, then the thick welding gloves, and finally the slender, almost delicate handpiece of the cutting torch.

There was a pause then, because one hand had to be removed from its protective glove to wipe away a single, minute tear before the specialist could fire up the cutting torch and begin the intricate and difficult job of dismembering the bicycle.

The job didn't need to be difficult, of course. But the specialist was, after all, just that—a specialist. Sloppy work could not be tolerated. Nor was it. When the task was completed, there was a carefully-arranged pile of blood-crimson pieces of space-age tubing on the workshop floor. Even the wheels had been first denuded of their spokes, then sectioned into precisely-measured small arcs.

The specialist gave the pile a few final adjustments, then devoted some time to carefully sweeping up the workshop floor until it was as pristine as it had been before the bicycle had arrived. As pristine as it had to be, because a sloppy workplace leads to sloppy work.

No great haste to dispose of the crimson heap, the specialist decided. The hard part of that job was over with, now. A glance at the wrist revealed it to be nearly dinner time anyway, and it was . . . appropriate . . . to have dinner before the fun job, the delightful job of disassembling the bicycle's rider.

A slow smile was followed by a tongue licking delicately at perfect white teeth. Anticipation, the specialist thought—certainly not for the first time—was often the best part. The very best part.

Dinner was simple; a small, hopping-off-the-plate-rare wallaby loin steak, an equally small baked Kennebec potato, and a fresh garden salad with just a tinge of olive oil. Tree-huggers and passionate, ill-educated greenies might scream blue murder about eating the country's national symbol, but wallaby—and kangaroo meat generally—was essentially cholesterol free and wondrous tasty in the bargain. Especially if personally harvested and properly dismembered into choice segments specific to their purpose. Whole saddles of young wallaby for roasting, loin and haunch steaks for the grill. Too many Tasmanians, thought the specialist, made far, far too much of the ubiquitous wallaby pattie. Vastly over-rated, but then, just about right for most Tasmanians and their decidedly pedestrian palates.

And with the simple meal, of course, the requisite, celebratory glass of Piper's Brook wine, the finest produced in

Tasmania and shockingly expensive at least by conservative local standards, but worth it. True quality could never be appropriately priced, the specialist mused, savoring each sip and making the glass last right through the meal.

Dessert was a small salad of hand-picked fruit, which the specialist savored while deciding where to start with the remaining, satisfying but also necessary, task of the evening. First, of course, knives to be honed. Nothing so crude as a meat-saw or cleaver; the specialist was a self-confessed neatness freak, a purist, and where possible always preferred hand-tools for any task they could deal with.

A final, delicious sip of the wine, just to cleanse the palate of the fruit syrup, and the time had come. First there was the vaguely undignified business of climbing into the disposable paper coveralls, but getting the knives perfect took enough time to forget that small issue. Then, out to the other workshop, where the already-occupied stainless steel table and its pleasures awaited.

The specialist stood outside for just a few moments, savoring the pleasures ahead while using every possible sense to scout the surroundings, ears cocked for unexpected sounds, eyes scanning what there was of the horizon for any hint of vehicle lights or some poacher or wallaby-hunter's spotlight. Almost wasted gestures, really; the risk of anyone wandering to this isolated spot even in daylight was remote enough. At night it was almost laughable. Still, the specialist took the time, expended the small, necessary effort. Carelessness has many faces, and succumbing to the lure of the bicycle would merely have been one of the obvious ones.

Field-dressing the body had also contained a modicum of risk, but once done, on an isolated bush track far from usual human travels, the elements of risk disappeared virtually overnight. This part of the country teemed with Tasmanian

Devils, truly world-class scavengers. By dawn, the specialist knew, there would be no sign of the gutting but a thrashed-up area where the devils had fought over the spoils.

Once eviscerated, the human carcass does not significantly differ from that of any other large quadruped. Broken down in meatworks terms, there are forequarters, hind quarters, loins, shanks, and all the other cuts. But the specialist deviated from meatworks procedure in that only surgically-sharp knives were used to dismember the young woman's body that graced the stainless steel table. And it was done, logically enough, with very deliberate precision.

First the head, tidily separated at the base of the neck, then placed on a convenient shelf to oversee the rest of the operation with sightless, ice-green eyes that were partly shrouded by still-splendid, tumbling masses of wavy blonde hair framing a face of once-exceptional beauty. Then . . .

Wrist and ankle joints first, then those of the knees and elbows, then the slightly more difficult shoulders. Each succumbed in its turn to the precision, and each was then placed, almost reverently, to one side as the butchery continued.

When only the torso and thighs were left, the specialist paused to run sensitive fingers down the nubbled spine to the still-remaining soft hollows above the buttocks, admiring the sleek, soft texture of the pale skin there. No nude bather; this specimen's tan paused where bike shorts had snugged the muscular buttocks.

The muscle tone was splendid, clearly the result of years spent cycling. The woman's passport, identifying her as one Hanne Larsen of Esbjerg, Denmark, revealed travels throughout Europe, North America, and northern Asia, and it was not difficult to believe she had done most of her traveling by bicycle.

A great deal of travel for someone only twenty-two, and

the specialist's mind went walkabout to speculate about how many men had shared this muscular body in how many countries. Certainly more than a few; the Larsen girl's bush had been pruned to a crisp shortness, edges carefully shaped to accentuate the labial lips.

She had probably enjoyed all the sex, too. At the peak of physical fitness, far from home in what, to her, must have appeared exotic, romantic places. Yes, there would have been men. The speculation shifted up a gear to march into the dozens, then back to precision as a latex-clad finger slipped into the short-cropped fur for a final, suddenly exciting check.

A virgin! Logic denied it; the firm pressure of an intact hymen against the finger shouted, "Yes . . . yes!"

Both disappointed and exultant now, the specialist looked over the dismembered sections of Hanne Larsen with new interest, this time surveying the various joints with the calculating vision of a proper butcher. And a thought.

What might they taste like . . . small medallions of tenderloin from close inside that spine? And could the rounded globes of that rump be properly slabbed into thick, succulent rump steaks with a crisping edge of fat to give just the right flavor? And how difficult might the skinning be? One thing to dismember a carcass, but skinning became an individual issue between species. A sheep, for instance, especially a youngish one, would yield its entire skin to a single knife-cut and a few well-place thumps of a fist on the inside, but a deer did not give up its hide so easily, and a 'roo or wallaby was more difficult yet to separate from its soft pelt.

But a human was more like a pig, the specialist mused, lips curving at a half-remembered written description of human flesh being termed, "long pig" by some totally forgotten cannibal tribe or another. That accepted, skinning became more a matter, then, of removing the rind just before cooking, or of slashing its edges and rubbing in salt and spices to make it crisp into crackling.

The specialist's eyes opened, fingers of one hand already reaching for the sharpest, most slender of the knives even as the other hand drew into focus one hip and thigh joint with the rounded knob of bone shining in the clean lamp-light.

The deed was harder than the thought, but . . . do-able. It took a few tries, but the final one produced a perfectly acceptable butterfly chop, if one slightly different in shape to what would be produced from a real pig in a real butcher shop. The rump proved more difficult, and both buttocks were in one- and two-inch slabs before a suitable, really acceptable, rump steak could be displayed.

The tenderloin was easy, once neatly removed from the surprisingly small lower ribs and the vertebrae. And with no skin to worry about, it sliced as neatly and easily as that of a deer, although the color was subtly different. More like pork tenderloin, which the specialist thought was somehow appropriate.

And the speculation about the skinning proved correct, too, although more difficult to judge now that the carcass had already been dismembered. It might have been considerably easier with it all in one piece and hanging by its heels. That might be the way to go next time—a quick kill, swift evisceration, then immediate hanging to cool and stretch the muscles and sinews. The specialist thought there would be insufficient useful cuts of meat in the forequarters; like those of a wallaby or kangaroo they were relatively minor by comparison to the rest. But . . . perhaps a small shoulder roast?

Not, it quickly became obvious, without a more traditional dismemberment, and probably the use of a meat saw, which offended the specialist's sense of routine. It could be done, but . . .

And the mind switched to the other problem, that of timing. Relatively exact temperature control was required for proper cooling and stabilization of such a large carcass, especially if the skin was to be left intact for later. And that might mean waiting until midwinter, which was far, far too long to wait.

Besides, while the theoretical season for this sort of game was open and year-round, the easiest and best times were certainly the Australian summer months between November and April. These were the months when potential was enhanced by the burgeoning flocks of backpacker and bicycle tourists, who fled the snows and cold of North America and Northern Europe for the warmth and sun of Australia.

The specialist's mind had already begun speculating about the design and specifics of a mobile cool-room as the first trip began to dispose of bicycle and rider into the unknown depths of the abandoned mine-shaft not far from the shack and sheds that had, themselves, only just survived the abandonment.

Essentially, it was a silent if prolonged operation, requiring surprisingly many trips from the dissection room and workshop. A few of the metal parts pinged once or twice off the sides of the shaft, but the meat and bones slid away to oblivion with a satisfactory silence. In no case could the sound of any actual landing be heard; the bottom was far, far below, where the shaft had encountered a natural fissure that extended God only knew how far below the plateau. And of course there were earlier disposals to cushion the landings. Last to be dropped were the woman's personal effects: the purse, the traveling gear, the jewelry.

The final cleanup, with brushes and brooms and lashings

of pure rainwater from the tanks, took substantially longer. It was rising dawn when the specialist—not in the slightest bit sleepy—headed back down off the escarpment. The powerful four-wheel-drive slithered and scrambled and bounced, often leaning precipitously as it descended along the virtually trackless route down a usually dry creek bed, then eventually moved cautiously across an overgrown paddock to where junction with a minor bush track could be accomplished with hardly a trace of its passage.

Once safely home in the large, federation-style house, resplendent with twelve-foot ceilings and far too large for one person living alone, the specialist plopped the tenderloin—the only cut to escape the mine shaft—straight from cooler to proper refrigerator.

Then it was time to shower quickly and change for work. It was while the even white teeth were being flossed and brushed that the mind made the transition to Monday morning . . . with faint overlays of that evening's anticipated filet mignon for tea—dinner, in North American terms. That thought provoked a brief interlude of futuristic planning, but it was only brief. First . . . today. A quick shopping trip would be needed, of course, but the croutons and fresh bacon could be got during lunch break, and it would be unthinkable to consider ruining a good filet with some jazzed-up sauce or another. The specialist wouldn't do that to any good steak, much less this exquisite offering.

# Two

Sergeant Charlie Banes paused his police vehicle at the entrance to the grounds of the newly-renovated estate now in use as a low-level mental health facility. A private facility, one of few in Tasmania, and the only one within his responsibility.

He hated being the bearer of bad news; if there was one element he wished could be removed—cut out like a cancer—from all his years of police work, it was situations like this. This specific one, particularly. One thing to be informing parents of a child's death, or searching for parts of somebody's loved one after an horrific vehicle accident. But this, this was even worse in its way, based not on fact but innuendo; not on logic but on fear and ignorance. And—worse—political. God, he hated politics.

But it had to be done, and done now, today. Running long fingers through his close-cropped hair as he emerged from the police car, he set his cap firmly in place and marched slowly to the front door of the institution, the appropriate words forming and reforming in his mind as he approached.

"I'm sorry, but Dr. Birch is away in America." The receptionist replied to his request in a tone that suggested he ought to have known. Which of course he ought to have known, indeed had known, but forgotten. Just as he'd forgotten the name of the American—no, Canadian—head doctor that David Birch had swapped with for half the year, just as he'd done the year before. He should have remembered; Dave had told him not that long ago.

His mind toyed with the thought, then he grimaced. It had, in fact, been months—not days—ago, and worse, he'd actually met this Canadian doctor the year before, and now couldn't even put a face to the forgotten name. Fortunately, the receptionist—whose name he did know—saved him from further embarrassment.

"So you'll be wanting Dr. Stafford," she said. "Ralph Stafford. I'll just see if I can find him for you."

Easier said than done; the Sergeant stood cap in hand for nearly ten minutes while Gladys Rainbird grew increasingly agitated at her futile efforts to locate the errant psychologist. Her shrill voice grew more and more shrill as she stabbed at the switchboard keys, first asking, then demanding that the institution's new top man be found.

"I'm really sorry, Sergeant," she finally said. "He's . . . he's . . ."

"A vexation, I'm certain. Sorry, Gladys, I was outside watching the weather." The voice came from beneath the Mexican-bandit moustache of a tall, lanky man, far younger than his iron-gray hair suggested. A man who'd approached from behind both of them in an approach so silent neither had noticed.

"But hardly a vexation for the police, I wouldn't have thought," the man continued, a puzzled expression sweeping across his face with meteoric speed.

"Not you, specifically, Sir," Banes replied, reaching out to shake hands as he introduced himself before Gladys Rainbird could begin. The doctor's eyes were hidden behind photosensitive lenses darkened by the sun, but his handshake was firm and positive without being overpowering. The fact he was nearly a head taller than the policeman put Sergeant Banes at no disadvantage; he'd been a copper too long to be easily intimidated.

"We met last year, if I remember right. Come on into the office," Stafford said.

They were in the office and the coffee ordered before the doctor's glasses gradually faded to reveal the palest gray eyes Charlie Banes had ever seen, eyes so pale they seemed to glimmer like ice from the tall doctor's well-tanned features. Coupled with the bandito moustache and strong, hawklike features, those eyes produced a strangely fierce effect that miraculously changed to one of empathy and compassion when the doctor smiled or spoke in his slow, deliberate voice, one as thick and soft as chocolate topping. A professional voice, Banes decided, but one used so long it was now the good doctor's natural way of speaking.

"Are you seriously suggesting our clients could be at risk?" Stafford asked after listening to the Sergeant's explanation with an intensity that even with Banes' experience and training drew out more information than he had originally planned to provide. Another trick; one he, himself, often used, but had never before had used against him so well. Tendrils of caution slithered round the base of the Sergeant's thick neck as he realized just how very good this foreigner was at eliciting information.

"Anybody in the wrong place at the wrong time is liable to wind up at risk," the Sergeant replied. "The whole town—the whole damned district—is all on edge, and that's without us knowing anything more than the fact that three tourists might—might!—have gone missing during the past few months."

"Just 'gone missing,' you say," Dr. Stafford said after a brief silence as he seemed to analyze each word, each nuance. "No evidence of violence, no evidence of unexpected changes in plans? And nobody local apparently affected by the whole thing at all?"

"No evidence of anything. Not one skerrick of bloody evidence," Banes replied, fingers again scrubbing nervously at his scalp. "That's half the bloody problem. It's as if these three women—there is that much common ground, for what it's worth—simply vanished into thin air somewhere along this stretch of coast. No evidence, no remains of them, their camping gear, their clothing . . . nothing!"

Banes paused as their coffee arrived, and stared for a moment into the steaming brew before continuing once they were alone again.

"But of course that hasn't stopped the flow of rumors—the bloody river of rumors," he said. "Whoever is doing whatever's being done, or been done, must, of course, be mad. Which in this country usually means crazy," he added, catching Stafford's flicker of misunderstanding in his peripheral vision.

"And this being the only 'madhouse' in the area, the whole setup is automatically under suspicion of everything from devil worship to mass mayhem and serial murder." The doctor's words could have been Banes' well-rehearsed next lines. "Hardly surprising," he said then with a deceptively casual shrug. "But from that point on I must admit to being a babe in the woods. What is it going to mean to me, to my patients, to my staff? And, of course, what's to be done about it, assuming you can't resolve the disappearances pretty damned quick?"

His radiant smile belied any anxiety at all, but those damned pale eyes were like frozen spit, revealing an unexpected hardness that Banes found himself realizing he probably should have expected. The next remark confirmed it.

"You're far more anxious about this than seems logical to me," the doctor said, voice dipping and slowing just a fraction into true professional mode. "Which means there's something here that you either haven't told me or don't want to tell me or merely just suspect and maybe can't tell me. Right?"

Banes didn't try to hide his own grin. Dr. Dave Birch, a friend of long standing, if seldom seen, had often had the same effect of apparent mind-reading, but it was difficult to accept with any ease. Especially from a total stranger. Especially for a policeman.

"Three young women, all foreigners, all either hiking or cycling round Tasmania, have apparently gone missing in this region during the last four months. All have been confirmed as having been in St. Helens or the vicinity just before their disappearances. All were traveling alone, or were alone at the time of their alleged vanishing. Not one has made any contact with family, friends, or ongoing travel destinations in any way. At least the first two had travelers' cheques and/or charge cards that have not been used since the approximate dates of their disappearance."

"Right. Too many coincidences. You get paid to be suspicious and it's probably second nature by now anyway." The doctor spoke into the silence the Sergeant's own whirling mind had created. "Well if it's any consolation I expect you're right about there being something damned strange going on, but you didn't come here for that. You didn't just come to ask me to keep my patients out of the public eye as much as possible, either, so let's have it out in the open. I only hope to God you're not thinking I've got any FBI-type profiling experience, because I haven't." He smiled that slow smile before adding, "For one thing, I'm a Canadian . . . not an American, although I realize the accents sound the same, this far away."

"Don't know if you don't ask," Banes replied without apology. "To be fair, I'd have expected that if you did, Dave would have mentioned it. He did give me a fairly thorough backgrounder, although to be honest I'd even forgotten when I arrived that you two had swapped jobs again, and the rest is gone from my mind like smoke."

"I'll find you a copy of my CV if you think it will help," Stafford said with a grin of his own. "But it won't. I'm just a plain old garden-variety psychologist, North American style. Weird, I sort of understand. Sometimes. Serial killing, or abduction, no."

"And you don't read palms or tea leaves or chicken guts, either," Banes said, finding to his surprise that he was coming to quite like this tall newcomer without having the faintest idea why.

"Not even that," Stafford said. "The one thing I think I can assure you of, however, is that none of our clients would likely be a part of what's bothering you. As Dave would have told you, I'm sure, these are people with relatively minor mental problems. Depression; easily treatable schizophrenia; bipolar disorders of course, but really, Sergeant, these people are hardly even a threat to themselves, much less anyone else. And none of them are really in a position to go about abducting or murdering young tourists. They're all in fairly time-consuming programs of rehabilitation, for starters."

"You know that and I know that, but this is a small community with more than its share of what you lot call rednecks," Banes replied. "They're suspicious of anything different, anything not totally local, anything at all, I sometimes think. That's one of the problems with Tasmania—if your ancestors didn't come off a convict ship you're a newcomer, and therefore suspect. You want to try and find a property to go shooting on if you doubt me."

"Pass on that, although I've done a bit of shooting in my time," said the doctor. "And I don't doubt you in the least. I'd only been here three days last trip before I'd heard the archetypical Tasmanian joke at least six times."

"About the boy who tells his mother that his fiancé is a virgin and she says, 'If she isn't good enough for her family, she isn't good enough for ours?' That's a transplanted North American joke and well you should know it," replied Banes, trying with a laugh to cover the defensive stiffness he felt. "Straight out of their hillbilly country, I suspect, although the parallels are close enough for it to fit here, too. There are things go on in the backblocks here you wouldn't really want to know about."

"I probably would, actually, but that raises the question of just what constitutes 'backblocks' as you describe them. Inland from here, for example, where I'm told families have lived almost since the first settlement, and with sufficient inbreeding that it seems every second Tasmanian is related to every third one?"

"It isn't quite that bad. Not anymore, anyway. I doubt we're any worse than any other part of the country in that regard. But I do take your point, and you can be sure there are people not that far from here I intend looking at quite closely. The problem is that without a shred of evidence, the worst I could do is charge the buggers with poaching, which is hardly even an offence in the 'country.' Half the people who live on the outskirts here regard poaching as almost a right."

"Been there; done that. It's much the same in B.C.—British Columbia, where I grew up. But let's cut to the chase, Sergeant. What do you suggest I do about my people here?

Keeping them confined to the estate isn't really feasible, as I'm sure you appreciate. They've always gone into town, albeit in groups and usually supervised. And of course, there is not a damned thing I can do if one of them wants to summarily discharge himself or herself; their presence here is voluntary, after all."

"There isn't much you can do, I'm afraid. Except maybe stop this business of having them in closely supervised groups. That, without doubt, draws attention. This town is used to tourists, but when you get groups who go about the ways your people do, not really shopping, not really sightseeing, but just . . . wandering . . . well, the locals damn soon get to know who's who, and that's what worries me. If nothing else, for God's sake keep them away from the town at night when the pubs are closing. I fear that will be the time we'll see trouble, and we are ready for that, for sure, but it will be easier to deal with if all your people are safe here at the time."

"I doubt if it'll be as simple as that. Unfortunately we have a couple of very, very attractive young women among our clients, and they have already drawn their share of attention in the town. Usually from men who don't seem to me to keep normal working hours, if I may say so."

"You may. And I could name each and every one of them. A girl would have to be madder than I think any of your people are to get within spitting distance of any of them," Banes said. But there was no grin with this comment. He knew only too well the layabouts who plagued the town's pubs and byways, usually drunk, usually obnoxious, but seldom sufficiently so that his small force could do much about it.

Of equal concern was the fact it was this same mob of tearaways that provided his most fertile hunting ground when it came to looking into the disappearances. At least three he knew of were convicted rapists and half a dozen others had been jailed for sexual assaults on women. Worse, several had lengthy histories with the government mental institutions in Hobart and Launceston, and were unstable at best.

"I doubt you'll find your serial killer, if that's what it turns out to be, among your local bunch of bad boys," Ralph Stafford remarked as if reading Banes' mind, and the Sergeant almost jumped at the shock of it.

"I'd appreciate knowing your logic; it might help."

The doctor shrugged. "Simply *not* logical," he replied. "If it was an unexplained murder, complete with corpse and evidence, then perhaps. But what we seem to be looking at here is well-planned, skillfully executed—if you'll pardon the word—and I simply doubt if your local rednecks would be up to the task. Not three times running. I know ours at home wouldn't, not without leaving some sort of trail."

"Okay. I'll buy that line of reasoning. But what are we looking for, then? I accept you're no profiler, but still . . ."

"A man, almost certainly. Probably young to middle-aged—unless he's been at this a lot longer than you know about—probably passably well educated, probably fairly fit, probably a loner, at least by the clinical definition. Don't have to be an FBI profiler to guess that much. It's after that the difficulties start, but let's see . . .

"Maybe another tourist, but it doesn't feel quite right to me unless it's a 'local' tourist, somebody raised here in the state who knows his way around. More likely somebody who lives here, or works here. Or works *through* here . . . somebody like a realtor, or a traveling sales rep. I mean let's face it, good-looking girl tourists damn soon learn to be pretty cautious about men they might let get close enough for an abduction attempt.

"I would be almost willing to bet that when you find him—if you can—he'll turn out to be wearing a tie. But then," and Stafford shrugged again with a deprecating smile, "he might just as easily be wearing board shorts and tattoos from one end to the other."

"Well that would make things just a helluva lot easier, I reckon," the Sergeant replied. "But let's not hold our breath. They're sending out a team from Hobart to take charge of that particular investigation, and it will be their problem more than mine, I expect. My problem is that I've only got a round dozen people to maintain control in a town and district where people are starting to get decidedly spooked. I've already got parents driving their kiddies to school and picking them up, stuff like that. And it hasn't really got much of a run in the media, yet, either. Let *that* mob of bastards get the bit in their teeth, and, well . . ."

"Yes, I know," Stafford said. And there was no grin now. Both men knew what a media circus could manage in creating chaos from mere difficulty. "Well, anything I can do to help, I will, of course. But remember I'm no real expert, although I expect your people will have a profiler involved anyway, fairly soon."

"They might, but it would end up being somebody from the mainland, because I don't think anybody here has had the training. And the bloody problem is that Tasmania isn't the mainland. It's a unique little place with some very, very unique aspects."

"Yes, so I've heard. Like blithering idiots chained to trees out on the back forty, or whatever you call it here, being fed like tame bears and treated not as well."

"If only it was that simple. Here, the blithering idiots are in the parliament, like as not. Or running the media."

Banes rose and reached out to shake hands. "Not that you

heard me say that, of course. Thanks for the coffee, and the chat. I expect I'll be seeing you again before this is over."

As Banes walked to his car, he let his eyes wander round the spacious grounds, absently noting the security difficulties that would arise if some of the local yobboes did decide to start trouble. It was not a reassuring sight; the institution had never been designed for the task it now had, much less one requiring security.

And as he reached the vehicle, it was to find himself face-to-face with one of the obvious problem people the good doctor had mentioned.

"Can I grab a lift to town with you?" asked a woman that under any other circumstances and in almost any other place could only have been described as a hooker. Tight bodice, short skirt, stockinged legs that seemed to go on forever . . . and a ravaged, once-pretty face with not-quite-right eyes that suddenly widened at the realization of his uniform before shooting a frightened glance to where needle tracks walked through the inside of an elbow.

"I . . . uh . . ." The voice grew tremulous, then slid into an outright stammer before the woman turned on her three-inch heels and fled toward the safety of the main entrance.

Banes could only shrug and get into the police car. He'd seen worse before. Far worse. But whatever other problems this woman had to bring her here, there was no doubt in his mind that drugs were or had been part of it. Which brought a new concern to mind as he drove back toward town.

# THREE

# Vancouver Island: Canada

## [Where there be . . . devils?]

Kirsten closed her eyes, then opened them again quickly, not wishing to reveal the turmoil that chewed away inside her, making her nauseous, light-headed and—most annoyingly—making her talk too much, too quickly, and with too little sense. What could it possibly matter that she was a jewelry designer and goldsmith, that her sister was something of an actress? That she hadn't seen Emma in nearly two years? She was worried about Emma, yes. But as much angry as worried, and that, too, emerged in the torrent of verbal diarrhea that gushed from her mouth.

Had he noticed? When she'd closed her eyes, the policeman across the desk from her had been looking at the picture of her errant sister, but when she opened them, he was looking at her, his expression calm, but expectant. Seeing . . . what, she wondered? A mid-thirties, underweight strawberry blonde who could neither say anything important nor shut herself up? A genuine nut-case who'd left her workshop on impulse, not bothering to change from her working garb of stained, well-worn t-shirt and jeans?

He said nothing, however, and finally Kirsten spoke, carefully choosing her words, hoping to overcome the impulsiveness that had brought her here in the first place.

"She was supposed to get here early last week, on the Nanaimo ferry," she said. "That's what her email said. And . . . well . . . she didn't. And now I'm worried . . . very worried."

The policeman nodded, the expression in his eyes urging her to continue. She thought he'd ask questions, but he merely waited; calm, placid, his eyes revealing nothing. Nice eyes, actually. Warm, a pleasant green-going-on-hazel coloring, and even, perhaps, compassionate. But impossible to read. Her imagination filled in the blanks, certain she must be coming across as some kind of deranged idiot. Kirsten bowed her head, fighting for composure, willing herself not to break into sobs of frustration and recrimination.

*Damn you, Emma! If you walked in this door right now I think I'd kill you just on principle.* And then shook her head at the ridiculousness of that thought, especially here . . . in this place, under these circumstances. She had never before set foot in the offices of the Royal Canadian Mounted Police in Duncan, and now regretted the impulse which had brought her.

This time, when she looked up, the policeman took pity on her.

"Let's go back to the beginning," he said, eyes flickering from the picture to Kirsten. Comparing, she wondered, the photogenic brunette actress with the scraggly woman in his office? Emma's mane of naturally sorrel hair with her own hastily ponytailed—if longer—cascade of curls neither blonde nor any recognized shade of red? Emma's enormous sky-blue eyes with her own, which her late husband had described as "shit-brindle" in color? Not that Ed was any judge; Kirsten had very quickly come to realize that a coke-head recognized only two colors—white for the powder and green for the money to buy it with.

The officer picked up a pen, dragged over a scratch-pad, and prepared to write. "Now, your name is spelled just how, exactly? You sort of lost me when you got to the 'K' in Nelson."

She almost laughed; would have under different circumstances. And once again regretted her penchant for irreverent comment. The first time he'd asked her name—clearly with no intention of writing it down at that point—she had flippantly given her usual reply to the question: "Nelsen . . . with a *K*." Now she was much more circumspect.

"Knelsen," she said, and went on to spell it: "K . . . N . . . E . . . L . . . S . . . E . . . N."

"First name?" He didn't even bother to look up, much less react to the spelling explanation.

"Kirsten," she said, then rushed on before her traitorous mind could add something stupid about that, too, being spelled with a *K*. "And that's my sister Emma—that picture you have. Well, her name's Emma but she goes by Emmaline, and her last name's not Knelsen, it's Zelichovsky. That's her married name, except she isn't anymore. Married, that is. She's . . . divorced. In fact, she might even have gone back to her maiden name, like I . . . did." And having faltered on that thread to a time better forgotten if only she *could* forget, she clamped her mouth shut, clenched her teeth, closed her eyes against the sudden shaft of bitterness that soured her throat.

If the policeman noticed her rapid-fire, breathless delivery, he gave no sign of it. Kirsten blinked again, and opened her eyes to see him still with the pen poised over the paper.

"Spelling?" he asked, not bothering to look up. Kirsten dutifully complied, then fell silent, not really trusting herself to speak without being prompted. The silence between them

land, Kirsten told the policeman, taking the Horseshoe Bay/Nanaimo Ferry with her touring bike, then making her way south to Duncan.

"She should have got here early last week," Kirsten said, realizing as she did so that she had already told him that, and that the very vagueness of the proposed arrival date gave little credence to her concerns. It wasn't until he followed up by asking if her sister mightn't have simply changed her mind that Kirsten's treacherous tongue once more took control, blathering out a litany of complaints about Emma's blatant disregard for anyone and everyone, her self-centeredness, rebelliousness, and total lack of reliability. The words just poured out, tumbling over one another in an uncontrollable torrent that hardly made sense even to her. And she couldn't stop!

She was half-certain his eyes actually did glaze over, at one point, but it didn't stop her diatribe. Neither did the fact he'd stopped writing, and merely sat there, apparently mesmerized by her outpourings. Finally she just clapped a hand over her mouth, forcing the tide of words to back up into her throat.

"Are you all right?" he said, then. And raised an eyebrow when she—still hand-over-mouth—nodded weakly. He waited patiently, then let a smile flicker across his mouth.

"I've a got a sister something like that; I sort of know how you feel," he said, and Kirsten could have whooped with relief had she dared move her hand. Then he continued, and the relief turned sour on her tongue.

"Now . . . this isn't going to make you happy, and I'm genuinely sorry about that. But I don't think at this stage I can help you at all," he said.

"But . . . but . . . she's missing!"

He sort of shrugged . . . not an actual movement, but an attitudinal one that was equally clear. "Missing, perhaps, but there's no law against that. Look, Ms . . . Knelsen, you must understand the constrictions we're up against here. OK, your sister is overdue, perhaps missing, but she's an adult, she's free to come and go as she pleases, and frankly, all I can be sure of here is that she is, as you've said, somewhat . . . inconsiderate."

"Damned inconsiderate!"

Again, that impression of a shrug. "Point is, failure to make contact with your relatives isn't a crime, and really, you haven't been able to give me any evidence there's been a crime of any sort. I understand your feelings, and I sympathize with your feelings . . . I really do. But . . ." He genuinely smiled, then, but it was a sad sort of smile, not encouraging at all. ". . . your sister has every right to go missing if that's her choice, and I have no right at all to go looking for her just because she has been . . . inconsiderate."

Kirsten heard the words, but couldn't . . . didn't want to . . . let herself believe what he was saying. She could feel the room somehow closing in around her, a ridiculous sensation, because she wasn't claustrophobic, never had been. Yet now . . . She shivered, feeling disturbingly strange. She had been caught in rat-hole tunnels deep underground while caving and never felt this confined. She shook her head vigorously, sending her ponytail flying from side to side, and blinked to clear her vision.

"But she's missing," she said again. "How long does she have to be missing before you can do something, for goodness' sake?"

This time, the shrug was visible . . . too visible.

"She has the right to go missing forever, if that's her choice and she isn't breaking any laws in the process, and hasn't left any sort of legal mess behind that would force us to look for her. I know that sounds ridiculous, but it's the . . ."

"It's a nonsense! Something's happened to her, or she would have been in touch by now. I know my sister. She might be extremely inconsiderate, but by now . . . well . . ." Kirsten couldn't hide the evidence of her anger; didn't try. The policeman clearly saw it, too, but he didn't, or couldn't, let it faze him.

"Like I said, it might sound ridiculous, but we are forced to consider her rights in all of this, as well. For all we know, she's deliberately decided to disappear, as she has every right to do."

"But she could be in danger. She could have been kidnapped, or in some sort of accident, or . . . or . . ."

"Or just have decided to drop out of sight for awhile, for reasons that make perfectly good sense to her, and are perfectly legal. But let's be fair, here . . . discussing the philosophy of it all isn't helping anyone. Have you made any attempt to check the various hospitals along the way, in case there might have been an accident of some kind?"

"No . . . I . . ."

"How about the ferry people, although I realize she needn't have identified herself, even if she was coming across as a foot passenger?" He glanced down at Emma's picture, then added, "Still, she's . . . memorable, eh?"

Kirsten could only shake her head, now beginning to feel increasingly foolish at having even started this with a visit to the police. Of course she should have checked such things, although . . .

"Surely you could check to see if there've been any accidents involving a bicycle," Kirsten said, forcing insistence into her voice, fighting the defeated feeling she could feel growing like a bad weed in her tummy.

"Yes. That I can do," he replied, rising to his feet. "If

you'll just wait a moment, I'll do that very thing." He was out the door before she could even thank him.

She bowed her head, eyes closed, and fought for better emotional control. A losing battle. Around her, the stark, institutional, impersonal flavor of the room did nothing to instill confidence. She wasn't at all surprised when he returned after a few minutes, shaking his head.

"Nothing at all," he said.

Kirsten sighed, seeing defeat but unwilling to recognize it, to give it substance. "So what do I do now? Go check the ferry terminal, I guess, but . . . that seems such a . . ."

"Long and difficult and frustrating approach," he concluded for her. "But no easier if we were to try and do it, and at least you can start now, while memories might be fresher. Otherwise, let's see . . . Do you have any way to contact any of her friends in Vancouver?"

Kirsten shook her head. "And I don't have access to her apartment, either. I don't even know where it is, except of course I have an address. But I don't know Vancouver at all. She's often talked about sending me over a set of keys, too, but . . . well . . ."

"The first thing you ought to do is stop beating yourself up over this," the policeman said. "Whatever's going on, you won't accomplish much by blaming yourself."

He handed back Emma's photograph as he rose from his chair . . . a clear signal he'd given her enough of his time, and Kirsten was out the office door almost before she knew it. She followed him through to the reception area, even remembered to shake his hand and thank him, but her mind was already out the door and headed to Nanaimo and the ferry terminal as she did so.

Fighting back tears of frustration, she pushed her way through the exit, her eyes blurred and her mind far ahead of her body as she smashed the door into a tall figure approaching the doorway from outside. The impact was a glancing blow; Kirsten recoiled to one side with a cry of surprise while the man she'd run into was sent almost to his knees, one hand still on the door handle.

"Sorry," she cried. And the word echoed as she repeated it, stumbling past and continuing her flight without even meeting the stranger's eyes. Out into the street, turning left to where her car was parked, she reeled like a drunkard, oblivious to the people she hardly noticed with her vision misted by tears. It wasn't until she reached the car, opened it, got in, sat, that she became suddenly aware she was in no shape to drive anywhere, much less all the way to Nanaimo.

*All the way to Nanaimo*. All of an hour's drive on the worst day ever! A shorter trip than most big-city commuters faced twice every working day. The sort of trip she had faced—and thought nothing of—before she'd forsaken the prairie winters and the baggage of her own brief, disastrous, long-ago marriage in favor of the milder climate on Vancouver Island. Kirsten sat hunched over the wheel of her disreputable old Honda Civic, her eyes still brimming with tears even though she felt more like laughing. Or screaming at the inanity of her thoughts.

No, she thought. Not Nanaimo. Not today. She would, instead, make the twenty-minute journey home—assuming she could manage that without incident—and tomorrow . . . well . . . tomorrow would be soon enough. Maybe she'd get home to find some message from Emma on her machine, or even Emma herself, lolling on the front stoop and building herself up for a theatrical arrival scene. Kirsten looked down at her scarred and faded jeans, gave herself a mental shake for having given in to impulse, for having rushed into this without dressing for the occasion.

Mom would turn over in her grave, she thought, and rightly so, too. Certainly Emma would have something to say about it, assuming she was home when Kirsten arrived. Emma—who could spend a week on the road cycle-touring and turn up looking like she'd just stepped out of a fashion advertisement.

*Damn Emma!*

# Four

Teague Kendall was merely trying to be polite when the door smashed open in his face. He clung to the police station door handle with one hand, the other flailing as he used brute strength to try and keep from falling. As he yanked himself upright, he felt the muscles pop in the small of his back. This bit of courtesy had come with a price tag.

"You're welcome," he muttered at the departing figure of the slim, reddish-haired woman who had flung herself blindly through the doorway just as he'd been preparing to open and hold it for a person approaching behind him. As he watched, she stumbled out onto the sidewalk, clearly distressed, her ponytail flying as she looked in all directions and none before turning abruptly left and lurching off down the street. Like an animal in pain, he thought.

His mind held a fleeting impression of enormous brown eyes—unusual for a redhead—and a distinct, if understated, attractiveness. Even with the strain of trying to keep from falling, he'd noticed how well she filled the worn and faded jeans she was wearing.

Teague cursed under his breath, then straightened and stretched, both hands going to the small of his back, where pain was spasming. He had a mental picture of his vertebrae throwing off sparks in some sort of pyrotechnic, spinal short-circuit. Then, the thought that electricity was used in some meat packing plants to relax dying muscles, make the meat more tender. A nonsense, on this evidence; his back felt like it was shrinking into a fiery core of pain, not relaxing in any way he could comprehend.

In his ears, the echo of the woman's hasty, over-the-shoulder "Sorry," which also did nothing to stop the feeling he'd just been clubbed across the kidneys with a four-by-two. No, came the unbidden mental correction—stop thinking Australian; you're back in North America . . . it's called a two-by-four, here.

He stretched again, then patted at his pockets, looked down to confirm he'd dropped nothing, and reached gingerly for the door handle, moving carefully, cautious to ensure he wasn't going to get knocked ass-over-teakettle yet again. It was unnerving, and a less-than ideal omen foreboding the success of his visit.

That thought was confirmed within minutes. All it took was two words—bicycle tourists—and *something* flickered across the green/hazel eyes of the policeman designated to deal with Teague's enquiries. Before that, the policeman had been predictably polite, even openly curious. He'd listened to Teague explain about being an author, about his wish to set his next book on Vancouver Island, now that he was living there. Mention that Teague wrote crime fiction had drawn only a slight upward flicker of one eyebrow; Teague had seen the same unconscious gesture when the policeman had scrutinized his business card, which had the cover of his latest thriller on the reverse.

They had inspected each other, Teague seeing a tallish, compactly-built, fairly typical policeman in his early thirties, with thinning, sandy hair and nothing very memorable except his eyes, which were strangely gentle. The policeman saw a man rising forty with the sort of looks often described as "black Irish"—light skin, bright blue eyes, with black-black hair and a five-o'clock shadow that no razor could conquer. Nearly six foot, compact rather than truly slender, and carrying the evidence of trying to maintain his fitness.

Then Teague said, "I had an email from a policeman friend of mine in Tasmania, mentioning they're still getting nowhere with a case from last summer . . . several cases, actually . . . involving missing tourist women. Bicycle tourists that just . . . vanished."

And saw that . . . *something* flicker in the policeman's eyes, felt the immediate sense of sudden alertness, couldn't help but think the man's ears would have perked had he been a dog, that his moustache would have quivered, his nostrils flared in search of a scent. Trying not to reveal he'd noticed—and not at all certain he succeeded—Teague continued speaking.

"Tassie and Vancouver Island are much alike, at least in some ways," he said. "Certainly both get their share of tourists on bikes, so I couldn't help thinking about it, and the more I thought, the better it sounded as a possible psycho-thriller. But I don't know enough about how things are done, here. I don't need police procedure in vast detail, but just . . . sort of generally. Like how you'd deal with an enquiry from, say, an overseas relative looking for such a person, for instance."

"Tasmania." The policeman sort of drawled it out, tasting the word like some foreign flavor. Or playing for time. Thinking . . .

"That little island off the bottom end of Australia," Teague said after it became clear the single word was perhaps a question. "It's where I've been living these last few years; I only moved back here permanently about nine months ago."

Which forced a nod, but didn't reduce that subtle odor of awareness.

"You're originally from here, then?"

"Victoria, but . . . yeah, sort of here, too. My grandparents were old-timers in this area, and I spent most of my summers up this way. It's Gran's house where I'm living now. That . . . well, I guess you'd call it a mansion, up north by the Somenos turnoff."

"Ah . . ." Finally a semblance of . . . comprehension? "You're the guy who's trying to promote the place as . . . what is it . . . some sort of exclusive restaurant?"

"Hardly that. I just invite what I hope will be an interesting mix of people for a simple, fixed-price, fixed-menu dinner party, occasionally. Lets me keep up my cooking skills and gives me at least a semblance of a social life. Being a novelist is a damned solitary existence, really. Not like being a journalist, where you're out dealing with real people most of the time."

The policeman's eyebrow flickered distinctly, then, and Teague knew it had been caused solely by mention of the word "journalist." He'd worked the police beat long enough—both in Canada and Australia—to know the delicate relationship that existed between police and the press.

"Anyway," he continued, rushing his words a tad in hopes of diverting the policeman from going down that slippery slope of thought, "I was just curious as to how such an enquiry might be handled here. In Tasmania, where the vast majority of tourists arrive either by air or on a ferry system that involves bookings and registration, it's fairly easy for police to follow up on such an enquiry, at least insofar as finding out if the person involved is actually there on the island. But here . . ."

"People come across with bicycles on the ferries all the time," said the policeman. "Especially in summer. Except for those who come via the ferries from The States, there are no records kept that I know of. Numbers, maybe, but that's of no use for what you're talking about."

"So if some mother in, say, Amsterdam, phones up and reports her touring daughter hasn't checked in for a week, what would you do about it? What could you do?"

The policeman thought for a moment, but his eyes continued to register wariness. "If it was an emergency situation—like, say, a death in the family or something—courtesy usually dictates that some effort be made to find the person. You'd know the drill, I expect . . . radio announcements asking them to make contact with the nearest police office. But apart from that, well . . . we have to have some reason to go looking for them. Some suspicion of a crime being committed, or actual danger, or something. I mean, I don't know what it's like in Australia, but here in Canada there's no law against a person failing to keep contact. People go missing all the time—more of them do it deliberately than you'd guess—and unless it's a kid or somebody mentally deficient or really old or something, there are . . . difficulties. If there is a reason—a legitimate one—we do the best we can, as you'd expect."

He paused a moment, chewing reflectively on a pencil stub and staring at Teague's business card. "Tasmania, eh? You have a lot of . . . friends in the police down there?"

"A few. I was a journalist. Covered police, courts, that sort of thing before my novels finally started to take off. But yeah . . . there are one or two I keep in occasional email contact with. Why?"

More chewing on the pencil. "Just curious. Coincidences do that to me." The policeman stared at Teague in silence for a moment, then seemed, somehow, to have made a sort of mental shrug, a silent decision of some kind. Then . . . "Your books are fiction, I assume. How do you like coincidences?"

An easy one to answer. "I don't, but I'd have to admit there've been plenty of times I've put something into a book without knowing, really, why, and then found out two hundred pages later that it . . . fit. Which isn't what you're getting at, I think?"

An infinitesimal shake of the head, again that . . . *something* in the eyes. And, again, that implied mental shrug. "That woman who nearly crowned you with the door? She was in here asking much the same questions you're asking . . . because she has a sister gone missing—a bicycle tourist."

Teague could feel the probing; the policeman made no attempt to disguise it. Interesting . . . the man had obviously seen the incident in the doorway, but Teague didn't recall noticing him. Must have returned to his office in the brief moment before Teague had actually entered the building. Even more interesting was the sudden surge of excitement the man's revelation produced in his own mind. Not the coincidence factor, exactly, but a familiar little *ping* that announced his arrival on the edge of something important. A mental wake-up call; he'd felt it before, learned it was worth trusting, even though it could turn on him like a vengeful woman.

Now he understood the unusual reactions he'd been conscious of with this policeman, who was clearly more intuitive than he looked.

"Oh," said Teague. Then fell silent. The two men stared at each other for a long moment, and Teague wondered if this nondescript policeman, too, felt the same *ping* he, himself, had just encountered. And why.

There was no reading the professional face. The man's eyes remained gentle, but Teague fancied he could perceive an edge to the expression, now; again there was that hint of wariness. The next remark, he was certain, would end this discussion, and he wanted more.

"I write fiction," he said, making it a statement stronger than just those three words. "Only fiction. So I hope there's nothing more to this than just some weird coincidence; I truly do."

"Amen to that," was the reply, but Teague emerged from the police station with the eerie feeling neither of them believed that. Which was a worry.

# FIVE

By the next morning, the whole thing seemed faintly ludicrous, and Kirsten was uncomfortable in the thought she'd accomplished nothing but to make a fool of herself.

As for driving to Nanaimo to try and glean information from ferry personnel . . . well . . . it was a daunting concept. Logic, she thought. Surely, if she just approached the whole thing logically, she could force it into something that might make some sense. So . . .

First, one final attempt to reach Emma by telephone. Which brought her to the ubiquitous answering machine.

Then she wracked her brain trying to remember the name of Emma's agent, fought her way through the directory assistance process to get a telephone number without having any more specific address than "Hollywood" with which to begin, and got—another answering machine.

"God, but I hate talking to machines," began a stammered, less-than-coherent message for the agent, followed by a second call because in the first, she had forgotten to leave her own telephone number.

Then she sorted her way through every possible written document she possessed in hopes of finding some way to contact the management of Emma's Vancouver apartment, only to find out she didn't even have the address! She was sure Emma must have written to her since moving there, but somehow she'd forgotten or neglected to make any note of her sister's address. She had nothing to work with but a telephone number and an email address.

Back to directory assistance, where she found that her sister's number was unlisted and no, sorry, she could not be provided with an address because that was, after all, one reason people paid extra for unlisted phone numbers. Kirsten's response to this was to remain polite, then—after hanging up—throw her telephone book across the room and stomp off to her workroom, where she sat and stared at her latest design project for what little remained of the morning. The design remained unchanged, her mind continued to flit about like a maniacal hummingbird, and nothing whatsoever was accomplished. Still . . .

Venting, she thought, was at least more satisfying than logic.

Come noon, hungry but not-hungry, unable to settle, she changed into clean, more-or-less tidy clothes—jeans, sweatshirt, sneakers—and nursed her geriatric automobile along the Island Highway to the Departure Bay terminus of the ferry to Horseshoe Bay. Assuming Emma had ever even begun her trip, Kirsten thought, surely somebody would remember seeing her. Emma was, as the policeman had said, memorable.

Memorable? The noon ferry was arriving even as Kirsten parked her car, and as she walked toward the terminal she saw no less than seven young women, sleek and svelte in their lycra cycling gear, wheeling heavily-laden bicycles off the ferry. From twenty paces, at least five of them could have been Emma, who would doubtless have shrieked with horror at such comparison, Kirsten thought. But wearing bicycle helmets—as required by law—it was difficult even to tell the hair color of the women, much less their faces. What was most evident—this made even clearer by the attention of various male bystanders—were the lengths of sleek, tanned, muscular legs as the women strode, individually and in pairs, to where they could mount their mechanized steeds and depart. Kirsten, doing a quick mental assessment of leg-length, cut her possibles to three, then one, then—as the women came closer—to none.

What followed then was what quickly became an endurance contest, an exercise in total, utter, insane-inane futility. Kirsten roamed the terminal area, showing Emma's photo to anyone who would look, asking her questions and occasionally inwardly cursing the result. Several male ferry and terminal employees took their own sweet time—deliberately, she was certain—looking at Emma's publicity photo, only to say they didn't/couldn't remember her and to make much of the fact that if they'd seen her, they certainly *would* remember. One or two devoted equal amounts of time trying to hustle Kirsten herself, an indignity she was forced to endure in hopes of gaining any relevant information.

She was the last one onto the departing ferry, having determined she might as well invest twenty dollars to travel to Horseshoe Bay and return as a walk-on passenger, hoping she could poll a substantial number of ferry staff during the voyages. Which she did, thrusting from her mind in the process that she was playing the proverbial needle-in-a-haystack game. A minimum eight sailings daily in each direction, with a potential fifteen hundred passengers and crew on each, she was told by one crew member. Nearly four hours later, Kirsten returned to her car, unsure if she had accomplished anything but the waste of an afternoon.

Several crew members on each run said they thought they

recognized Emma; one was morally certain, although he couldn't remember what day he'd seen her, or which sailing, or even which direction the ship was going at the time. Everyone was patient, polite, trying—many of them too hard—to be helpful, but Kirsten had written the trip off as a bad job even before it ended. Especially when several more female cycle tourists disembarked, and she realized she hadn't even seen them during the voyage, lycra or no.

The real highlight of the trip, she decided during the drive home, was the new ring design that had been coalescing in her head amongst all that futility. With a fleeting spurt of hindsight, she wished she'd taken the time to just relax and enjoy the scenery; she hadn't been on a ferry since moving to the island.

# SIX

Kirsten's answering machine and Emma's agent's voice mail flirted for over a week, playing strange, often hypnotic word games that might have been amusing, were the issue not so serious. But it was an ill-fated romance that died like a bad blind date when it suddenly became clear the agent hadn't heard from Emma and didn't especially care.

And since nothing else she tried got her much further toward finding Emma, Kirsten was pleased almost beyond belief to be invited on a serious caving expedition during the coming weekend. If nothing else, she thought, it would take her mind off worrying about Emma—at least for a little while—and besides, this expedition had the potential to be even more exciting than usual. A member of her caving club had been told of a possible "new" cave, so this would be an opportunity to be among the discovery team, to help with the initial survey. It was her first such opportunity, and she was surprised at just how much excitement she felt. Kirsten had become involved in the sport almost two years earlier after impulse led her to join a guided cave tour, and although she still couldn't adequately put into words the attraction it held for her, she did know it was fascinating beyond all logic.

There was something elemental, almost magical, in being

deep beneath the surface, totally dependent upon artificial light, seeing, touching, feeling, what she sometimes thought of as the soul of the world. She had never been totally alone at sea, or in outer space, but Kirsten imagined similarities, illogical as it might seem.

Phil Whitfield, a veteran British Columbia caver, was quoted as describing it as, "like mountain climbing, only inside-out and backward, and in the dark." Kirsten thought that rather poetic; certainly more so than her own words when she'd once been silly enough to try and explain caving's fascination to a non-caver acquaintance.

She had been relating her weekend's adventures—at length—when she found herself fascinated by the transformation in her listener's face, which went like a speeded-up movie through mild disinterest, sort-of-interested, really interested, then mild disbelief, total disbelief, and finally repugnance as Kirsten described crawling around in pitch darkness through claustrophobic tunnels paved with mud and water and sometimes—if rarely—even bat guano, while ignoring giant crickets, spiders, and various other insects and crustaceans. Mention of the fabulous calcite formations—stalactites and stalagmites, moon milk, and flowstone—were wasted, she realized, the instant she mentioned the bat shit.

"How . . . interesting," was the final response, and the woman left Kirsten's studio patting at her hair and clothing as if she could somehow have become contaminated. She might have been leaving a leper colony.

More than a year later, Kirsten could still get a chuckle out of recalling that incident, and she did exactly that while gathering her gear in preparation for Saturday's departure. She was ready when the distinctive sound of Jimmy Norris' battered four-wheel-drive announced the arrival of her fellow caving enthusiasts.

They rumbled off, westward and ever upward, banging and clattering their way along a labyrinth of logging roads, forestry tracks, and abandoned access tracks, often having to backtrack, always thankful for the four-wheel-drive as they negotiated washouts and steep inclines. Navigation was partly by topographical map, partly by odometer, and when they finally reached what they assumed to be the point to move in on foot, it was a gully that looked no different than a hundred others they'd already passed, just one more watermark through a series of limestone ridges that loomed more than a thousand meters above them.

Several hours later, they were stumbling single file along a dry—at least for now—creek bed, surrounded by old-growth forest, way back in the hills behind Lake Cowichan, and Kirsten was half-seriously wondering why anyone would endure such things in the name of sport. The terrain was shockingly rough: no trail at all and every step was risky on the unstable footing. Devil's club, with its fierce thorns that seemed to leap out and grab for the unwary, had to be gingerly avoided, and anything that might have been easy going was littered with blown-down timber and forest litter and innocent-looking rocks that turned treacherous as soon as a human foot touched them.

Kirsten was third in the line of four led by the tall, lanky figure of Sid Drew, a tiling contractor in real life and possessed of the largest hands Kirsten had ever seen on a man. Her other two companions, Les Green and Jimmy Norris, were co-workers and twins in temperament; they operated heavy equipment in the forest industry to finance their obsession for underground exploration. All were loaded down with the gear they hoped would be required this day—heavy coveralls, safety helmets, sturdy waterproofed boots, ropes, battery-operated lights of varying types, camping gear in the optimistic assumption they'd find something worth staying the weekend to explore, food, water, and the tools they expected to use in exposing this potential new cave.

All—or none—of which might be needed. Vancouver Island might have the largest concentration of caves in all of Canada, but only a quarter of the thousand-or-so known caves have ever been mapped, and the odds of finding a completely new system that would allow significant human access were . . . odds. Still, Sid had told them his information about this possibility had come from a friend in the wildlife service, who'd negotiated this very gully while tracking an elk wounded by poachers.

"He said he could feel the earth breathing, so there's some damned thing there," Sid said. "Only one way to find out, so we might as well give it a shot; better than spending the weekend staring at the boob tube."

Kirsten occasionally wondered at such poetic comments from Sid, who was the epitome of the rugged, outdoors type and generally taciturn with it. But when he eventually called a halt to their safari and waved one huge hand at the sidehill to their left, it became immediately obvious they were going to search not for a gaping hole in the ground, but for the earth's breath.

# SEVEN

## "Karst"

### [Where there be caves]

About four per cent of Vancouver Island is underlaid by soluble carbonate bedrock, usually limestone, dolomite, or marble. It is this factor, along with exceptional rainfall, the right sort of forest cover, and the right geological and glacial history, which creates the phenomenon known as "karst"—which is a unique and distinctive topography. Caves are the result of rainwater moving through this bedrock, ever-so-gradually dissolving the rock itself by a simple yet complex chemical process.

Rainwater contains carbon dioxide already, and as it percolates through the soil and leaf-litter of old-growth forest, it picks up even more, eventually creating a weak solution of carbonic acid, which dissolves the carbonic bedrock.

Over thousands of years, the process results in a landscape where streams disappear into sinkholes, emerging sometimes miles away after traveling through subterranean cave systems . . . or sometimes never emerging at all. Where a dimple of the land's surface can suddenly collapse, exposing a sinkhole a foot across, or big enough to swallow a bulldozer. The cause can be an earth tremor or a sudden freshet or a discarded tree limb falling onto the fragile ground cover roofing the cave system below, a system that might stretch through miles, to depths unmeasurable. Thanksgiving Cave, on the northern part of Vancouver Island, has more than 7000 meters of surveyed passage, to depths of more than 200 meters, one of the longest and deepest in Canada. It may have that much again, or more, that no human has ever seen.

Sometimes the evidence of underground caves is obvious—at least to the trained, experienced eye—right on the surface. In places, the karst is exposed. In places, streams visibly plunge into the unknown through obvious cave openings. In places, sub-surface collapses have exposed obvious cave mouths, some huge, some small. Logging equipment has exposed some cave openings; wandering hunters, bushmen, and fishermen have stumbled upon others.

And sometimes the earth just . . . breathes.

# EIGHT

It was Kirsten who found it.

The four cavers had spread out, moving slowly across the steep hillside. They quartered the ground like hunting dogs, picking their way carefully and methodically over the treacherous terrain, pausing at every hollow beneath a gigantic hemlock or spruce, occasionally cupping their hands at the edge of some huge rock that was partially exposed from the moss-covered, leaf-littered, blackberry-plagued, rock-strewn hillside. They touched, listened, opened their senses.

Kirsten had, for whatever reason, begun moving uphill and to her left, going back along the sidehill in the direction from which they'd approached. Everyone was on the move, but in silence, all concentrating on trying to read the terrain, to understand it, to decipher whatever clues might exist to reveal the presence of a cave hidden . . . somewhere.

She paused near a visible, vertical run of exposed limestone: rough, gray, smoothed by exposure, but broken in places. She took a step forward, then another, leaned down to look more closely.

And the earth blew in her ear.

". . . and I'll follow you anywhere," she exclaimed, eyes widening with delight as she realized the significance.

The others swarmed to join her, drawn by her cries of excitement and anticipation. Each man clambered up the slope, each in turn moving precisely as she had first done, peering at the exposed limestone, stepping closer, then smiling as the hidden cave breathed upon them. Cool air—almost cold, indeed—emerged from the cracks and crevices in the limestone. Once noticed, it was something they could almost smell and taste. But move only a few feet away and it was gone.

"Well done, Kirsten," sighed Sid, his tall body bent almost in half, his ear and cheek inches from the outcropping his long fingers caressed with a lover's touch. He was the most experienced caver among them, which made his excitement all the more contagious, but Kirsten knew that she would be the one to actually start the exposure of what lay beneath, might even—if safety allowed it—be first to enter, assuming they'd found a cave system that could be explored, that was large enough to allow human entry.

They whooped their way down to where the packs were stowed, grabbed up the required tools—shovels, slings, a strong fencing crowbar—then returned to pause reflectively before the work began. For serious cavers, entering any cave requires adherence to a strict code of conduct, partly for safety reasons, but also to ensure absolute minimum disruption or damage. Fair enough to open an entrance to a hitherto-unknown cave system, but it was a task that must be done right. Here, Sid's long experience came to the fore, and he took charge with constant reminders of the care that must be taken.

Kirsten was impressed at how he seemed able to read the rock, to know that moving *this* segment would release *that* segment, that insertion of the crowbar just *here* would begin a whole sequence of events, that prying loose *that* particular rock would loosen an entire structure of collapsed limestone outcropping, until, finally, the last piece of loosed rock thudded down, and an entryway—of sorts—was revealed. It wasn't much, a narrow slot that started in almost sideways, invisible from any distance. But from it issued the earth's breathing, air that had gone into the cave system somewhere, meters or miles away, and was being exhaled here.

"Lunch," said Sid. Then relented, if only a little, and after a skeptical and probing look at the top of the cave mouth they'd created. "Okay, Kirsten, I guess you deserve a look, at least, but we are not going one step inside until after lunch."

Kirsten fairly flew down the hillside to her pack, grabbed up the most powerful of her flashlights, and raced back up to where she could shine the light through the narrow entrance gap they had created. The gap was a sort of slot in the limestone, perhaps a foot across and twice that high—the size dictated by Sid's strict adherence to minimum disruption and the possible future need to restore the site.

Kirsten wedged herself into the opening, closed her eyes for a moment to try and adjust her vision to the darkness inside, then flicked on the flashlight and opened her eyes, virtually at the same time. She also held her breath, as if to expand the surprise factor. But when she exhaled, there wasn't all that much to be seen.

Their opening-up work had created a new twilight zone, where outside light revealed evidence that this had, indeed, at some point in the dim and distant past, been a legitimate cave entrance, then been blocked by rock slippage, possibly due to earthquake. The floor of their new entryway was a mixture of rubble and sediment, proof that water had once flowed through the system, and that some of the hillside scree had tumbled back into the cave mouth when the landslip had covered it. Kirsten's light went beyond, into a transition zone that showed an expansion of the entry slot, an area which had not seen natural light in perhaps centuries. And it went on! The darkness seemed to shrink around her narrow flashlight beam, absorbing it, swallowing it whole into a narrowing blackness the light simply could not defeat.

"It goes!" she heard herself say, and was somehow surprised at the sound of her own voice, even more surprised at the echo of excitement she could both feel and hear.

"Good. You can be first to find out how far." Sid's voice sounded in her ear as he peered over her head into the infinite darkness beyond the light's beam. "But first, lunch."

He got no argument; Kirsten's ears heard him, but her mind was already far in front of them, floating like the dust particles in the narrow beam of light. It wasn't until Sid physically tugged at her sleeve, drawing her away from the entrance, that she shook herself back to the present and turned to follow him down to where the packs were stowed.

Lunch was a brief affair. Nobody wanted to take the trouble to actually cook anything, so they all dined on energy bars and still-warm coffee from their thermos flasks. Then they busied themselves preparing for an entry into what Kirsten already thought of as her own personal cave. It was much the same gear for each of them, with variations to suit personal taste—warm underwear in layers beneath sturdy nylon oversuits with Velcro-closing pockets or none at all, sturdy waterproof boots, knee and elbow pads in the almost certain likelihood they'd be crawling, stout but flexible gloves, the all-important mining-type helmets with built-in headlights. And each also carried at least two backup lights in the form of small but powerful flashlights, along with packs carrying spare batteries, snack food, first-aid gear, and basic climbing apparatus in case that be needed. Sid, ever the optimist and a believer in being prepared for anything, also carried more sophisticated climbing gear . . . just in case. He also got to bring the mapping necessities: survey tape, pencils, paper, compass, and clinometer.

Staying warm and dry were significant considerations; once they got any distance inside the cave, they'd be moving in virtually one hundred per cent humidity and a temperature constant just a few degrees above freezing. Getting properly dressed and prepared became a finicky but necessary precaution, and when all were finally ready, they clambered back uphill to the entrance and began maneuvering their way inside in the order designated by Sid. Kirsten led the way.

The going was, at first, relatively straightforward. The passage twisted and turned, narrowed and widened, forced them in places to move stooped over, and in some sections was muddy and slick underfoot, but easy going for all that. No crawling needed, for which they were suitably thankful. Then Kirsten hit an almost right-angle bend that required her to squeeze through sideways, and when she emerged, it was to see her light beam altered as it revealed a slick downslope into a low-ceilinged, generally smooth-floored chamber with walls that seemed honeycombed with holes and cracks and fissures.

Getting down into it required team effort. Any misstep on the descent held the risk of a serious fall, or—worse—a slippery slide into the broad pit that dominated the center of the otherwise smooth floor. Water seeped and trickled across the floor from several of the other openings, and even from the edge of the room it could be heard tinkling down into the abyss. The sound became more obvious as they crept their way down to the floor level and eased over to observe the well.

"Not a pleasant place for a swim," Sid remarked in typical understatement. The water level inside the pit was several feet below the rim, although the cave floor suggested it overflowed on some occasions, probably when heavy rains at the surface sent sufficient water to this point in the cave system.

They spent some time rigging a light, weighted line and testing for depth, mildly surprised to find the water was only a few feet deep. Or appeared to be; it was impossible to be certain their makeshift device had touched every part of the bottom. One thing was abundantly clear. Anyone falling into this well would have little or no chance of getting out without help from above. The walls were smooth as glass, slick, greasy with mud-like slime.

Moving carefully, the team worked their way past the pool, testing in turn each of the various openings in the wall of the room, listening for sounds, sniffing, testing for the breeze that would reveal the most likely route to continue their exploration. They also scanned the low roof for possible avens, shafts leading upward out of the room, but found nothing accessible. In the end, they settled on what appeared the most obvious exit, almost directly across from where they'd slithered down into the forty-foot-across chamber.

It was the broadest of three possible passages which air movement suggested had to go somewhere, but it became increasingly constricted as they explored, and after several twists and turns and some clearing of long-ago-fallen rock, it petered out into a tunnel that was a sort of long funnel. They could feel the breeze, but there was no way through. Backtracking, they tried the second possibility, and found that it, too, narrowed quickly into a rubble-filled, impassable opening. Here, too, the cave breathed, but they were shallow breaths.

Their final choice was the least promising. It began as a crawl, quickly narrowed to make the journey a slither. Kirsten, the smallest of the four cavers and still first in line, managed to keep moving through the claustrophobic tunnel, inching forward over the cold floor, wriggling and slithering, as she pushed her helmet and light ahead of her, her face so close to the floor she could barely find space to squint ahead. She was reaching the point where she'd begun worrying if any of the men could reach her—should she actually get stuck like a cork in a bottleneck—when the passage suddenly opened again. Then things got really tricky.

She'd struck a fault line of some sort, and found herself on hands and knees, facing a smooth-edged slash in the floor ahead of her, like a huge knife-cut, a water-filled ditch that extended out from the wall on her left and disappeared into darkness on the other side of her. It wasn't that wide; she probably could have stepped across, had there been room to stand. But in her current position, she wasn't even sure she could get turned around, and she didn't dare proceed without knowing the men would have room to get through. If they did, and could somehow cross the chasm, she could see that the passage broadened ahead, spreading quickly into what looked from her side to be pretty good going.

Somehow, contorting herself like a nylon-clad orange worm, she managed to get partly turned, and shouted back toward the crawl. "I'd better come back. There's a really tricky bit ahead of me, and I'm not sure you'll be able to get this far. It's awfully tight."

Sid's voice replied from so close it surprised her, and was followed by one huge hand clamping down on her ankle. "I *am* this far, what hasn't been scraped off in the crawl. But damned if I think I'd be able to back out of this. Squeeze over a bit and let's see if I can't look past you."

Which she did, sufficiently at least that he was able to suggest she crawl right to the edge of the chasm while he held her trailing foot to ensure against her sliding over the edge. Then she had to listen to his laughter echoing through the narrow passage as she explained that the channel was only a few inches deep, a minuscule problem magnified by her imagination and the tricky artificial lighting.

"Let's push on, then," he said. "The boys will have no trouble getting this far, and it looks to broaden out ahead. We'll see if we can't find a comfy place to take a break and let my geriatric bones settle back into place, eh?"

Kirsten moved ahead to where the passage widened, and Sid popped like a fat orange cork from the crawl she'd just exited. They moved ahead easily after crossing the shallow ditch. Kirsten—thankful nobody could see—blushed as Sid warned the two men behind him to beware "Kirsten's Chasm," a name she knew would stick to the virtually nonexistent hazard. Such naming of features inside caves provided a ready-reference for future trips or discussions of past ones, and all caves and their maps contained such names. Many were humorous, others merely descriptive, some bordering on the profane, but they were a testament to those who'd first explored these underground frontiers. Names like "the gravel grovel," "the belly-up squeeze," "nun's nightmare," "the giant's staircase," and "the dinosaur's backbone" were usually self-explanatory to those familiar with the unique caving vocabulary, incomprehensible to almost anybody else.

The further they went, the more the passage opened, until suddenly Kirsten found herself leading the men into a huge, sprawling cavern—no—a series of caverns that sprawled amoeba-like, with tentacle passages going every which-way. A honeycomb of rock formations and passages cried out for exploration wherever they looked; it was like a scene from a monster-movie set . . . only real. And they were the first to see it!

"We'll take a break, I think," said Sid. "Or at least you

guys will; I want to have a quickie scout of Kirsten's Chasm, because I think it might give us an easier way back . . . if I'm right." He turned back along their route and within moments was gone, disappearing into the blackness beyond, leaving his companions to seek places to sprawl out in relative comfort, eat and drink a little, and discuss what they'd seen. And what might be ahead, which was far more important.

"Good thing we brought camping gear. I'll bet Sid decides to stay the night," said Jimmy Norris. "It'll be nice to get warm and fed and stretched out properly, after going back through that dirty little crawl."

"Hell, that was an easy one," Les responded, and the two of them launched into a vivid discussion about earlier, different trips and the unique obstacles and hazards they'd faced. Kirsten, knowing herself the novice in this company, was content to listen, examining her surroundings as she mentally followed tales of abseils into unknown, bottomless pits, climbs up muddy, treacherous ledges beside waterfalls, under waterfalls, neck deep in subterranean rivers.

She had yet to experience a caving trip that involved serious rock climbing or—and she wasn't sure about even wanting this one—diving to follow rivers that somehow magically dipped underground, popping up with fanciful illogic where least expected. Many surveys used dyes to follow such underground rivers, and almost every such expedition wound up with unexpected, surprising results, like a stream that shot underground in one ravine only to emerge not further along, but in a totally different ravine and from what logic said must be the wrong direction.

"You're a good girl, Kirsten; we'll keep you." Sid's voice interrupted them on his return, and his explanation for the cryptic remark made all of them smile. Kirsten's Chasm, it seemed, looped back—as Sid's uncanny cave savvy had made him suspect—until it had brought him to where the removal of just a bit of rubble had given him easy access to the well chamber.

"Piece of cake, getting in and out this far now," he reported. "We'll still have to bend a little, but it's better than crawling on our bellies; I do hate that part of this business. But the other thing I hate," he said—his voice suddenly serious, ominous—"is getting caught in a cave when I don't know the weather turns, and that's what's happened, I think. You don't notice it in this chamber, but there's a helluva lot more water in those passages we just came through than there was. And with all our gear lying out there in the open, I think we'd best get ourselves out there with it, because we can't even guess what might happen in here if there's a big storm outside."

Sid's expertise and authority brooked no argument; within minutes they were moving as quickly as possible back toward the outside, all the more thankful for him having found a way to bypass the crawl on the other side of Kirsten's chasm. Even so, it took them the better part of two hours, during which it became abundantly clear that Sid's observations had been right. Portions of passage that had been bone dry were now dripping, where there had been damp sand there was sopping wet slop underfoot, and in places they had to wade through flowing, knee-deep water.

They emerged from the narrow cave mouth to find themselves facing a typical Vancouver Island deluge. Their ravine wore a cloak of dripping fog, rent by lashings of downpour. Their gear was already soaked, and so were they by the time they slipped and staggered their way out to the road, their vehicles, and the slithery drive back to town.

"We'll have another bash at it next weekend, if the weather comes good," Sid said at one point, obviously in response to a look of disappointment on Kirsten's face. How he could see any expression at all beyond her exhaustion and the smears of mud that begrimed every inch of her, she couldn't imagine, but it was . . . nice.

After all, this was *her* cave, although in the fullness of time she realized it would end up with a proper name of its own, at least the beginnings of a proper survey and examination by half the island's caving fraternity. But for now . . .

She whiled away the remainder of the homeward journey composing possible names for the cave. Whimsical ones, like "Dragon's Breath Cave" and "Lungs of the Earth" vied with more prosaic titles, but eventually she just admitted to a secret vanity. "Kirsten's Cave," she decided, would do just fine.

# NINE

The abrupt change in the weather caught the specialist by surprise, and he cursed himself for the carelessness it spawned when he almost got disabled by one of his own traps. The slippery scree slope he had to negotiate to get back to the forestry track was difficult enough in dry weather; during a heavy downpour like this, it became a nightmare. Damn Vancouver Island weather!

A rock popped out from beneath one front wheel, causing the sports utility to careen dangerously. Correction caused the other front wheel to spit out shards of rock and greasy leaf litter, and the next thing he knew, the vehicle was sliding out of control, then bouncing over an unexpected pile of rubble before drifting into yet another skid. He only just managed to avoid sliding headlong into the "tank trap" ditch he'd prepared to keep unwanted visitors from using the old track to his aerie near the top of the ridge.

Gasping from the sudden exertion of fighting the wheel, he sat for long moments after the vehicle stopped, then plunged out into the deluge to begin the laborious process of laying down home-made ramps which would allow him to cross the ditch. Not an easy job, this time; he'd skidded slightly off-track, and didn't dare try to back up and try again.

Getting the ramps secured ended up being an hour's work with pick, shovel, and crowbar instead of the few minutes it usually required. He was saturated from both the rain and the sweat inside his rain gear before it was done, and much of the pleasure he'd gained from his experience with the pudgy theatre director earlier in the day had been sluiced away.

Eventually, though, he got the vehicle across, the ramps re-stowed, and as much of his tracks as possible erased from the area behind the tank trap. He'd have to return the next day—weather permitting—and complete that job; it was vital that the trail to the old molybdenum mine on the ridge be kept as obscure as possible.

It wasn't until he'd finished stowing his tools and was about to climb back into the driver's seat that he noticed that the camp cooler, obviously jolted off the back seat during his precipitous slide, had bounced to the floor and now lay on its side with carefully-wrapped parcels of meat scattered all over the place.

"Damn it," he snarled, instinctively glancing round to ensure he was really alone on this isolated road, that nobody had seen his disastrous driving, his efforts to disguise his passage, and—most importantly—this final humiliation, all his choice cuts of meat lying helter-skelter, and—worse—not even labeled yet. He forced himself to patience, replacing them into the camp cooler in an orderly fashion. And smiled at knowing that one package, at least, didn't really need labeling. It was smaller than the rest, containing as it did only two choice wee morsels. They would have to be frozen—something he'd have preferred to avoid—until he'd somehow managed to gather a few more. He contemplated that as he drove carefully down the isolated forestry track, thoroughly enjoying the mental debate about just how many such morsels he'd need to make a suitable appetizer.

And what to call such a dish? Terms like "prairie oyster" and "mountain oyster" were common enough wherever sheep and cattle were castrated in the name of good animal husbandry. He'd heard the terms used throughout the Canadian and American west and on sheep and cattle stations in Australia, could even remember the first time he'd tasted the delicate flavor of calves' testicles quickly seared in hot oil. Absolutely no resemblance to the salty taste of oysters, of course, but . . . unique. Sort of like tiny cubes of tenderloin cooked in the hot oil of a fondue.

Of course the tiny package in his cooler was . . . subtly different. He was contemplating a variety of suitable names when he rounded a bend and saw where another vehicle had slewed from the roadside to leave obvious, fresh tracks in the deteriorating forestry road that led down to the better, more traveled roads around Lake Cowichan.

He wondered about the tracks, but only briefly. Even contemplated checking out the place where the vehicle must have been parked, but it was well behind him by then, and reversing uphill in the teeming rain held no appeal whatsoever.

# TEN

Mother Nature was kind to the cavers. Each of the next three weekends arrived with good weather that allowed them to revisit the cave and explore ever deeper into the labyrinth system, which seemed to honeycomb the underground beneath the high ridge. Passages went everywhere, some to dead-end against old fault lines, others to narrow into impassible cracks in the limestone. But some opened into vast chambers, filled with beautiful calcite formations created by the water percolating from above, dissolving and reforming the chemicals into works of natural art.

They even found a second entryway, or at least what might turn out to be one if they could ever find it from outside on the surface. From inside, it was little more than a slot between two massive rock faces; outside it seemed overgrown and almost obscured by a clump of devil's club, fiercely protected by the plant's evil thorns.

Kirsten made several attempts to toss a rock wrapped in bright surveying tape out through the thorny barrier, but eventually she and Les—her partner on that day—turned back without actually trying to force a way through.

"You might make it, stripped down to nothing and greased like a pig," Les said. "Although I hate to even think what the thorns would do to you in the process. You'd be leaving a fair few bits behind, eh? I doubt there'd be room for me without some help on the outside, like maybe from blasting, and somebody to clear away the damned devil's club. Still, worth trying to find it, if you got enough of that surveyor's tape out so we could see it. We'll send Fred out to look for it when his curiosity gets the better of him and he can't resist the temptation to come see this area for himself."

And, indeed, they were a party of five the next weekend, when Fred Hollis joined them for another exploration of Kirsten's cave. Not that he'd be going underground with them; word was that Fred didn't do that anymore. His preference these days was to stay on the surface, poking about on explorations of his own, maintaining a radio watch, acting as a safety back-up.

Kirsten wasn't at all sure how long it had been since Fred had been an active caver, except that it had apparently been years. She knew he was considered invaluable as web-master for caving groups all over Vancouver Island, knew he had some sort of connection with Tasmania and caving groups there—rumored to be an old girlfriend, but who really knew?—and made regular trips there, ostensibly to avoid the worst of Canadian winter weather. He was reputed to know as much about the sport of caving as almost anyone, except perhaps Sid, who professed himself delighted to have Fred along.

"I just wish you'd develop a computer program to make surveying a bit easier," he joked as they drove along the shore of Lake Cowichan en route to the forestry track they would take to the higher elevations. "Maybe something that would tell us whether we're going to need wetsuits or not? That would be nice."

"You're not likely to need wetsuits here unless it starts

raining again like it did last month," Fred replied. "You know that as well as I do. The caves down this way aren't nearly as wet as the ones further up-island."

"This one might surprise us," Sid replied. "Just where we had to turn back last time it was opening out nicely, and I can tell you the signs said it carries a pile of water when conditions are right. I think it draws from all over that big ridge in back of it, and there could be water sluicing through there from miles away."

"And probably sheds it just as quick, too. I'll bet you twenty bucks that well you mentioned has the same amount of water in it today as it did the first time you saw it."

"I know better than to bet with you," said Sid. Which was just as well, because when the four of them reached the well chamber, they found Fred's prediction exactly correct. In fact, their entire journey through to where they'd turned back on that first trip was boringly similar, if sufficiently tiring to necessitate a rest when they got there.

Their rest break over, it was determined that Kirsten and Les would form one exploration team, now, while Sid and Jimmy went off on their own tour. This chamber—dubbed the "coffee shop"—would be their rendezvous, and Sid gave them specific instructions as to timing for that, too. Back in three hours . . . max!

"And be damned careful," he said with a meaningful look at Les. "When a cave starts opening out like this you never know what the hell you'll find. No fancy stuff . . . no risks . . . right?"

Kirsten bowed her head to hide a grin. Les and Jimmy were notorious practical jokers, especially with each other, and she knew Sid had separated them for safety's sake as much as anything. Working as a team, the duo could achieve amazing feats, but they also got into a lot of trouble through their shenanigans and had lost more than one job in the outside world because of it.

There was room, even a necessity at times, for such rapscallion sense of humor in caving. Being stuck in a narrow crawl with one's chin in the mud and bat shit and nowhere to go but forward—somehow—demanded more than just perseverance. But the risks inherent to the sport called for niceties of control the boys seldom exhibited, and Kirsten could remember previous trips in which they'd been strongly criticized. Yet each—without the other to egg him on into dangerous behavior—was a stout and welcome companion underground.

Sid and Jimmy wandered off into the most obvious of the right-hand outlets, and Les bowed in mock gallantry to let Kirsten lead the way into the maze of passages which exited the cavern on the left. All pretext of serious surveying had been abandoned. There was simply so much to see that everyone wanted to cover as much ground as possible; they could always do a survey after the thrill of first exploration had been satisfied or they'd run out of new routes to follow. Kirsten made the mental decision to take the easiest, most obvious ones first.

This decision led them increasingly deeper within the cave system, moving sometimes slowly—sometimes quickly—by caving standards, anyway, through a system of passages that required careful negotiation but no serious climbing or crawling. They moved quietly, seldom speaking but using touch and hand signals to point out the various features of interest as they noticed them. A little natural nest filled with cave pearls drew the eye at one niche; substantial sheets and strips of speleothem decorated nooks and crannies along the way, some striped, warped into grotesque patterns, while others looked like icing on an inside-out cake.

They passed one low-ceilinged area the size of Kirsten's dining room that was so filled with straws—miniature stalactites growing down from the ceiling to meet smaller, less substantial stalagmites growing upward—that it was like peering into a heavy rainstorm in shades of bronze. Eventually, given thousands upon thousands of years and a lot of luck, too, these formations might grow sufficiently to touch each other, mating to form columns and even, perhaps, fill the small room entirely.

Everywhere they moved, there was vivid, clear evidence that the cave system was still strongly affected by percolation water, and occasional serious flooding as well. Their boots moved across smooth limestone, sand both dry and damp, and occasionally through patches of greasy mud and pools of standing water. They were nearing the limit of their time, but apparently nowhere even near the limits of potential exploration when Les tapped Kirsten on the shoulder and indicated with gestures that he needed to make a pit stop.

"I'll just go back around the last bend," he said, already reaching for the empty bottle he carried for just such a purpose. One of the foremost rules within caving etiquette . . . leave nothing at all behind, and certainly not human waste, but Kirsten found herself wishing he hadn't told her, because it caused similar thoughts she could happily have done without.

There aren't many disadvantages to being female, but having to struggle out of a heavy nylon jumpsuit and several layers of undergarments so you can try to pee in a bottle in subterranean darkness has to be high on the list, she thought. And tried to put it out of her mind. Fat chance! She moved further along the passage, convinced she could actually *hear* Les filling his waste bottle. She knew it was her imagination, but couldn't help being cranky at how damned easy such an exercise was for male cavers; hell—they could even see what they were doing, the lucky buggers. Then she had a mental image of Les huddled back in the passage, cocking his head around like some demented crow so he could see what he was doing while he piddled in a bottle, and the sudden surge of laughter almost brought her undone.

*Stop it . . . stop it . . . stop it.* She moved farther, turned to peer inside a long, narrow chamber, her eye drawn by the run of a sediment-filled trench that spewed into, but mostly across, the passage she was in. Another Kirsten's chasm, she wondered, or perhaps the beginning of the one they'd encountered further back? Certainly it looked similar, and further evidence of flooding within the cave system at some times.

This chamber, her light revealed, was different from most they'd come across. It was higher; she had to tip her head to put light toward the ceiling in several places and still couldn't be certain where it topped out. And one wall, miraculously sculpted by the vagaries of nature, looked for all the world like an antique roman wall, complete with a flowing trough that made a tiny waterfall—now dry—which would spill into a unique, cone-like formation on the floor below. Moving closer, stepping carefully to avoid marring any of the flowstone on the floor, she bent to peer into the small pool, wondering what unique formations might have been formed by the percolated water. Cave pearls, gleaming calcite formations rounded by the water passing over them, would be possible, if not always likely. Equally probable would be nothing more than sand and silt.

But what her headlamp revealed in the depths of the little pool wasn't some esoteric limestone or calcite formation—it was an impossibility! All her logic, all common sense told her she could not be seeing this. It was something that could not, should not exist in this place. But . . . it did.

Kirsten propped on her heels and stared into the bowl formation, unwilling to believe her eyes—unable not to! What she was seeing made no sense at all, yet it was there, within reach. All she had to do was reach down and . . .

She stripped off a glove, quickly reached into the water which filled the bowl, and as quickly yanked her hand away as the liquid swirled into opaqueness and the object she'd been reaching for disappeared. It happened so unexpectedly, so without warning, that it startled her, and she nearly fell.

It's all the mud dissolved in the water, she thought, and sure enough . . . as she watched, the turbidity faded and she once again found herself looking down at exactly what she'd seen the first time—the bottom portion of a gold ring sticking up from the sediment at the bottom of the formation. Still impossible, still unbelievable, but . . . it was there, she could see it, she could . . .

This time she was more careful. Moving with infinite care, she dipped two fingers into the bowl, trying in the reflected light to allow for refraction, easing her fingers downward until—swift as a heron's strike—she was able to plunge her entire hand into the icy liquid and grasp the ring even as the turbidity returned to cloud the water and hide everything again.

"Gotcha!" she cried, and lifted the ring to where it gleamed in the beam of her headlamp, to where she could turn it in cold fingers that suddenly went numb just as her brain seemed to go numb, recognition smashing like a blow to the head. This time she did fall, any semblance of balance destroyed by the impossibility her eyes revealed and her brain refused to accept. She simply sagged, collapsing on the damp, hard floor like a discarded rag doll. She slumped onto her side, lay for a moment until her equilibrium returned, then pushed herself back up to a kneeling position and held out her cold, clenched fist to the light from her headlamp.

Kirsten slowly opened her chill fingers, but first closed her eyes, half afraid her hand would be empty, even more afraid—illogically—that she would once again see this thing that could not be.

This ring. This gold ring with the unique, hand-engraved bezel around an oddly-shaped chunk of Australian boulder opal. Hand engraved by her own hand; it was the first really good ring she had ever made.

Emma's ring, the ring she had given her kid sister more than ten years ago. And which, to her almost certain knowledge, Emma had worn ever since, worn as a sort of talisman, a good luck charm, a totem.

It could not be here! Kirsten's brain seemed filled with static, the words, "It can't be" echoing in her head . . . or perhaps in the very cave itself as she spoke them over and over and over.

Then she heard her name penetrate the echoes, Les' voice asking if she was all right. She shook her head, eyes swimming as the headlamp slashed through the shadows around her, then quickly fumbled open her coveralls to reach an inner pocket and deposited the ring there, feeling the coldness next her skin. Safe, hidden!

She couldn't explain her sudden feeling of panic, of total paranoia. Didn't try. She simply secreted the ring, struggled to her feet, and was halfway out of the chamber by the time Les got to her. She even—miraculously—got her head together enough to explain away the shouts he thought he'd heard from her.

"I've never felt anything like it before," she explained, not daring to meet his eyes, thankful for not having to because of their opposing headlamps. "I just sat down for a moment to rest and I must have drifted off or something. And I had . . . well . . . a nightmare, I guess you'd call it. And because I'd turned my headlamp off to save the batteries, I woke up into darkness and I sort of . . . freaked. I don't remember shouting, though. Are you sure you really heard me?"

Les just shook his head, perhaps in disbelief, perhaps in sheer astonishment. He was—Kirsten knew full well—a world-class male chauvinist; anything strange done by a woman could never be allowed to surprise him for long. Indeed, by the time they rejoined the others, then made their exit from the cave, he seemed to have forgotten the incident. Or at least said nothing more about it.

Kirsten said nothing either. She could feel the ring, tucked hard in against her ribs in that inner pocket, but nowhere could she find words to mention her discovery, much less the paranoid air of secrecy that enveloped her like the damp darkness of a claustrophobic cavern.

She went through the motions, doing her share of work during the packing-up process, but throughout the entire journey back to town, she had the eerie sense of being outside-looking-in, of watching herself and her companions from some sort of adjacent universe. Her entire focus was on the ring in her pocket, on getting home to her workshop where she could examine it properly, and alone.

# Eleven

Three days later Kirsten was no further ahead, except for being certain beyond any question that this was, indeed, Emma's ring—the ring she herself had crafted by hand. But how in the name of anything at all rational could it have been where she had found it? Where she knew she had found it, despite the insanity of it all?

"It makes no sense at all to me." Sid Drew prowled her studio cautiously, moving as carefully as she'd seen him move through a cavern strewn with delicate, fragile calcite formations. His tall, lanky form seemed too big for the room, and he kept reaching out as if to touch the tiny jeweler's tools and delicate bits of material, only to pull back again, as if to make sure he didn't inadvertently break anything. Kirsten had finally, in sheer desperation, called upon Sid's expertise because her own mind was incapable of finding any logical explanation, but it seemed he was equally flummoxed.

All manner of unusual things are discovered in caves. Vancouver Island cavers have discovered fossils, calcified evidence of prehistoric sea life, animal bones both relatively new and incredibly old. At the bottom of one shaft—nearly a hundred and fifty feet deep—a ten-thousand-year-old bear skull was once found. The lightless world of the underground claimed a variety of visitors and victims; one cave had even captured a bulldozer that fell through the cave roof, doing extensive environmental damage in the process.

But nowhere in caving lore or legend was there mention of a find like this . . . especially not a cave newly discovered, previously unknown, unexplored, inaccessible until she, herself, had discovered the entrance.

"Well it had to get there somehow," she insisted. "I know I didn't take it in with me, and I can't imagine how you or Les or Jimmy could have anything to do with it." Then she plumped down on her stool and let herself slump forward, eyes on the floor and Sid's enormous, stocking-clad feet. She had told him it wasn't necessary to remove his boots at the entry, but he'd insisted.

"And nobody but us even knew about the cave . . . that's what makes it so . . . so weird."

"Not true. The guy who told me about it knew, although I can't imagine him having anything to do with this," Sid replied. "And Fred was there when he told me, but Fred doesn't go into caves anymore. Hasn't in years; since he . . . did his back in." The hesitation was so slight she wouldn't have even noticed had she not been concentrating so deeply, but he didn't explain and she couldn't find the words to ask. "And Fred hadn't actually been there until he went with us; I specifically remember him mentioning that," Sid concluded.

He paused, then, running huge fingers through his thick but short-cut hair. "Did I tell you, by the way, that he located that other exit you found? He must have had himself quite a little wander while we were messing around underground. And so did you; that other exit's way to hell back in a sort of little side canyon. A lot higher up than where we went in, too, and according to Fred, in a jungly little crevice that's absolutely choked with devil's club. Said he'd never have found it except a little tiny end of the survey tape you poked out was showing."

Kirsten shivered, remembering the interminable crawl that was needed to reach the narrow slot in the limestone, how she'd had to squirm on her belly through mud and bat or bird droppings to reach the opening, how even from underground she'd somehow sensed the devil's club reaching for her with those vicious, evil thorns.

"Well you can be fairly sure nobody used that entrance to get in and put this ring there," she replied, hearing bitterness in her voice. "Les and I decided I might be able to squeeze through if I starved for a week and slathered myself in grease or something . . . but not with that devil's club blocking things from outside."

She looked again at the ring she'd been fiddling with while they talked. Sid had inspected it briefly, but that served only to illustrate that it wouldn't have fit on the smallest of his fingers.

"I don't know what to make of it all," he said. "But given your sister's still not got in touch—and now this—I think your next step has to be a visit to the cops."

"Another visit," she corrected him. "And I guess you're right, although I can't imagine what good it might do. If *we* can't even come up with any sort of explanation for how the ring got into my . . . that . . . cave, then . . ." Kirsten shook her head, suddenly aware that the fingers holding her sister's ring were visibly trembling. She clenched her fist, feeling the metal bite into her flesh, but it served only to emphasize the effect.

"Last time, they said there was nothing to be done because there was no evidence Emma hadn't just changed her plans, gone off on her own without bothering to let me know. Which could have been true enough, God only knows. But if I show up with this, and the story behind it, they'll think I'm crazy, to boot! I mean really, Sid . . . I can't even explain it to myself!"

"Which doesn't mean there isn't an explanation," he replied with typical pragmatism. "Just means we don't know what it is. I think you have to at least try. Don't forget that they've got people trained to investigate things like this."

"Yeah, sure. CSI Vancouver Island," she replied, and could feel the hysteria building as she did so. "Can't you see it . . . an entire crime scene investigation unit crawling around in there with fingerprint kits and those fancy lights that show blood stains and their tweezers and flimsy little rubber gloves and . . . and . . ." Then she had a mental picture of a crime scene investigator having to piddle in his own specimen bottle while another held the light so he could see what he was doing, and she laughed. And then began to cry, the tears pushed out by a feeling of such hopelessness that it wracked her slender body.

Strong, large hands reached out to gather her in, pulling her against Sid's stomach before she could fall from her stool. He held her in silence, just . . . being there, and eventually she regained control, or at least a semblance of it. What actually stopped her reactive performance was another mental picture—one of her friend staring upward and silently praying. *Why me, Lord? Why me?*

"Okay, I'll try again," she said after wiping away tears with her sleeve. And did so—or tried to—that very afternoon, only to find that the officer she'd originally spoken to was away for several days, wouldn't be available until Monday. Unable and unwilling to face starting her explanations from scratch, Kirsten decided to wait. She was home again within the hour, seated at her workbench, staring into space and totally unable to focus on anything that even resembled work. Her thoughts were deep in the cave of her mind, and her mind was deep in the cave she had discovered, staring into a pool at a ring that couldn't, shouldn't, be there . . . but was!

# TWELVE

"This is tailor-made for you. You never get out enough and you know it, Kirsten, much less to something where you can get all dolled up like a forty-shilling pisspot and do something really different, for a change. Honestly, you've got less social life than one of your cave bats."

"Bats are extremely social animals," Kirsten retorted, and might have saved her breath.

Pauline Corrigan, Kirsten's oldest and dearest friend, was in full cry, fairly dancing with excitement as she described the dinner party she was insisting they both attend the following night. A special dinner party, invitation only and—best of all—free, since Pauline's boss, Dr. Ralph Stafford, would be picking up the tab.

"This guy who does these affairs is a writer, which makes him artistic, like you, so you'll have that much in common right from the start," her friend continued, totally unwavering in the face of Kirsten's skeptical scowl. "He's supposed to be a real gourmet, a really fantastic cook, or chef, or . . . whatever. And they say he does things up really posh—that's English for very *very* fancy—and his house is, like, to die for . . . a real, old-fashioned mansion. And you've got that absolutely fab lilac dress we got you at that really excellent sale in Victoria that time, and I've never yet seen you wear it, and . . ."

Her friend stepped back a pace and ran a jaundiced eye over Kirsten's day-to-day outfit of faded jeans, sneakers, and sweatshirt. ". . . and God knows it wouldn't hurt you to dress up for a change," Pauline continued. "It's a good thing you never have to actually sell the jewelry you design, because . . . looking like this . . . well . . . it isn't what I'd call the clothes for power-selling." Pauline paused for dramatic effect, then threw in the kicker, bringing tears to her wide gray eyes with the intensity of it all. "And besides—you promised!"

She had, and Kirsten had already admitted to herself that she would accompany her over-enthusiastic friend to the gala dinner party. Even in the relative isolation of her studio existence, she'd heard the rumors surrounding these unusual affairs, hosted by a recent arrival to the district. No, she thought, not recently arrived . . . recently returned. This . . . Teague Kendall was a native islander who'd spent many years away in Australia, or New Zealand, or some obscure tropical island somewhere, depending on which version of the story you heard. As for the fact of him being a writer giving them anything at all in common . . . well . . . she wouldn't hold her breath on that score. She'd heard his books were thrillers, rather than conventional mysteries, and very *very*—to use Pauline's phraseology—bloody and violent. Not her preferred bedtime reading.

Still, curiosity was among her most vivid character flaws, and the chance to eat anybody else's cooking oughtn't be sneered at. Besides, in the mood she was in right now, waiting impatiently for her policeman to return on Monday, anything that might take her mind off Emma's ring and its implications would be welcome. Assuming, of course, that she could get her mind off the mystery. It had consumed her ever since she'd got home, cleaned up the ring, and begun puzzling over the circumstances of having found it. After Sid had left, and her abortive visit to the police station, she'd threaded the ring onto a long, fine gold chain; it now nestled between her breasts, and she was constantly aware of its presence, could almost hear the puzzle and the mystery of it screaming out to be solved.

She also found it quietly amusing that Pauline was so intent on linking her up to their soon-to-be-host, a man neither had ever seen, but made no mention at all of her tall, handsome, bachelor boss, who had made such a success of his privately-run mental health clinic that he could put it in the hands of a colleague every winter while he traipsed off to follow the sun. Of course, Pauline had her own cap set for the good doctor, Kirsten thought, and smothered a smile at the thought of a match between her five-foot-nothing, lovable but hopelessly disorganized best friend and the extremely tall, extremely well organized man she worked for. The attraction of opposites, she wondered? Or just her friend away with the fairies, as usual? Pauline was a delightful, warm, and genuine person, but her imagination and downright flightiness was, occasionally, a worry. She was as much a flibbertigibbet as was Emma, but without Emma's lack of consideration.

"Okay, I'll go," Kirsten finally said, as much to put an end to Pauline's incessant nudging as anything else. "But you have to drive; I'm in a cranky mood and I might decide to have a drink or two. Especially if the food isn't to my taste; I've heard you don't get an awful lot of choice at these affairs."

"Only enough so you know what wine to bring," Pauline replied. "Tomorrow night is beef . . . and fowl, so it'll be red wine and white, won't it? But we don't have to worry about that, because Ralph . . . Dr. Stafford . . . is bringing enough for everybody. He brought a whole bunch back from his last visit to Tasmania, really top grade stuff, too. Apparently they have a really excellent wine industry there. I just adore red wine," she prattled on, "but it doesn't like me at all, so I won't be sorry to be the designated driver. It's better than having a screaming hangover headache the next day. Or worse," she added with a mischievous smirk.

Kirsten, whose taste in wine ran more to cold, white varieties that came in cardboard boxes, merely raised an eyebrow at the suggestiveness. She seldom drank, but had learned she simply couldn't tell the difference between cheap cask wine and the finest bottled variety. A peasant palate, Ed had called . . . *No,* she thought with a shake of her ponytail. *No. I will not go there. Not ever again. Never.*

But she would go to the dinner party. The concept intrigued her, for starters . . . this notion of somebody inviting a group of total strangers to his own house, expecting them to get all gussied up, pay for the privilege of sampling his cooking, bring their own wine, and have no choices about what they were to be served. Certainly it gave the term "pot luck" a whole new meaning, and somehow this Teague Kendall person had promoted the concept into being flavor-of-the-month, she thought, then grinned at the unintended puns.

"And I'm not going to be anybody's date, either," was her final condition. One easily fulfilled, as things turned out, since she was expected only to make up the numbers because the wife of the clinic's administrator was out of town on business. Pauline's employer, it seemed, was a stickler for protocol, and having booked for four, he would have four!

# THIRTEEN

The theater director made a splendid pot roast, the specialist decided. Even after a month in the freezer, the slight marbling of fat within the section of the man's flabby buttock responded perfectly to many hours in a crockpot, surrounded by vegetables and garnished with a myriad of spices.

Mopping up the last of the gravy with a home-baked biscuit, the specialist privately determined that this was more due to the man having spent years sitting on his rather broad-beamed ass than because of any real theatrical talent . . . if he'd been any kind of decent director he wouldn't—after all—have become a pot roast in the first place. Although . . . the steaks had been pretty good, too, if a trifle tough.

The specialist was marginally worried about the impetuousness of it all; giving way to spontaneous impulse wasn't normal for him, and therefore *should* be worrying. Then he thought of what a hash the director had made of Karshner's *The Man with the Plastic Sandwich*, and stopped worrying. The man was lucky not to have been ground up for hamburger meat. Dog food, even.

Besides, it had been remarkably easy, far easier than sitting through the ghastly performance. The specialist sipped at his second glass of Piper's Brook—almost his last bottle of that splendid vintage and no more available until winter; now *that* was worth worrying about!—and allowed himself to relive the adventure.

The director, a pudgy, prematurely-gray man in his middle years, with that sort of broad, flabby rump usually associated with trailer-trash matrons, had brought the play from somewhere else. Probably, thought the specialist, in search of a less sophisticated audience. From Saltspring Island, or Victoria . . . not important, really, except that it should have been left there. The specialist, having coffee in town one morning, had overheard some of the cast and crew decrying a decision by the director to sack one of the actors [a perfectly competent actor, by all accounts] and assume the role himself. "Megalomaniac," "control freak," and "damned fool" were among the nicer things his people were saying about the man, and their private opinions of the play and its direction were even less flattering. Enough to make most people give it a miss, but the specialist prided himself on fairness; he determined to go and see for himself. A mistake! The show was worse than he ever could have imagined.

But even mistakes can have their bright sides. Having determined by the end of Act 2 that the director should have stuck to acting—which he did with some competence and even a degree of flair—and let somebody else—*anybody else*—take on the directing, the specialist was enjoying an illicit smoke outside the theatre when the director, himself, emerged with one of the stage crew.

The man was, not surprisingly, bitching and complaining about everything except his own incompetence, and proceeded to add to his sins by cadging a smoke from the hapless stagehand, then ungraciously mentioning that he really preferred American cigarettes.

"That'd be right . . . bludge a bloody smoke and then complain because it isn't your brand of choice," the specialist muttered under his breath, slipping into Australian thinking and vernacular as he did so. "You don't half fancy yourself, do you, little mate?"

He was finishing his own cigarette [European, by preference . . . but at least he bought his own!] when he suddenly realized the stagehand had returned inside, as had those few audience members who'd taken the interval break outside. Only he and the director remained in the deserted alley beside the theatre. Just the two of them, standing within meters of the specialist's SUV, deliberately parked handy in case of rain. Convenience, he wondered, or . . . coincidence?

Impulse struck like lightning. A moment later he was giving the director outrageous compliments about the play and thinking it a measure of the man's ego that he sopped up the lies without even wondering why anyone would utter such rubbish.

The rest might have been planned, it went so smoothly. Offer a smoke. Hold the light for it a touch low to make his victim stoop and offer his neck with an almost pathetic innocence. A swift, single blow delivered with studied precision. And had anybody observed, they'd have seen one gentleman helping another, perhaps intoxicated, into a darkened vehicle. Then . . . gone. Halfway to Lake Cowichan before the final curtain. The director was being professionally field-dressed on a lonely, remote bush track before anybody even began to take his disappearance seriously.

The specialist would dearly have liked the opportunity to have spent more time in actual conversation with the pudgy incompetent, but the perfection of that single blow forestalled that pleasure. The director never awoke, could never have imagined the delights his scarce-cooled remains would provide . . . even without conversation. No great loss to the theatre, but still . . . useful.

And the specialist was himself surprised. He could never have imagined just how different a flabby, middle-aged, masculine carcass might be, compared to the svelte, trim-taut-'n'-terrific female specimens of earlier experiments. Ignoring the obvious, of course . . . things like the tender testicles now waiting in his freezer for enough companions to make at least a decent starter course. The entire musculature was subtly different, the flesh itself . . . not as firm. Noticeably more coarse, although that might be just his imagination.

By the time the weather broke on that month-ago weekend, giving the specialist such annoying problems in leaving his secretive retreat, only those few choice cuts of meat remained to stir memories like this. The director's head, bones, and accoutrements had disappeared down the shaft of the abandoned molybdenum mine, joining their female counterparts from earlier expeditions. It was an example of his feelings for the man that he discarded the director's wallet and ID without even bothering to look at it. Which even now brought a sort of smug satisfaction; surely the ultimate insult to an actor—dying at the hands of somebody who didn't even know his name and couldn't care less. Of course the man got abundant media play after his disappearance, but still . . .

"Not all that hard an act to follow," he mused now, sipping at the epitome of great Tasmanian wine and pondering his choice of desserts. There was fruit—the earliest of the local crop; but also a tub of locally-made "Death by Chocolate—The Ultimate Decadence" ice cream. *Surely appropriate, but perhaps . . . overkill?* Indecision annoyed him as much as word play delighted. Tomorrow night promised new treats for both mind and palate, so he contented himself with ten plump, fresh, green grapes.

At least he hadn't been forced to ruin a perfectly good bicycle. He always hated that part.

# FOURTEEN

"Fair warning. This first appetizer course is purely optional and I shall take no offense if anybody decides to give it a miss. I've another one coming that's . . . well . . . more conventional, let's say."

Teague Kendall tossed off the remark casually, but Kirsten couldn't miss the twinkle in his eye. She wasn't entirely surprised. The man was a bundle of contradictions, and clearly believed entertainment to be an important factor when it came to dinner parties. He was also something of an actor; he'd flitted between the roles of maitre d', ebullient "mine host," and temperamental chef ever since his guests' arrival, and did it with a smooth, natural charm that was disarming, if sometimes extravagant.

They were thirteen—a surprise in itself, that—at table, a massive oaken structure that could have seated two dozen with ease. Three separate parties, actually, but divided and rearranged by Kendall as he seated them according to some formula of his own devising. Kirsten, Pauline, Dr. Ralph Stafford, and John North, the clinic's chief administrator, had begun as one party; the others involved people whose names Kirsten had already forgotten despite being introduced and now being seated between two of them.

Kendall had no such problem, and proved it by addressing each of them as he placed a large, oil-filled fondue at each end of the table. He'd been on a first-name basis with everybody almost before they were through the front door of his aging but still-gracious mansion, and she found herself wondering if he'd been given a guest list to study. Still, it helped her now; she followed his voice around the table and tried to fix names to faces. A wasted effort, probably—Kirsten was hopeless with names and knew it—but still she couldn't help but follow his voice, which was like that of her friend's boss in having a unique, seductive quality. Dr. Ralph Stafford's voice was deep and thick, like rich, dark chocolate, but Teague Kendall's—while equally deep—held a different sort of richness, more like velvet, or the whisper of silk, like her lavender dress. She was glad to have worn it . . . no sense even trying to deny that! Teague Kendall was an unusually handsome man. Not quite as tall as the good doctor, and a bit stockier, but actually more handsome, in a rough-hewn sort of way. And his warm, open good-humored manner only enhanced that, giving him a devil-may-care, what-you-see-is-what-you-get aura . . . like that of a mischievous child.

Dinner-wear suited him, she thought. He looked comfortable, totally at ease. She remembered the author photo on the book cover she'd seen, one in which he'd been in casual, outdoor gear, and looked equally comfortable. She watched as he left the room, then returned within moments, bearing trays of what appeared to be meat diced into small chunks.

*Hardly original. Surely he isn't trying to re-invent fondues as something new and chic and modern?* Kirsten had no idea why she didn't quite believe her own thoughts, until Kendall set down the trays and explained.

"What we have here are prairie oysters. Or mountain oysters, depending on who's doing the naming and where," he said, and she saw again that hint of mischievous grin. "Certainly not to everybody's taste—if they think about it too much—given that what they really are is calves' testicles. But on cattle ranches in many countries I could name, this is the ultimate delicacy at round-up time and the basis for half a dozen traditional recipes."

Kirsten watched him scan his audience, as if trying to decide in advance who was going to try his offering, who might think it all some sort of prank, and who . . .

"And yes, I've heard all the tales about how this is purely a dish used to deflate the egos of wandering city-slickers—who are not told what they're eating until after they've eaten it. Effective, too; I've been there and seen it done. But that is not what's going on here, because you've all been given fair warning."

Once again, he surveyed the audience. "Of course, for all I know there isn't a city-slicker among you, and if that's the case it's probably just as well I diced up some prime tenderloin to pad out the supply. And if anyone thinks they can discern the difference . . . well, be my guest." And he laughed. So did everyone else, including one or two who—Kirsten thought with sudden irreverence—had been eying the globules of meat as if expecting them to suddenly leap up and start fornicating.

The mental picture was too much! She had to bow her head and try to hide the guffaw that bubbled in her own throat, and almost missed Kendall's next remark.

"So I'm going to mix metaphors tonight, so to speak, and go get you some real oysters, along with some prawns and veggies, and you can do your tempura exactly as it suits you," he said. But his eyes were on Kirsten; he'd noticed her reaction and one raised dark eyebrow suggested he might even have understood the reason for it.

He was a cunning manipulator, she thought during the brief interval in which Kendall left the room, then returned bearing trays of "proper" oysters, prawns, cubes of finely diced seafood of some sort, and various bits of vegetable artistically sculpted into a variety of shapes. Everything was delivered to table with an air of flamboyance that stopped just short of parody, then Kendall seated himself in the host's chair and spread both hands in an invitation to begin. Which they did, if somewhat tentatively at first.

Kirsten had no problem dealing with Kendall's unusual starter course; she'd been raised on the prairies, and nobody growing up in Swift Current, Saskatchewan—known as Speedy Creek in the local vernacular—could do so without knowing what prairie oysters were and how tasty they were! Taste, of course, wasn't the point of the issue. Kirsten twigged to that immediately and gave Kendall full marks for inventiveness, if not for choice. What he'd created was a surefire method of ensuring that his guests had an immediate topic of dinner conversation that couldn't help but interest them all, and which also forced them to observe their fellow diners more closely than otherwise might have been the case.

It was simply impossible—at least in the beginning—not to pay attention to who chose which morsels from the trays, impossible not to pause in one's own chewing and taste sensations to see the reactions of all the others. Unfortunately, it did not help Kirsten's inability to remember names. Which was distracting when she found herself watching one woman at the far end of the table spear up a piece of meat with her fondue fork, then sit staring at it, mesmerized, seemingly unwilling to commit the morsel to the hot oil, but equally unable to just . . . put it back.

*What are you thinking? And why can't I remember your name? I heard it not ten minutes ago and it's gone . . . disap-*

*peared. Come on, lady . . . at least put the damned thing into the oil; you can't sit there staring at it all night. It won't bite you unless you bite it first.*

Kirsten suddenly realized she was sitting in exactly the same position, her own—already cooked—morsel cooling on the fork. Other than that, and a small matter of age difference, they could have been twins. Kirsten had already eaten several of the delicacies by this time; it was the other woman everyone was watching. But no . . . not quite everyone. She glanced around to meet the piercing blue eyes of her host, eyes that fairly danced with an amusement he could obviously tell she was sharing.

*I'll bet you watch "Survivor." In fact I think you've been taking lessons from Jeff Probst. I'll bet you could give Pauline's esteemed boss a run for his money when it comes to knowing about human behavior, too.*

Kendall's eyes danced, and when his lips parted in a stunningly white grin, she found herself wanting to try and follow the music and steps, to somehow get into *his* mind and understand this brilliant game he was playing. He radiated that impression of good-humored openness, a sort of boyish welcome-to-my-world that Kirsten found startlingly attractive, but she thought the mind behind it all must be astonishingly creative and cunning.

They shared the experience of watching the other woman, nodding in unison as she finally emerged from her trance and placed her tidbit into the fondue, and Kirsten fancied she could hear his silent cheer as it was finally retrieved, cautiously tasted, and ultimately accepted. When the woman reached avidly for another piece, Kirsten thought she could actually feel Kendall's attention drift round the table . . . *knew* she could feel it return to focus on her. Then he gave a brief shake of his head and turned again to his duties as their host, guiding the conversation, making sure everyone was being catered to. Occasionally, in response to some unobtrusive signal, staff would emerge to clear away plates, refresh the wine supplies, and generally tidy up, but overall, the meal was surprisingly casual.

The next course—actually several all-in-one—was only marginally more conventional. Kendall had somehow contrived to cook an enormous turkey in the fashion usually reserved for Peking Duck, and served first the white meat, then the dark, and finally the crispy, decadently-delicious skin, each portion provided with a variety of dipping sauces, tangy, tasty vegetables, and his own unique turkey stuffing . . . but tortillas instead of Chinese pancakes to wrap it all in. The effect was, of course, almost identical, but . . . tortillas? He'd done it for effect, Kirsten decided, also willing to concede that his turkey stuffing was ample compensation for any whimsy.

Throughout, Kendall guided and steered the conversation without seeming to . . . a question here, a subtle redirected comment there, all with the assured confidence of an orchestra conductor. The conversation ranged through all manner of topics, from the man's own books to great literature to the mystery of the still-missing theatre director to great mysteries of the modern age and ages gone by. Even religion and politics, normally considered taboo subjects for the dinner table. At one point, Kendall and Pauline's doctor boss exchanged interesting and entertaining reflections about life in Tasmania, where both had spent considerable time. Wine was consumed in large but acceptable quantities, and Kirsten had noticed earlier that their host had ensured each party had a designated driver, and voiced his insistence on that convention.

When nobody could manage another sliver of turkey, he

announced a break before dessert, directing the smokers to a roofed patio off the huge dining room and inviting everyone else to wander at will through the main floor of the mansion, or the gardens if they'd prefer, while he attended to preparations for a dessert that Kirsten was certain she had no room for, and equally certain she was not alone in this.

Teague Kendall's home was a striking testimonial to its era, a time when craftsmen and materials were expected to be of the highest quality, and little or no expense was spared in the creation of such masterpieces. It was the woodwork that caught Kirsten's eye: ornate cornices, mantelpieces, bookshelves [of course!], and paneling that glowed from years of polishing and care. The house, Kendall had told them, had belonged to his grandmother, whose husband had made his fortune in a range of ventures, including timbering and mining all over Vancouver Island and the adjacent mainland. The current owner had obviously done his best to maintain the graciousness of the place, but also had imprinted his own taste when it came to decorating. West coast native art shared space with traditional—and sometimes similar—art from Polynesia and New Guinea and Australia. Teague Kendall clearly loved good woodcarving, and the décor reflected his taste.

Kirsten wandered from room to room on the main floor, pausing to peruse the contents of the bookshelves which vied for space with the artworks. It was all a finely-balanced marriage of library and art gallery, and she found it suited her own taste and artistic temperament very well indeed. Then she stepped into what had perhaps been the old gentleman's study, or office, and stopped dead in her tracks. Not a study . . . a billiard room. At least it had been.

The walls were floor-to-ceiling bookcases that seemed to have been designed around the artworks in the room, with specific gaps for specific pictures, others to allow display of various ornaments, carvings, and statuary. And one corner held a gigantic leather armchair, a side table, and the sort of reading light a dedicated reader would insist upon. But the center of the room was what caught her eye—a full-sized billiard table, used not for billiards but as the workspace on which a gigantic jigsaw puzzle was being put together. Dead center was a piece of cardboard with the edges of the puzzle already in place, along with half a dozen bits and pieces already fitted together. And surrounding that, the remaining pieces were laid out in neat, tidy rows, face up. But the crowning touch was the shade on the obligatory suspended, pool table light fitting—a rectangular shade with the words: ONLY ONE on every facet.

Only one? She stood there, mesmerized by the concept of being able to fit only one piece into the puzzle, then having to—what?—quit and do something else? Her eyes were already scanning the expanse of upturned shapes, seeking a color, a nuance of shape. Only one? It would be like an order to eat only one salted peanut . . . the ultimate in self-control . . . or self-torture. Clearly the man was a highly disciplined person, or a masochist. Kirsten stood shock-still, letting her eyes wander, her subconscious do the work. She loved jigsaw puzzles, had never seen one this huge, this complicated. Or this irresistible. Her own work demanded a good eye for color, detail. Even from all these choices, she knew that sooner or later one piece would reveal its rightness. When the mental command arrived, she was ready, and her fingers flashed out, lizard-tongue-quick, to snatch that one piece from the array of thousands and fit it into place.

Only one? She found herself wanting to glance round, to ensure her privacy while she disobeyed the injunction. Already she'd seen another possible match, perhaps not . . .

quite right, but still . . . She poised, fingers flicking as she contemplated the choice, all her attention focused on the intricate display.

"Was it Oscar Wilde who said the only way to deal with temptation is to give in to it?" Her host's voice was a seductive whisper, but his grin, when she turned—startled—was the mischievous grin of a childhood playmate, a co-conspirator. "I make exceptions for visitors," Teague Kendall said. "The rule is really just there for me, because I need it to keep me honest."

"I'm not sure I understand," Kirsten replied. "I mean . . . what difference could it make? It's your puzzle, after all . . . or is it?"

"Mine, for sure. But it's more than a puzzle . . . it's a tool. What you're looking at is my writer's-block-buster, and it's a powerful tool that has to be used wisely and well or it loses its usefulness. Except as a de-stressor, of course. But any sort of puzzle does that, just by changing your focus."

"You mean by taking your mind off your problems. But how can limiting yourself to just one piece do that? And how can it fix writer's block?"

Now his grin was infectious. "Doesn't matter if it's one piece or twenty, the focus gets shifted anyway. Which is the point, for me. If I can't figure out where I want to go with a scene, or a conversation, for instance . . . I walk down here from my office—which is upstairs, so I get the added benefit of a wee bit of exercise, at least going back—and allow myself the fun of playing with the puzzle until I've got one more piece fitted. But only one . . . that's all it takes to have the desired effect. Then I go back to work, and by some miracle or another, whatever's been blocking me has disappeared. Works every time."

Kirsten found her eyes drawn to the second piece she'd

noticed, and her fingers automatically reached for it, then stopped as she realized what she was doing.

"But what if there are . . . say, two pieces that you see that should fit? Or do you enjoy putting off temptation?" she asked.

"Close your eyes."

"I'm sorry . . ."

"Close 'em . . . quick."

She obeyed, but it was more a slow blink than anything. So of course she saw his hand flash out to mix up the pieces, shifting them, altering the color and shape pattern she'd been fixing in her mind. The second piece she'd focused upon disappeared in the new mix so quickly it surprised her. She could, of course, find it again, but it would take time.

"See . . . magic!"

"And you . . . do that? To yourself?"

"Every time. Well, almost every time. I have to . . . otherwise I'd be spending eight hours a day here instead of working, which would make my publisher unhappy and me as well, at least in the long term."

Kendall paused, letting his bright blue eyes move from looking at her to looking at the broad muddle of jigsaw pieces. And when he continued, there was almost a sadness in his silk-smooth voice. "But don't think it's always easy. I have a sort of addictive personality, and there are times I'd give almost anything to just do one of these things from start to finish without so much as thinking of anything else. I'm the same way with big crossword puzzles, occasionally."

"I can only do the ones that come without any possibility of cheating," Kristen replied. "Once I know there are answers I can get to, my patience evaporates. I just want to get on with it, and next thing you know the fun's gone out of it all. So . . . how long does it take you for, say, a puzzle like this?"

Kendall shrugged. "Depends how much trouble I'm having with my writing, obviously, and on how I start. I cheated with this one, to the extent of doing the entire outside edge in one hit, but only because I was between books at the time. The one before was a ten-thousand-piece puzzle, like this one, only a different picture. And not the easiest of books, the one I was working on, so it worked out at about twenty pieces a day. They both got done at pretty much the same time."

"A year and a half?" Kirsten was suitably impressed, both by the timing and the incredible discipline it must have called for. She looked at the vast array of puzzle pieces, then back into Kendall's eyes, seeking to see the hardness, the evidence of the fierce determination that had to exist. It might have been there, but it was disguised. All she saw was two bright eyes looking back at her, one from beneath a slightly raised eyebrow that suggested Kendall, too, was looking for something beyond the superficial. But the expression was there, then gone almost before she noticed it, and his voice betrayed nothing.

"You've got a good eye," he said. "Not that I'd expect otherwise . . . you're a jewelry designer. Good hands, too, I expect." And without warning, he reached out to lift one of Kirsten's work-roughened hands for inspection. He didn't comment on the roughness, nor did he hold her hand overlong, or suggestively, merely inspected and . . . nodded.

"I'd best get back to being *mine host,*" he said with an infinitesimal shake of his head. "The best, as they say, is yet to come . . . but only if I take charge. You go ahead and play if you want." He nodded toward the puzzle table. "Or you might be firm with yourself, in which case I can recommend the real library, which is the next room over." And with a gracious, if somewhat self-mocking half bow, he was gone.

Kirsten shook her head, half wondering if this incredible conversation had really taken place or if she'd taken too much wine aboard. It seemed, in retrospect, sort of . . . mystical, ethereal, otherworldly.

*And if those are the best words you can think of, you'd best go see if his library has a decent dictionary or thesaurus. Good thing he's the writer and not you.*

Kendall's "real" library was as eclectic as Kirsten might have expected, and she was not surprised at how organized it was, either. Proper floor-to-ceiling bookcases, here, and while some shelves held ornaments, the room was clearly devoted specifically to books. No Dewey Decimal system, but certainly an organizational pattern he'd worked out for himself, with research books grouped by subject and ranked by author, but the fiction running the gamut of that genre . . . only the author's names to differentiate sci-fi from black murder mystery, contemporary literature from historical.

Kirsten browsed idly, finding that even the seemingly newest appeared to have been read, and some showed evidence of being read and reread and reread yet again. He appeared to have everything by James Lee Burke and James W. Hall, had the complete works of John D. MacDonald, obviously liked Sharyn McCrumb's "Appalachian" novels, but not her other work. He had a complete collection of Peter O'Donnell's "Modesty Blaise," but confined his Thomas Perry to the "Jane Whitefield" novels. Only Jan Burke's *NINE*, but all of Sandford's "Prey" books. None of this surprised her much; all logical enough reading for a thriller writer.

There were oddball inclusions, also. Denise Dietz, a name Kirsten certainly recognized, since her own bookshelf held three of the provocative titles—*Throw Darts at a Cheesecake*,

*Beat up a Cookie, Footprints in the Butter.* Jenny Maxwell's "Blacksmith" trilogy, the bleak, black works of Australian writer Gabrielle Lord, who Kirsten had once tried to read. She shuddered at the memory.

And there were unexpected exclusions, also. Not a single copy of Kendall's own books graced these shelves, nor had she noticed any in the puzzle room. Still . . . what a superb collection! If he willed this all to the local library, he'd have to watch his back, she thought, and chuckled at the vision of a tiny, gray-haired librarian studying esoteric murder mysteries, seeing a safe, sure-fire method of doing away with Kendall just to get his collection of books.

"Kirsten! You're going to miss dessert." Pauline's voice brought Kirsten back to reality with a tangible snap, and she allowed herself to be literally dragged away, her friend's chatterbox voice setting their pace as they hurried back to the dining room. Trying to move so quickly in unaccustomed high heels nearly brought her undone . . . she stumbled and almost fell as they turned the corner by the puzzle room, where most of Kendall's guests had gathered. Kirsten was brought almost to her knees, and it was while trying to find her balance that she caught, from the corner of her vision, an occurrence she didn't at first believe she'd actually seen.

The problem was, it happened too quickly, and amidst the milling of people herding together to join Kirsten and Pauline en route to the dining room. The men were gathered together like so many penguins, so alike in their dark dinner-wear it was difficult to tell one from another. Even harder to identify the hand that swooped down to pluck up a single jigsaw piece and transfer it to the man's pocket—and the act was so unexpected, so illogical, that Kirsten was seated in her chair, awaiting dessert, before she could convince herself she'd actually seen it, not just imagined the whole thing.

But she had! By closing her eyes, she could see it again. A man's hand—the right hand—without any jewelry. No! There had been jewelry. Must have been. The man had been wearing French cuffs, so there must have been a cufflink. Kirsten squinched her eyes tightly shut, fighting to bring back the mental picture, then sighed as she realized the cuff hadn't been exposed sufficiently to give her any sight of the cufflink.

"Are you all right?"

The voice came from her left, a man named . . . Tom? His wife, Sharon, was sitting near the other end of the table, and Kirsten winced at being able to remember her name, but not his. She stared at him blankly for an instant, then skirted the problem entirely.

"I'm fine, really," she said. "Just . . . perhaps a touch too much wine, earlier." It was difficult not to look down at his hand, his wrist. Was he wearing French cuffs? He was . . . they all were. Every man in the place, including their host, who entered at that moment bearing a tray of local, seasonal fruits cunningly arrayed and displayed like a piece of artwork. He was followed by a stunning young woman who carried the "real" dessert—a large ice-cream cake that had been sculpted into the shape of a mournful-looking bull moose with enormous but saggy antlers and his tongue hanging out. The sight brought chuckles and sighs of appreciation as the moose was paraded round the table before being given pride of place in the center. This was no commercial, Dairy Queen offering; this was art for the sake of art, deliberately made cute, but not quite too pretty to eat.

"This splendid creation is not, as you might imagine, some esoteric variation of chocolate mousse," their host said with a wry grin. "If this lad were a race-horse, he'd be named *Ultimate Decadence, out of Death by Chocolate.* And for sure, he'd be a winner . . . except for tonight. Tonight, he gets eaten, or melted. I suggest the former. Dig in and try him while he's frozen." Whereupon he assaulted the poor moose with a deftly-handled slice-and-serve gizmo designed for proper cakes. In moments the animal was dismembered and distributed, reminding Kirsten of some sort of prehistoric tribal rite—choicest cuts to the hunters, the rest allotted according to rank. A most grisly thought, but the dessert was delicious for all that.

Coffee and liqueurs followed, and their host waited for a suitable silence, then offered Kirsten the perfect opportunity to raise the issue of the stolen jigsaw piece. But could she? She had been considering mentioning the matter privately to Kendall; that seemed only fair—she could imagine the frustration of getting that close to the finish of such a puzzle, only to find that crucial piece missing.

*Anyone could imagine that! I expect it's happened to all of us, one time or another in our lives. But . . .*

But, she wondered, what sort of person could actually do a thing like that? She glanced round the table once more, seeing seven men, all seeming perfectly normal, typical people, and felt ice run down her spine at the realization that one of these men was seriously . . . twisted. There was a maliciousness in stealing that puzzle piece—unless it was some strange sort of practical joke—that seemed to Kirsten somehow . . . malignant. It smacked of mind games: cunning, devious, and totally nasty. Dirty, somehow. Tainted.

She thought of that even as she listened to Kendall speak, her mind half with his comments, half with the thought that she was suddenly very, very uncomfortable in this company.

It was almost as if he'd somehow been reading her mind, or following her gaze round the table throughout dessert, as she confirmed that any of the male diners could have been the one who'd snitched the puzzle piece. Almost as if he knew she'd seen the piece stolen . . . perhaps had picked it up himself as some sort of test, or trap. No doubt in her mind that his words were ultimately aimed squarely at her . . . he said as much, if not directly.

And then it got worse.

# FIFTEEN

"It's time to tip the chef," Kendall told his audience. "What I'd like from you now, if you fancy sharing, is grist for my professional mill—the writing of mystery thrillers. And tonight's topic is *coincidence in mystery,* sort of stretching the adage that once is chance, twice is coincidence, and three times is conspiracy, if you will. I'm sure we've all been through circumstances where hindsight has revealed inexplicable links, things we couldn't have known about or understood without the benefit of coincidences we didn't know about at the time."

Kendall took a sip of liqueur, glanced round the table. "I'll begin," he said. "Show you the kind of thing I'm after. It started with a visit to the local cop shop about a month ago . . ."

He went on to relate his adventures, giving an overblown and humorous account of having been assaulted by the door, of watching a "stunningly beautiful" stranger "dressed like a skid row bum" disappear in the aftermath, of asking his questions of the police, of being told about his mysterious assailant and her inquiries on a subject so specifically like his own.

"The meeting—if we can call it that—was chance," he

said. "But having both of us enquiring about a subject so . . . distinct, I think we might agree was coincidence. So what do we call it when that person turns up again in my life? Unknown, until . . . very recently. Totally unexpected. Not someone I'd gone looking for, although I freely admit I would have if I'd had the slightest idea where to start. But now . . . found! Is that simply more coincidence . . . or is it some sort of cosmic conspiracy? I certainly don't know, and I don't mind admitting it worries me just a bit."

The question brought a wide range of answers from around the table, most leaning to the coincidence theory. Kirsten listened, utterly fascinated by the logic, and lack of it, which emerged. But more fascinated by the way Teague Kendall managed to avoid making any sort of eye contact with her, by the way he avoided tying his unusual little tale to this night, this place, this group of people, her!

But it was aimed at her. He knew it. She knew it. Although she didn't know what he expected of her . . . was she expected to follow his lead, or to pass? He'd given her the choice. What would she say when it came her turn to comment? And then it was, and her mouth opened, and as usual, she lost control of her tongue.

"Our host is too gracious by far," she began, reaching for the words, seeking caution in an attempt at humor. "No proper woman, of course, could pass up the chance of being identified publicly as *stunningly beautiful*. Thank you for that, Teague, although I'm less pleased with the comment about my clothes. Still, Pauline would agree with you . . . she's always on at me about that."

Kirsten reached into her décolletage, fumbling with suddenly clumsy fingers as she lifted out her sister's ring and held it out where the diners could see. "Our host has given you a sort of a puzzle," she said. "Now I'm giving you a tougher one. I'm going to tell you all a story that's not about coincidence or chance, but about impossibility."

And she did. Once started, she simply couldn't stop, and what poured from her lips was given in such detail, and—somehow—in something that must have been coherency, must have made some sort of sense. Because everybody listened in total, rapt silence, right through to the very end. Not a cough, not a sigh, not a sideways glance interrupted her as she spoke. Instead, two dozen eyes peered at her, prompting, imploring, entreating, silently begging for more and more detail. Like baby birds . . . only silent.

She told them about her inconsiderate sister, about that final email, about her visit to the police. She told them about her caving expeditions, about the finding of the ring . . . Emma's ring . . . her ring! Her treacherous tongue blatted out personal details, private thoughts that had no place here, no place anywhere, dammit!

Until finally, when she'd brought the tale full circle, ending it here at this very table. And paused, gulping, half ashamed of having let her mouth run away with her yet again. Mentally cursing herself, almost in tears. Then they erupted in applause, and Kirsten sat there, stunned, held in place by Teague Kendall's startling blue eyes and the realization everyone thought she'd been part of the entertainment!

The mercifully short remainder of the evening passed in a sort of hazy blur for Kirsten. Emma's ring was duly passed round the table and duly admired, but—she was certain—more for the craftsmanship and uniqueness than for the mystery surrounding its finding in the cave. Her sister's apparent disappearance raised once again the equally mysterious disappearance of the hapless theatre director, who at least had spurred some public interest. Rumors of every sort abounded . . . he'd run off with a gay lover, run off with a woman, fled the ignominy of a truly awful production of a truly great play, fled a bad marriage, suffered amnesia, suffered some death-dealing illness and fled to buy time and circumstance for suicide. It went on and on and on. Yet Kirsten's own mystery hardly merited comment, by comparison, either because nobody took it seriously, or because it was simply *too* mysterious.

None of which mattered all that much to her. She had vented, almost certainly made a great fool of herself, and really wanted nothing more than for the evening to end so she could go home and hear no more about mysterious disappearances. Until Monday, of course, when it would be discussed in a suitable time and circumstance. But first, she had to endure the drive home and the barrage of questions from her closest friend.

"Why didn't you tell me about your sister?" was how that began. And—surprisingly—ended. Pauline wasn't interested in the details; she was Kirsten's friend, and saw her role as being a comfort-giver. Once Kirsten had fumbled her way through answering the first question—"I don't know, really. I just . . . didn't"—Pauline simply said, "Well if I can help, I will. I'm here for you if you need me. You know that." And the remainder of their journey home was driven in blessed silence.

Even in her muddle-headed confusion, Kirsten thought it had to be a record . . . twenty consecutive minutes of Pauline in silence. She was actually glad when—on reaching her home—Pauline reverted to normal by asking how Kirsten could have got close enough to knock Teague Kendall over and "not" remembered?

"I think he's just the coolest thing since white sliced bread," her friend cooed. "*I'd* have remembered, I can tell you that much. Oh well, at least now you've got my point about going around in your work clothes all the time. I'm surprised he remembered you . . . and he did—don't forget that!"

# SIXTEEN

The specialist awoke late on Sunday into a world subtly altered, minutely changed, out of focus, no longer totally in control. It was . . . disconcerting. Annoying, even, although not as annoying as the fact that the public library wasn't open on Sundays, which forced him to the Internet for answers. He hated the Internet, because it, too, was not in control. It offered so much in the way of information, but finding that information required the mindset of a computer geek, the time to click through myriads of links, and the patience to sift through even greater myriads of informational chaff to find just one kernel of actual knowledge.

Time! He quelled the impulse to throw the computer mouse across the room, and tried to surf and think at the same time. Part of his mind was already high in the hills . . . double, triple, quadruple-checking his aerie for trace evidence that might cause problems. The rest of his attention was on the screen, frustratingly scanning reference after reference, document after document, knowing the answer was out there somewhere in cyberspace, if only he could find the right keyword, the right link. If only he could find anything at all significant before his temper boiled over!

What had happened was simple enough to decipher—one

didn't require a PhD to figure out that Kirsten's sister's damned ring had somehow made its way from the abandoned mine-shaft where he'd discarded it, down through some opening, some tunnel or system of tunnels in the ridge below, to emerge far below and far away in a cave. Carried by water, perhaps . . . that might make as much sense as anything else. It was a concept so ridiculous as to be possible, even believable. Believable, indeed, because it had happened! He had seen the ring, heard the incredible story of an impossibility he knew—now—to be only too possible.

And . . . if the ring—what else? Would the almost inevitable police investigation turn up others of his discards that had followed the ring on its subterranean journey? A wallet? A watch? Some fragment of bicycle? Any one of a hundred bones? His mind reeled with visions of disconnected bones swimming in darkness like so many hapless sperm, and he couldn't stop the words and music of "Dem Bones" thundering around inside his head.

Funny. Hilarious, if this wasn't so potentially serious. He would have to check out things up in the hills, but not today. It couldn't be today . . . too many people would be wandering the back-roads on a Sunday, too much chance of being noticed. But tonight, or better yet tomorrow morning early . . . ? He could be in and out before dawn, with any sort of luck. Which thought brought him to the real problem, the impossible maze of coincidence involved with all this. The specialist was not superstitious; superstition was for ignorant fools. Nor did he believe in omens, which only served to make ignorant fools superstitious. But . . .

*Once is chance, twice is coincidence, and three times is conspiracy.*

This situation had gone far beyond all of those. It was speeding headlong into the realm of myth and legend, illogic and incomprehension . . . and he didn't believe in those, either. But this astonishing chain of coincidence was disconcerting, the more so for the randomness of it all. Worse than any conspiracy. A conspiracy at least suggested a plan, logic. This was more like the much-vaunted chaos theory, and he hated it. What he hated most was not being in control . . . total control.

The word "karst" popped up, and he almost clicked past it, except there was a reference to Tasmania that caught his eye. Another random factor chucked into the stew! Perhaps . . . ?

The downloading seemed to take forever, but eventually he found the Tasmanian mineral maps, found indeed a pleasingly familiar topographical map, with an even more pleasant pinpoint he could hardly fail to recognize. Maps . . . and karst . . . He clicked, scanned, double-clicked, scanned, clicked, then halted in almost smug satisfaction as the B.C. government Web site began to disgorge links that led to links that led to . . . pictures. Computer-generated pictures that showed how rainwater percolated through the limestone, the four per cent of Vancouver Island's surface underlaid by soluble bedrock. How that same drainage water etched passages, fissures, entire mountains spider-webbed with underground hydraulics systems, caves.

This was better! This at least made some sense, revealing an unlikely but at least possible way in which that damned ring had made its incredible journey. The skeletal music in his head died, replaced by a mental image of the torrential rains that had followed his experience with the director. Then, absurdly, pictures of bleached skulls bobbing in an underground torrent, bouncing off walls of stone where policemen bobbed for them like apples. He looked again at the pictures, sighed, then smiled as another memory intruded with the recalled smell of pot roast. All of which led to another thought, and he sat there, staring blindly at the computer screen as he visualized the way Kirsten's lilac dress had hugged a taut, muscular rump. Sisters, although not looking all that similar. But in the genes, the structure, the very flesh? The taste?

*I can find out. I can do that! Now that I know who she is and where she is . . .*

It was worth doing, too. The screen-saver flowed in to cover his screen, but he wasn't looking at it anymore; eyes closed, he wrung his supple fingers together, dry-washing his hands as his mind roamed a universe larger than the Internet. Kirsten's sister had tasted different from the director. Not vividly so, but noticeably, and it wasn't a matter of spices, he now realized, but of . . . gender, of youth, vitality.

More important . . . he still had one entire Emma rump roast in his freezer, and . . . yes, he was almost certain . . . a two-inch-thick slab of choice steak, as well. Cut square across the grain to ensure maximum tenderness. His tongue slid across already-moistened lips as he pictured Kirsten biting down into a piece of that steak, devouring it with the same eagerness she'd displayed with the prairie oysters the night before. When should she be told, though? Before might necessitate force-feeding, a . . . distasteful possibility.

*Now there's a rather appropriate choice of words.* The thought brought the slenderest of grins.

So . . . after. Yes. After, when it was too late, when she couldn't change her mind. And he would have to make a special produce-buying expedition, too. Real Idaho potatoes for baking, only the freshest of accompanying vegetables. Because this would be an occasion . . . something very, very special indeed.

Then a sudden, worrying thought. Illogical, but . . .

What if Kirsten's ingestion of her sister's flesh somehow tainted his experiment? It seemed ridiculous, on the surface of it all. She would herself be . . . prepared for the table well before her digestive system could cope with what she'd eaten, before it could really become . . . part of her. He thought . . . decided not to worry on that score. It would have to wait awhile anyway; better to plan it all most thoroughly, to ensure no missteps, no mistakes. Better to stretch out the silky threads of anticipation.

Opening his eyes, the specialist returned to the computer screen, did a fast double-check of the circumstances and possibilities about the ring and its amazing travels. Logic said it was a one-off situation, that no other single item of his discards could have made such an incredible journey. Unless, of course, the abandoned molybdenum mine itself bottomed out in a cave that might be reached from below, and that seemed unlikely. Kirsten had said the ring was in a chamber, all on its own, with no indication even of how it got there. Indeed, she had seemed to think the ring must have been brought into the cave after her party had discovered it, was obviously vaguely suspicious even of her caving companions.

This, then, would be the logical police attitude to the riddle . . . the likelihood somebody else had entered the cave, deposited the ring, then left again. At first glance, that certainly would seem the most likely scenario . . . unlikely the police would ever even guess at what had really happened. And, of course, they would find no further evidence, because there simply was none! He had never been in the cave, didn't even know where it was—although he had a fair idea; memory of those tracks on the road that rainy day provided a likely location.

So . . . what to do now? Already he had discarded the thought of simply dumping an explosive charge down his mine shaft. Collapse the shaft, then burn the buildings and just walk away. Find another center of operations once the dust had settled. It was the obvious solution, so of course it was highly suspect. Lord only knew what sort of demons such an action might release! All it could possibly do was attract even more attention to the area.

And yet . . . what if the old mine shaft did bottom out in a cave that might one day be found? Sooner or later, it would be found; these caving people—if the Internet was to be believed—liked nothing better than to explore, to survey, as they laughingly called it, until every nook and cranny had been exposed, every secret place violated, robbed of all mystique. And now, given the finding of Kirsten's ring, exploration would be more intense, not less. Worse, it would bring increased numbers of people to wander the region around his aerie . . . and that simply would not do!

Again, he sighed. But logic had spoken and must be obeyed. He would have to move, and fairly quickly, too. Not all that complicated a situation, except that without an aerie, without the total privacy he wanted, needed, *had to have* . . . his most favorite activities would have to be put on hold. Unacceptable! And worse . . . having to deal with Kirsten anywhere but in the exact place he'd dealt with her sister would diminish the experience. Not much, but any diminishment was too much! He would go into the hills tonight, check and recheck and double-check to ensure his aerie was safe, but he would keep it until after Kirsten's . . . visit.

After that bit of rather tasty business, it would be almost time for another junket to Tasmania, anyway. Surely he could put things on hold until then; no sense in building up a store of meat that he daren't leave behind and couldn't very well take with him. Not that it mattered, Tasmania in summer offered abundant opportunity to restock the larder.

Decision made, the specialist switched off the computer and abruptly turned his attention to brunch. Two fresh farm eggs, he decided. Free-range, of course, brown and possibly double-yolked, with a bit of luck. And some of that Danish, beautifully-smoked bacon. Back bacon, which the Americans with their usual perverted logic called "Canadian" bacon.

He should have his own smoker, the specialist decided. It would come in very handy. That was one thing he could do today . . . check out the sporting goods stores and see what was available. It would have to be portable, given the change in circumstance, but that was fine so long as it could make proper bacon.

Cold smoking, or hot? He decided cold would be best, although it took longer and the equipment was probably less portable. Excitement, then, surpassed annoyance, and after the dishes were done, he returned to the hated, ubiquitous Internet.

*Information is power.*

# SEVENTEEN

## Tasmania

Old Viv Purcell's eyes were going, though they served him marginally better than his three remaining teeth. Still good enough, at any rate, to see that the thigh bone his dog had just brought him was human. Or had been. And despite a reputation—fairly earned and unmatched by those few Tasmanians anywhere near his age—of being a "rum'n," a thoroughly disreputable character, old Viv knew there were times when doing the right thing was the wisest and maybe the only choice. So he took the bone to Sergeant Charlie Banes, who promptly scolded him for doing so, for not leaving it where it had been found. Untouched!

Or maybe it was just because he marched into the cop shop waving the grisly trophy like a baton; either way, he wasn't about to take a lot of rubbish from any damned copper, and said so.

"I've done me duty, I have," he said. "Now do yez want me to show you where old Bluey found the damned thing, or not?" Bluey, the Jack Russell terrier in question, wasn't quite as ugly as Viv, and had more and better teeth, but his disposition was infinitely worse, and Charlie Banes kept an eye on the beast as it prowled the anteroom of the police office. Dealing with old Viv was one thing . . . he'd been doing that for years . . . but Bluey was famous for leaving tooth marks in those silly enough to turn their backs on him.

"I'll 'ave you know I've given up a day's work just to bring this in," the old man continued. "Had to walk three mile afore I could bludge a ride, too. 'Course I'll be expecting you to drive me back. All the way, too, mate. Right to me flaming door."

Banes sighed and shook his head. No getting out of this, and he'd end up buying the old man a beer—or more probably several—before they got there. That was a given. So . . . several hours cooped up with the two of them in his police vehicle. Not a pleasant prospect . . . the dog stunk, but the old man was worse. Already he was pondering where best to stop for the beer. It would have to be somewhere they could drink it outside, because he daren't leave that damned dog alone in his vehicle, where it would either eat the upholstery or crap all over everything.

"Right. Let's be away, then," he said. Decision made. Best get on with this before it got even more complicated. If nothing else, he knew the bone had been found somewhere near where Viv was wintering, an old stockman's hut on "Misery" bush run, back in at the foot of Blue Tier.

Viv lived by himself . . . a matter of choice by any and all concerned. There had been a time it was otherwise—the randy old bugger was reputed to have children all over Tasmania and even a few on the mainland—but even the few who knew he existed wouldn't put up with him. By all rights, he should have been in some aged care facility, but no government official was game enough even to suggest that, much less try to enforce it.

So Viv took his pension, supplemented it with a bit of poaching, a bit of tin and gold prospecting, and various bits of itinerant labor when he found somebody desperate enough to hire him. In his youth he'd been a man of sound reputation—at least as a worker—but he was pushing ninety, now, and the rough edges were rougher than ever. Most people reckoned he was uglier than his dog, and meaner in the bargain, and they expected he'd wake up dead one morning, likely in the damned dog's belly. Mongrels, the both of them.

Charlie Banes had a more charitable attitude, having had years of dealing with the irascible old curmudgeon. He knew the old man poached the occasional deer and trout, but only for his own use and never, ever, allowed any waste. Half the bushies in Tasmania were poachers, but the more modern crew had none of the old man's morals or strength of character.

Or his pungency. The Sergeant kept all the vehicle windows wide open as they drove back toward the escarpment. If Bluey decided to dive out after a rabbit or road-killed possum . . . too damned bad!

*No, strike that. It'd break the old bugger's heart . . . assuming he's still got one. Still, I wish both of them would bathe a bit more often.*

Actually, Banes quite liked old Viv. Sometimes. And at all times, he respected the old geezer's knowledge of all things relative to bush life in Tasmania. Banes had, in his younger years, served as the resident copper in every rural station throughout the state's northeast, and had to admit old Viv's knowledge of the land, the people, and the issues outstripped his own a thousand-fold.

Taking the course of least resistance, he picked up a six-pack at the first pub they passed, then changed his mind before driving away and went back for another, even adding a small flask of rum. He dreaded the thought of some passing motorist reporting old Viv happily tippling inside a police cruiser, but it was safer and faster than any alternative.

"A little discretion, if you please," he advised old Viv, who responded with a toothless grin and a half-hearted attempt to wave the beer can at the first car they met. Charlie Banes could only laugh.

Soon enough, they reached the turnoff to Goulds Country and the maze of forestry tracks that run north along the Great Musselroe River, then onto progressively more remote tracks edging in under Blue Tier, tracks that became rougher and narrower as they went along. Banes was mentally congratulating himself for having turned a six-tinnie trip into one requiring merely four—his own single beer not being allowed to count—when old Viv suddenly shouted at him to stop, screaming the command as if they were in danger of hitting some unseen obstacle. Banes stomped on the brake pedal, spilling the remainder of that single beer, and skidded to a halt. The track at this point had switchbacked almost under the imposing bulk of the tier, which actually overhung it in places.

"Should be about here, I reckon. Bit hard to tell. Light's not the same as 'twas then. Wish you'd let me bring the damned bone . . . dog'd know what he's supposed to be looking for, if you had." The bone had been placed immediately in an evidence bag for eventual shipment to Hobart, then perhaps on to the mainland, for forensic testing. Both men knew it was indisputably human, but procedure required that some scientist confirm it.

"Probably take it off someplace and bury it," Banes replied, clambering down from the cruiser and wondering if old Viv was fit enough for any extended search . . . assuming they could even determine where to begin searching. He needn't have worried on that score; the old man was like a wombat in the scrub. Bent low, he scurried along shouting slurred encouragements to the dog, who might or might not be paying any attention. Banes was hard put just to keep up.

He lost sight of both for a time, and was forced to follow the sound of the old man's curses and the terrier's incessant yapping. Then he caught up once again, just in time to view the dog's rump sticking out of a tiny crack in the rock wall, and old Viv glaring impatiently at him for taking so long.

"That slow and you didn't even think to bring along the beer," he said, waving the nearly empty tin he'd obviously carried along with him. "Slack . . . that's the only word for it."

"Never mind the compliments. What's that bloody mongrel up to?" Banes replied, watching with amazement as the agile terrier squeezed further into the rock crevice, then disappeared entirely from sight.

"Don't insult me dog; he's got more brains than both of us together," was the reply. "You wanted more bones and that's what he's getting for you. I hope."

Banes stepped back and surveyed the terrain where the dog had disappeared, noting that it appeared to be almost solid rock. Certainly, he thought, there was no evidence here of any buried body, and no evidence of one having simply been dumped. Ridiculous place to dump a body anyway, he thought, given the effort it had taken them to reach this spot. Nobody would go to the trouble; probably nobody could. He knew he'd be incapable of carrying a body here from the track, even assuming he knew the place existed.

"Dog's off after a bandicoot," he muttered, squatting on his heels and wishing he had brought along the beer. He knew Bluey's breed—they could be here an hour before the dog decided to return, assuming it made such a decision at all. Hot on the track of some bandicoot or rodent, it might stay inside there for hours.

*Make a liar out of me, you bloody obnoxious little mongrel.*

And, to his astonishment, the aged dog's ugly face emerged from the crevice as if in answer to the thought. Even better, the creature held a bone, which it duly spat out before switching ends and returning into the rock before either man could speak.

It was old Viv who scurried forward to grab up the bone, and he was already handing it over before the Sergeant's objection was fully voiced.

"There!" he chortled. "What'd I tell you? G'wan, you little beauty . . . bring us out the rest and show old doubting Thomas here what a real dog can do."

And the stinky little terrier obliged, returning again and again to deposit random bits of what had once been a human skeleton, then squeezing back into the crevice on another foray. Within half an hour they had several ribs, an ulna, and various smaller bones that could have been—to Banes' eye—the remains of anything from a bush rat to a wombat. Old Viv was more discerning.

"Some poor bugger's talking to Him upstairs," he remarked. "Now if me lovely wee dog would just get on with it, we could get back to the vehicle. Getting fair dry, I am."

What Charlie Banes wanted too, but even more, he wanted a skull, or at least a jawbone. With teeth. Something that might—might being the operative word—help them somehow in identifying this skeleton. And he was silly enough to say so, which brought wheezing gasps of laughter from his geriatric companion.

"You tell the dog, then," Viv said. "I'd like to hear what he answers back, but I'm going back for the beer, since you're too damned lazy. And mind you ask him nicely. He'd like as not take a chunk out of you if you don't show proper respect." The old bushie was already departing when he threw the clincher over his shoulder . . . "And don't, for Christ's sake, try to take one of them damned bones away from him, not if you fancy keeping all your fingers."

Banes cursed under his breath and moved over to where he could sit, back against a towering stringy-bark, and watch the grotty little terrier as it made trip after trip, returning each time to spit out another bone and throw a fierce, evil, yellow-fanged smirk in his direction. He was, however, mindful of the owner's caution; this was no proper retrieving dog, trained to sit and deliver tenderly to hand. Even old Viv had occasionally felt the little dog's teeth.

That thought grew stronger as Bluey finally did what Banes had wanted . . . he emerged with a toothy lower jawbone in his mouth, spat it out, then sprawled down on his belly and stared at the policeman as if daring him to even move, much less try to pick up the dog's sacred object. When he picked up the jawbone again, the look in his mad, terrier eyes said he was about to chew it to shreds before Banes' very eyes, and the Sergeant had to close those eyes and pray. He didn't dare think of the consequences, even less follow through on the thought to shoot the damned ugly mongrel to preserve the grisly evidence. The two were engaged in a staring contest—Banes losing and knowing it—when the old man tapped him on the shoulder with a still-cool tin of beer. How he could have made the trip so quickly, not to mention so quietly, Banes didn't stop to question. He merely accepted the tinnie and thanked his lucky stars when Bluey dropped the jawbone and began a demented dance around his master's feet.

"Either he's tuckered out or there's nothing more he can find," Viv said. "Should be plenty enough for you, anyway. How's about you pick it all up while I have a bo-peep and see if there's anything else about we ought to know about?" He didn't wait for a reply, merely disappeared into the scrub with the dog on his heels, leaving the Sergeant to follow instructions, collecting the bones in a plastic bag he'd brought on the vague chance it might be needed.

They were back at the vehicle, the bag-o'-bones safely stowed where the damned dog couldn't reach it, before Banes could voice the question that had been niggling at him since long before their incredible discovery.

"You've been having a lend of me, Viv. Telling me bloody whoppers, you have. You didn't bludge a ride within three miles of here; not within thirty miles, I reckon, 'cause there's nobody at all much closer than that. So how the hell did you and that amazing bloody dog get out here in the first place?"

He knew the answer almost before the words were past his lips. Viv's reply confirmed it.

"I said I walked three miles and I did. From home to Axton's place, which is where you'll be taking me now," the old man said with a cunning smirk. "Never once said I walked from here, 'cause I didn't. 'Sides, would I lie to a copper?"

He had in the past and he doubtless would again, and both men knew it and accepted that, but in this case, Banes knew the explanation was a bold-faced truth, if one that blandly ignored the obvious. Viv, who'd lost his driving license before his dog had been born, most likely, was still driving round the back blocks in his rust-bucket of a utility, knowing the odds of meeting any authority way out here were remote at best.

"You're a rum'n, Viv Purcell," he replied, shaking his head in admiration at the old man's sheer gall. "You don't deserve a glorious wee dog like that."

"Is that the best you can do? Ask stupid questions instead of the one you should be asking?" The old man's attitude was strangely truculent, and Banes hesitated, falling squarely into Viv's trap. "What you should be asking is how that body got to where it was," the old bushie growled, then turned his back on the policeman and began clambering up into the police cruiser. He settled himself comfortably, whistled up the dog, and opened another tinnie before continuing.

"You won't be telling him, will you, darling?" he said to the wriggling mongrel. "But you know, don't you? And so do I!"

*But you're not going to tell me until I beg, are you? Well bugger that for a joke. You'll have had a bath before it happens. That's how long it'll take; mark my words! You'll tell me in the end, just so you can rub my nose in it. You won't be able to help yourself.*

Banes held to that dream through all the long, rough miles back to the turning that would lead them to the property where old Viv was living. No easy task; the usually voluble old bushie was silent as the sphinx throughout the trip, speaking only to his dog and not much of that. His only words to the policeman were couched in a feeble attempt to distract his attention in hopes Banes would miss seeing Viv's ancient utility parked behind a shed at the main homestead. The Sergeant might have laughed, but he was no longer really in the mood.

*So much for that three-mile walk, although I expect you got the distance right. Damn it, old man. Speak to me!*

They traveled that final three miles at a snail's pace, Banes still dreaming and his passenger's victory smirk as annoying as the damned dog's grin. When they got to the decrepit shack where Viv was camped, the policeman offered the remaining tinnies. They were graciously accepted, but bought nothing. Sighing, he offered the flask of rum, and that, too, was received . . . this time even with a formal bow. But the smirk was now one of utter and total elation.

Angered, Banes mentioned the long walk Viv faced to return for his truck, then added careful words about driving with no license. The smirk became outright laughter that even the dog seemed to share.

So he begged.

# EIGHTEEN

*In the cold gray light of dawn . . . Hummph! Even Mr. Teague Kendall couldn't put it much more appropriately than that, I guess. Pity.*

Kirsten was at her workbench, staring at Emma's ring and half wishing she'd never attended that damned dinner party, never met rising literary star and host Teague Kendall, and—most of all—never been seduced into shooting her big mouth off about the mystery of Emma's ring and all it entailed.

This morning it all seemed . . . uncomfortable, like having been caught telling tales out of school. Not least because of her realization that even now, after more than a month of angst and worry, she'd be no more surprised if Emma walked in the door than if she found out her errant sister had run off with a rock star. Except for this business of the ring! Or run off with Teague-bloody-Kendall, for that matter, although Kirsten was honest enough to admit that thought merely reflected and fought with her own attraction to the man.

*You need another man like another hole in the head. Not that there'd be much chance he fancied you—not after last night's performance!* The voice in her head spat acid-flavored words. The vibes Kendall had awakened in her did nothing to improve her mood.

It was six o'clock, she'd hardly slept, had yet to even scrub off the minimal makeup she'd worn the night before. Her mind was going at warp speed, but her body reflected her own mood and that of the world outside, where low clouds drizzled wearily, not making much of an effort . . . just enough to wash what little light there was, forcing everything into monotone.

Kirsten looked at the ring again, then down at the ancient chenille robe she'd been wearing most of the night, at the huge, floppy, bear's paw slippers—a long-ago gift from Emma, who'd called them "Sasquatch Feet." She didn't think of looking in a mirror. Wouldn't dare! Didn't want to think about how she looked. Didn't want to think about anything, but couldn't stop herself. What was she going to tell her policeman the next day? *Her* policeman? . . . she didn't even know his name! Well . . . she did know it, except for the life of her she couldn't remember it, and worse, couldn't remember where she'd put the card it was written on.

*So you go in and ask for the constable with the sympathetic, green-going-on-hazel eyes. About thirty. Sandy hair that's thinner than he is. Surely there can't be that many cops in the place matching that description.*

It wouldn't be that simple, she knew. Simply couldn't be that simple, not the way everything was spinning into the realm of the impossible, the unbelievable. What had Kendall said? *Once is chance, twice is coincidence, and three times is conspiracy.* By that standard, things had passed conspiracy in the last curve and moved into the straight toward outright chaos.

Which brought to mind the other thing that had niggled her all night, disrupting her attempts to sleep with the intensity of a single mosquito that had survived the bug spray, slipped under the net, and was now intent on inflicting all possible torment before biting. That damned jigsaw piece.

*Somebody took it. I saw that. I know I saw it. But it could have been Kendall himself. Or at least I suppose it could, although I can't imagine why. And if not him, then who? Or should that be whom? Oh, damn, damn, damn . . . now he's got me thinking about grammar!*

It was, she thought, adding insult to injury. She didn't want to think about Teague Kendall at all, but he had somehow stepped into her world, and now he was moving through it with all the grace of the proverbial bull in the china shop.

*Go away! I don't want you. I don't need you. You're too glib, too charming, and definitely too damned handsome. And cunning and devious; I'd almost bet you took that piece yourself.* Except . . . she wasn't sure at all. Nor was she entirely certain why such an inconsequential act should bother her so much, except that it signified a level of underhanded sneakiness and cruelty—yes, that was the word that fit best—cruelty! Anyone who would do a thing like that had to be cruel . . . it was simple as that.

*Bitter and twisted. Oh, damn that Kendall . . . now he's got me thinking like a character in one of his novels. No . . . no . . . no. You stay out of my world, boyo, and I'll have the decency to stay out of yours.*

The clarity of that thought got her off the stool, out of the workshop and into the shower, then got swished away by the shampoo. Soured by the lyrics she couldn't "not" hear.

*Gonna wash that man right outa my hair . . . Oh, damn it . . . damn it . . . damn it!*

By the time she was dry, Kirsten knew she would have to tell Kendall about the missing jigsaw piece. She simply couldn't "not," no matter how much she told herself it would be far, far safer . . . far, far more logical . . . to just let the whole thing go. What difference could it make, anyway? The piece was gone, now, and unless Kendall himself had taken it—*why do I keep thinking that?*—it was probably gone forever. He would eventually finish his book, eventually finish the puzzle. Then he'd know without her having to tell him, without her having to move into that ever-so-interesting, tantalizing, dangerous aura.

*Stunningly beautiful! You're getting worse than Pauline, mooning over her damned doctor. Who is very nearly as handsome and charming and . . . dangerous, maybe . . . as Teague Kendall. I guess . . .*

Now thoroughly annoyed with herself, Kirsten pulled a brush through her hair, dressed quickly in the first thing that came to hand—Thursday's jeans, sweatshirt right out of the dirty laundry hamper—tugged on her sneakers, and rushed out of the house, tugging her hair through the back-band of a baseball cap as she went.

She returned an hour later, hair wetter than when she'd left and her body singing with the exercise of deliberately seeking hills to climb on her bike, which had been neglected lately and must, she thought, be grateful for the use. Her mind, unfortunately, was still as jumbled as when she started . . . locked in a will I won't I tug-o'-war about Kendall's damned puzzle. Head down into the home stretch, she was halfway into her driveway before she noticed the parcel sitting on the front stoop. A big box, long and vaguely familiar. The sort of box flowers get delivered in.

*On a Sunday?* That was Kirsten's first thought as she halted, balancing on the ball of one foot, and just stared at the parcel. The second thought was that it must be a mistake, especially if it really was flowers. The third was that it had been so long since anybody had sent her flowers, she probably wouldn't recognize the container anyway. Putting the bike away, she walked back round the house, collected the parcel, and somehow managed to refrain from examining it too closely, just enough to be sure it really was addressed to her, until she'd let herself into the house. Then she opened it and thought—not too seriously—that she might faint with surprise.

*Swooned. Kendall would surely say "swooned." And he must be selling tons of books if he can afford a bouquet like this!* Even to her unpracticed eye, it was a display that registered colors in dollar signs. Kirsten was suitably impressed. She moved through to the kitchen, laid the box on the table, and tentatively reached for the card envelope inside. An embossed envelope. "Thank You," it said in rich, flowing script. She sat down to open it and a moment later was glad she had, because now the risk of swooning was real!

> My dear Kirsten. This is just to thank you for stepping in at the last minute to make up our party last night. And—of course—for adding so much to the entertainment with your wondrous tale.
>
> Ralph Stafford

Kirsten sat there, stupefied, staring at the words, comprehending but not understanding, so confused she could only vaguely be aware of the tiny disappointment the flowers hadn't come from Teague Kendall. Then she giggled.

*Awful neat handwriting for a doctor. I thought they were supposed to write in incomprehensible hieroglyphics. All this for shooting off my big mouth? Jeez . . . I'm ashamed to wonder what Pauline got.* But she did wonder, and was suitably ashamed, especially when her giggling subsided and she began to wonder if her friend had received anything at all. Maybe Pauline was, in the good doctor's eyes, merely an employee? Or worse, a hired convenience . . . a thought she immediately dismissed as unfair and insulting to Pauline. But . . .

That issue was solved when the telephone rang and she picked up to hear her friend's voice fairly screaming with excitement and delight about the flowers and card which had just arrived for her, too. Kirsten felt herself relax as she listened to Pauline rattle on a mile-a-minute, sharing—as only Pauline could—the bubbling emotions which made her . . . Pauline. Kirsten listened, inserted appreciative oohs and aahs in appropriate places, and didn't mention her own bouquet and note.

Even Pauline, thankfully, couldn't go on forever. Eventually her friend's exuberance ran down and she turned to somewhat more serious issues. It couldn't be avoided; Kirsten didn't even try.

"Listen . . . about last night, Kirsten . . . Are you sure you're all right? You went all . . . strange, there toward the end."

"I'm fine, really. It's just that it's been . . . sort of emotional for me. I'm worried about Emma, of course, but she is just so damned unpredictable that I've kept thinking I'm worrying for nothing. But finding that ring . . ."

"Well you're going to the police about that tomorrow, aren't you?"

*If I can ever find that nice cop's damned business card!*

"I was going to, but . . . I'm just not sure, Pauline. I mean . . . what can I expect them to do, send an expedition into a cave to look for evidence?"

"Well I'd certainly hope so!"

"Give me one good reason."

"Well because . . . because . . ." Pauline, for once, stumped for words. But not for long. "Because that's what they're there for . . . that's why. To investigate mysteries, to look for missing people. You have to tell them that. And if I was you, Kirsten, I'd try and con Teague Kendall into going with you when you talk to them. He's a big name . . . they might just listen a bit better to him, if you don't mind me saying so."

"Take . . . Kendall? Did you start drinking as soon as you got home? Did you even go home after you dropped me . . . or shouldn't I be asking that?"

"Well of course take Kendall. I mean . . . look at all these coincidences and stuff. It's just . . . weird, but he did say that . . . whatever he said . . . about coincidence and conspiracies and all that."

"Once is chance, twice is coincidence, and three times is conspiracy. That's what he said, and I seriously doubt it's a saying he coined himself. Probably got it out of somebody else's book, for goodness' sake. Really, Pauline . . . we're not talking about some international conspiracy, here. We're talking about Emma being . . . well . . . missing, or whatever the hell she is. And a ring that turned up where it shouldn't have been. Or at least not for any reason I can think of."

"All of which sounds like the plot for a mystery, and isn't that what Teague Kendall is famous for, after all?" Pauline was unperturbed by Kirsten's logic. She launched into a convoluted logic of her own, one so intricately zany that Kirsten didn't even bother to try and follow it. So she listened. And listened. And finally, in desperation, resorted to a lie.

"I have to go," she finally interrupted. "Somebody's at the door."

Kirsten hung up the phone and just sat there, head in her hands, exhausted as she so often was after a conversation with Pauline. But it only lasted an instant before her doorbell did, indeed, ring.

*Am I getting psychic? Or is this going to be God's revenge for that lie?*

Thoughts that seemed appropriate enough when she opened the door and found herself face-to-face with Teague Kendall.

# NINETEEN

Kendall saw the flowers. He didn't say anything, but Kirsten noticed his flicker of observation as they entered her kitchen, and was glad, without knowing exactly why, that she'd already put the card away in the kitchen table's drawer.

She was less glad about him arriving unexpectedly. Less pleased, still, that he'd caught her disheveled from her bike ride and mentally off-balance because of the flowers from Pauline's doctor. The fact that Teague Kendall, even dressed casually in a flannel shirt and jeans, still somehow managed to look like an ad for men's outdoor wear didn't help.

"I should have called first. I know that and I apologize," he'd said when she answered the door . . . and seemed to mean it. "Actually, apologizing seems to be the name of the game, today, because that's the entire purpose of my being here." This, once they were in the kitchen, where his gaze wandered, seeming to survey and catalogue the room while at the same time "not" noticing her personal disarray.

"What do you have to apologize for? Certainly not your cooking . . . that's a fact. Speaking of which, do you want coffee? I was just about to have some."

*Coffee, tea, or me? Well, not looking like this, I expect.*

She couldn't help it. The thought sprang into her head

without warning, and curled her lips into a smile. Kirsten ducked her head, hoping to hide the smile, but it was too late. Kendall raised a questioning eyebrow, and she had to stammer out the first excuse that came to mind.

"Instant. That's all I have . . . what I usually drink. Oh, hell . . . what I always drink," she said. "Except for times like last night. You serve good coffee, too, by the way."

"Instant is fine. Black, please." Kendall—damn him for being so observant—had already figured out where she usually sat at her kitchen table, and without being asked, he crossed to the opposite side and sat down. "And if it's any consolation, I usually drink instant myself, except on occasions like . . . last night."

Whereupon he flashed that killer grin before adding, "And while you're boiling the jug, maybe you could explain why I'm making you so nervous. Have I come at a bad time? Boyfriend asleep in the back room or something?" The question was casual, obviously intended to sound as if he were joking. Maybe. She was seeking the words for a suitable reply, but got no chance.

"After last night, I'm not surprised if I make you nervous. That's what I came to apologize for, actually. Honest. I didn't mean to put you on the spot like that. It's just that . . . well . . . you were there, and it was on my own mind, and it fit so well with my usual dinner party repartee, and . . . well . . . it just popped out. I mean . . . I was going to ask you about it anyway—but at a more . . . appropriate time."

Kirsten was astonished. It was the least suave, least Teague Kendall–style, most out-of-character statement she'd ever heard. She peered closely, half expecting him to blush. Then she giggled. And he scowled.

"What's so funny?"

"You. Teague Kendall . . . at a loss for words?"

"I am never at a loss for words. Never." And she could see the scowl fighting against being transformed into that damned killer smile. "Sometimes I wix my murds," he said—the smile winning—"but I always, always find them."

"Just as well, I suppose," she replied, fighting to keep her own smile under control.

*Pauline was right. You are just the niftiest thing since white sliced bread. Or was it the coolest? Either or both, and silky smooth as that damned seductive voice, too. So what's the kicker line, here? You obviously want something, and unless it's my body, you just might get it, too. And maybe even . . . NO!*

"Now that we've got that sorted out, are you going to accept my apology, or not? And your jug's boiled, by the way."

"I'll . . . think on it over coffee. Can't think proper when in caffeine deprivation." She rose and turned her back on him while she prepared the cups. "You did say black?"

"I did, but I'll change my mind and have milk and two sugars if it's okay. In fact maybe three sugars would be better. I think I might need the energy."

That remark surprised her, but Kirsten managed not to show it. She busied herself preparing the coffees, and held her tongue until she'd put them on the table and sat herself down. Kendall's verbal incoherence had eased all her embarrassment at having been caught looking far less than her best, and she was actually beginning to feel quite comfortable in his presence. Besides, this was her house, and he was the one apologizing. She sipped at her coffee, winced, blew on it, put it down, picked it up, blew on it again, finally dared a second sip. Kendall watched her performance, didn't even try to test the temperature of his coffee.

Nor did he say anything. Just . . . looked. It was vaguely disconcerting to see the intensity in his stare, and all of a sudden she began to feel all disheveled again. Kirsten looked away, down into her coffee, but when she lifted her gaze again it seemed he hadn't moved a muscle.

She tipped her head, then tipped it the other way, and suddenly realized he wasn't staring at her, but off into space, into some netherworld that only he could see.

"Hey!" She waved her hand, watched the slow return to the here-and-now. Wondered where he'd been. And why? Didn't ask, nor did he volunteer the answer. "Do you always ask your dinner guests to help provide you with stories?"

She asked the question as much to see if he was really there, really listening, than because she wanted to know the answer, although . . .

"Usually. I'm a story-teller, after all . . . and that's where storytellers get the stories they tell—from other people." Then he grinned, and she saw again that boyish exuberance she'd noticed the evening before. "You'd be amazed what people will tell you after they've had a jar or two and you've filled their bellies with good tucker. I have to be a bit careful, though, if last night's to be any sort of example. I really didn't think before I led you into it all, and with hindsight, it was incredibly insensitive."

Now it was Kirsten's turn to smile. "I really can't imagine you as a sensitive New-Age guy," she said. "But I'll be honest and admit that judgment comes without even having read one of your books, which I understand are extremely . . . violent."

Kendall nodded, his eyes alive with laughter. "And extremely well-written. Don't forget that part," he said. Then, more seriously, "Certainly not in the category mystery fans call 'cozy,' that's a fact, but they're not as bloody and violent as you might suspect from the covers . . . over which I have little control. Sometimes extremely dark and brooding, I guess, which accounts for my usual sunny disposition—I write away my angst and demons and violent urges, which is a passably safe way of dealing with them."

Violent? Just the thought sent an inner shiver, and sensitive New-Age guy or not, Kendall saw it, and Kirsten saw him see it, saw the flicker of concern that flashed across his eyes. She waited, expecting some comment, but had to speak herself when it became clear he wasn't about to.

"If I want violence, I only have to turn on the television news," she said. "I . . ."

". . . don't need to sit down and deliberately read about it," he finished for her. "Nor should you, if it isn't to your taste. So what do you read? And don't tell me you don't, because I wouldn't believe you. I saw the way you looked at my bookshelves."

"What you saw there was pure, naked envy. And before you ask . . . no! You cannot see my bookshelves. Not because of what's on them, but because they're . . . you're! . . . so damned well organized! And I've always wanted to be, but I'm not and never will be, I guess. And because . . . well . . ."

"Because I'd learn too much about you just by looking at them?" And he laughed. "No prize for that guess, dear lady . . . it was written all over your face." And laughed again, but it was the sort of laughter she could share, and which drew her into sharing it. Gentle, comfortable . . . seductive. Kendall returned his attention to the now-cooled coffee, draining it in a single draught. Then came the surprise, the trap, and Kirsten walked into it blindfolded, despite the fact she ought to have known better.

"Tell you what. I will bet you that I can sit right here and name three authors with a place on your bookshelves. I'll even trust you to play fair, if you're that self-conscious about not letting me see for myself. Are you game for that?"

"Not without knowing the stakes. What do I get if I win,

and what does it cost me if I lose?" She spoke bravely enough, but inside there was a frisson of caution she couldn't deny. Teague Kendall was a dangerous man . . . far too confident for her liking, far too . . . charming, damn it!

"If I'm wrong . . . let's see . . . do you like theatre?" When Kirsten nodded, he went on. "OK, I'll take you to see this new play, called *Stumped*, that's coming next month. It's by a guy down in Sidney, an author, in fact, whom I know quite well. And just to sweeten the pot, I'll throw in dinner beforehand and coffee or a drink afterwards. How about it? Can't lose either way, I'd say. Oh, and this time I promise you won't have to sing for your supper."

*This isn't a real bet . . . he's hustling me for a date.* The thought was so surprising, so unusually provocative, that she almost fell for it. Almost, indeed forgot the rest of the agreement. Almost . . .

Kirsten allowed herself a hidden smile, then shook her head and tried her best to look skeptical. "But if I lose?"

Kendall had the grace to look at least a teensy bit sheepish. Then he shrugged. "I was hoping to persuade you to let me come with you when you take this ring problem back to Dick Mooney."

*Mooney? The cop, of course! How could I forget a name like that?*

She found herself staring across the table as if Kendall was some sort of mind-reading alien. He, for his part, met her stare with an expression bland almost to the point of smugness. It was infuriating . . . and confusing.

"How . . . how do you know his name?"

Now it was Kendall's turn to look confused. "It was him I talked to right after you tried to brain me with the door. I told you that last night. Told everybody. Of course he wouldn't tell me who you were, nor should he have, but he did tell me enough for me to put it all together when I saw you again. Are you all right?"

*Stupid, stupid woman. Of course he told you last night. God! A man looks at you . . . that way . . . and you just fall apart. Idiot!*

"I am fine. Except I do not like coincidences and I do not like sucker bets." Anger was riding roughshod over her confusion, now. Somehow, she was being set up. The problem was . . . she couldn't imagine how. "Why would you want to come with me? What's in it for you? Because I don't mind admitting I can't see anything in it for me! Or do you think I need my hand held, or something?"

"Perish the thought. Not that I'd mind, you understand."

*Don't you dare patronize me, you . . . snake-oil salesman.*

"What's in it for me is obvious. I'm planning a book on circumstances that are . . . pretty damned similar. Knowing first-hand how the police react to your situation, actually being there, hearing the words, seeing the attitudes, is an obvious benefit. And . . . well, hell . . . I'm going to be asking him all about it anyway, so I might as well be there from the get-go."

Kendall took a deep breath. Held it while he looked at her ceiling. Held it a very long time, it seemed to Kirsten. She fought the temptation to look up, to try and see what he was looking at. A stain on the ceiling? Spider webs? He exhaled before she had to succumb.

"As for what's in it for you . . . not much, I guess. Just . . . somebody to be there for you, somebody to lean on if you need it. I don't know." He shook his head. "You don't need me there, obviously don't want me there, so let's just forget I asked, okay? It was just . . . an idea, that's all. Call it a good intention, which I know . . . the road to hell is paved with them." He was rising to his feet, obviously ready to give up and go home, when she stopped him with a gesture.

"So you did want to come and hold my hand?"

"No, damn it. I did not! It's just that . . . well . . . I've dealt with police a lot, over the years. I know how intimidating they can be. I know the way they go round and round the mulberry bush with their questioning. It's annoying, it's frustrating and . . . Damn it, woman . . . you know how upset you got the last time! So . . . okay, let's say I did want to go along for moral support, to hold your hand, if that's the words you want to use. My words aren't making any sort of sense, here, so let's use yours. I've told you what would be in it for me. What's in it for you is the only thing I have to give . . . somebody to just . . . be there for you! What's so bloody wrong with that?"

*Nothing. Nothing at all and you know it, Kirsten, you silly twit. Except . . .*

She could see Kendall's anger, feel his frustration almost like a heat wave across the table between them. What she didn't feel was any sense it was actually directed at her. He was angry with himself, maybe for not using the right words, maybe for having approached such a sensitive subject so lightly. He wasn't even being manipulative. She knew that without bothering to question how she knew.

Ed would have banged on the table with his fist, or the coffee cup, or—more likely—a beer bottle. Gone all red in the face, towered over her like some sort of ogre. Would have tried to intimidate her with his anger, would have called her insensitive, stupid, and worse for putting him into such a situation. Would have dumped on her the moment he heard she'd been to the police in the first place, adding to the shit heap every chance he got until she finally, in desperation to just end it, would have given in, hoping he'd forgive, knowing he wouldn't forget. Ed would no more have uttered the term "be there for you" than fly to the moon . . . unless it would be another step on another power trip. And having got this far, he would have demanded she accept the bet, knowing he would win, knowing . . .

"You know, don't you?"

Teague met her accusation calmly, but seemed unsure what it was about.

"Know what? About the ring mystery? Only what you've told me. How could I possibly . . ."

"The books, damn it! And don't you dare try to lie to me."

"I wouldn't think of it."

"In a pig's eye you wouldn't. Come on . . . which three authors? As if I couldn't guess all by myself . . . and no, I'm not about to try."

"Okay. Denise Dietz, Lou Allin, and Victoria Gordon." All she needed to hear to realize Pauline had been the tattletale.

*I will kill you, Pauline Corrigan. With my own two hands, I will strangle you! No . . . better . . . I'll go to your damned doctor and tell lies about you. Or your weight-watchers' group and tell the truth!*

For an instant, Kirsten actually believed the expression about seeing red. Could almost see how a person could be reduced to violence just through sheer frustration! And friends like Pauline, who'd no more think before she spoke than . . . than . . .

"You have my permission to put Pauline in your next book . . . as a victim. As the bloodiest, most tortured, most suffering victim in fictional history. It was her, wasn't it? Well of course it was . . . she's bought me books by all those authors, and . . . and . . ."

"And knowing they were gifts from a friend, I knew they'd still be there on your bookshelf, however much in disarray. But please, Kirsten . . . don't go cranky on Pauline. All she did was answer me when I asked her what you like to read."

"I'll give you cranky . . ." She was on her feet, now, fighting for control. Not knowing if she wanted to cry or throw up or throw something, already reaching for the electric kettle in case the decision went that way. Then stopped. She had never thrown anything at anyone in her entire life. Not even as a child. Not even at Emma, who all too often deserved it, assuming anyone ever did. Not even at Ed!

She stood there, then, visibly trembling and not caring who could see her. Knowing Teague Kendall could see it, knowing somehow that he wanted to get up and provide comfort, to somehow make it all go away . . . but was afraid to startle her, to somehow make things worse.

*How could you know that, you idiot? The man's as cunning as a shithouse rat!*

But she did know, just as she knew it when the epiphany came . . . that stray, errant thought which solved everything. Like a miracle. It stopped the trembling, let Kirsten square her shoulders, take a deep, powerful breath, then turn to face Kendall. Indeed, to march over, take him by the hand, almost lift him to his feet.

"I'll deal with Pauline my own way, and in my own time. But you," she said, "are coming with me. Now."

There ought to have been sparks, then, just as their hands touched, their eyes met in some mute understanding. *In any proper romance novel, there would have been, anyway.*

But at this moment Kirsten didn't feel any sparks, and she didn't know—or care very much, either—whether Teague Kendall felt sparks or not as she led him, meek as a lamb, to her bedroom.

# TWENTY

The look on his face was reward enough all by itself.

He showed total, utter confusion when she pulled him into the room, looked even more confused when she pointed at the rumpled, unmade bed . . . *Mom's probably spinning in her grave!* . . . and firmly demanded, "See!"

But he kept his cool. She had to give him that much.

"I see a bed. With a book on it." A flat, simple, statement of the obvious. Then he began to look intently around the room as if expecting to see . . . what? A naked man leap out of the closet? Singing, perhaps? Dangly bits bouncing in tune? She wanted to laugh, had to force herself to keep sounding stern, in control. Which she was!

"Right! You agree, then. That is a bed? With a book on it? And over there . . ." pointing with what she hoped was a suitably haughty, imperious gesture . . . "What is that?"

"A bookcase?" Making a question out of what should have been a statement. Good . . . she was winning, here. And Teague Kendall, cunning, devious, trickster that he might be, was losing. Would lose!

"Book . . . shelves! Right! So you admit that?" Pointing again, her finger directing his vision from one to the other. "This is a bed . . . it is not a bookshelf? That . . . is a bookshelf. Admit it!"

"Okay . . . I admit it. Now what? Are you going to magically levitate the book from the bed to the bookcase? Sorry . . . bookshelf. I mean, I know there's a trick in all of this, but . . ."

"Please do not interrupt. Just admit, once and for all, that the bed is a bed and the book is on the bed and NOT on the bookshelf. Go on . . . do it, dammit!"

"Fine. I admit it. Do you want me to swear it on the Bible—which is on the damned bookcase . . . bookshelf . . . whatever the hell it is? Now what, pray tell, is the point?"

"I am getting to the point," she replied, stifling the glee, choking down the burble of laughter that threatened to escape and ruin her entire performance. "Now, if you'd be so kind, please pick up the book."

He did. Stood there, holding it as if it might bite him. Looked at the book, looked at her . . .

"And please, note the title of the book—*Blackflies Are Murder*—and also note the author—Lou Allin. You can ignore the fact that it was nominated for an Arthur Ellis award."

Kendall shook his head, then did what he'd been told. Looked at Kirsten, looked back at the book. Scowled. Shook his head again. Then Kirsten saw his lips begin to twist from scowl to just the tiniest hint of a smile, saw the smile race through infancy on its way to become a gusting hoot of undisguised adult laughter.

"You are one . . . weird . . . woman," he said when he'd managed to control the laughter sufficiently that he could speak. "If I were a cannibal, I'd chop you up for dinner, just to ingest your memory capabilities. Unbelievable!"

Then, somewhat to her surprise, he bent to replace the book on the bed, carefully, almost tenderly, assuring it ended up in exactly the position he'd taken it from. There was something . . . just . . . nice, about that gesture.

"And of course it's the only book in the entire house by Lou Allin, and of course I have already admitted it wasn't ON your bookshelf, and I had to name three books that were ON the bookshelf, so okay, lady . . . YOU WIN!"

Then she had to follow as he stumbled from the room, wiping at the tears of laughter that blurred his vision and mumbling, "Semantics . . . bloody semantics. I will never, ever live this down. A world-famous author done in by semantics! And by a woman who doesn't even bother to organize her bookshelves. Probably couldn't organize them!"

Down the hall, he plunged, through the kitchen, laughing so hard he could hardly walk, but somehow finding his way back along the route by which he'd entered. When he reached the front door, reached out to fumble for the knob, Kirsten suddenly feared he was just going to leave without . . .

*Without what? Without giving you a chance to gloat some more? Without giving you the chance to really rub his nose in it? Is that what you want? Is that what you really want?*

She could have saved her concerns. Kendall opened the door, even stepped out onto the front stoop, but there he halted, blocking her own exit. With his back to her, Kirsten couldn't figure out what he was thinking, what he planned to do. When he turned abruptly to face her, her eyes saw Teague Kendall, his entire face alight with good humor. But her mind saw Ed, and she recoiled instinctively.

Kendall's face altered, though the smile remained. And quick as she'd been to respond to habit so thoroughly instilled by her former husband, Teague Kendall was equally quick. He stepped back, hands held low and open . . . placatory, appeasing, totally non-threatening. Stepped back so far he lost his balance, back-pedaled down the steps, fell flat on his back with an almighty thud, arms windmilling uselessly as his head mashed a thick clump of path-side flowers.

Then he lay there. Unmoving. Unconscious? His eyes were closed. Dead, for all she knew! Kirsten flew down the steps to kneel beside him, exchanging one form of panic with another as she fought for control, tried to think just what she should do. *Check his pulse . . . see if he's breathing . . . phone 911 . . . lift up his head . . . no, don't do that . . . he might have neck injuries, head injuries, might have broken his back, might . . .* She was leaning down, her eyes inches from his own closed eyelids, her fingers fluttering at his collar, his shirt buttons, when his voice rumbled in her ear.

"Don't you dare touch me." And those amazing blue eyes opened, capturing her gaze even as one hand whipped out to lock around her wrist, immobilizing her. Kirsten could feel the warmth of his breath, was suddenly aware of the faint, but unmistakable tobacco flavor there, mixed with coffee and not—for some reason—at all objectionable. She couldn't move, couldn't even think effectively, so she just stayed still. Very still, for a very long time. Hours, it seemed, during which she saw expressions whirl through his eyes like cloud formations, or swirling, ever-changing seascapes.

"And don't try to kiss me, either." The words startled her; his gesture of pushing her away while he tried to regain his own footing in the same motion would have been ridiculous, had there been any humor left in all of this. Kirsten nearly fell backward, was only saved when Kendall grabbed her hand again to steady her. "My mother warned me there'd be days like this," he said gruffly, tugging until she was erect and they stood, face-to-face.

"I'm . . . sorry," she said. "Really I am."

"You're a menace . . . that's what you are." But his gruffness was clearly feigned, as proved by his next words. "Are you all right?" The concern was legitimate, genuine. Kirsten chose to ignore the meaning of his question.

"Why wouldn't I be? You're the one who fell. I'm . . . sorry." Repeating herself wouldn't improve anything, but she didn't know what else to say. Except what she didn't want to say, would not say.

Teague Kendall let go her hand, stepped back—cautiously—along the sidewalk, wincing slightly as he moved. And limping a bit, too; he must have twisted his ankle in the fall, she thought. Still holding her gaze, he brushed absently at the rear of his jeans, the back of his head, flower petals going everywhere. Then he twisted his shoulders . . . back and forth, from side to side. He looked to be in pain, but there was a different sort of pain in his voice when he finally spoke.

"Guess we're not going there, eh? Fair enough; we each fight our own demons in our own way. I'll be in touch when I know more about that play."

He turned away, was five uneven paces down the sidewalk, five steps further away from her attempts to apologize, to somehow . . . make it right, before Kirsten managed to speak.

"Wait!"

Kendall paused, and she could see from his body language that at first he wasn't even going to look around, but he changed his mind, turned back to face her. Silently . . . not looking as much angry as just cautious. Kirsten sought frantically for the right words, finally settled for the easiest.

"What about tomorrow?"

Kendall raised one dark eyebrow, his lip twisting in the beginning of a sneer. "What about it? You won the bet, remember?"

"I'd like to have you . . . with me."

"What for? You don't need anybody to hold your hand.

Dangerous even to try. Although that poor copper might welcome some help if you happen to get riled."

*Riled? I don't believe I heard that! Riled? In this day and age?*

"Where do you get words like that? Do you eat dictionaries? I'm not surprised you lose bets because of semantics. And I wasn't 'riled' . . . I was . . ."

"Terrified. Don't bother trying to deny it and I already know you're not about to explain it, either, so let's just drop that bit, okay? Right . . . you want me to be there, I'll be there. Nine o'clock? Fine? Now I'm off home to lick my wounds, have a drink and probably the second of the two cigarettes I allow myself each day. I was supposed to wait until after dinner for that, but today I think I'll make an exception."

He turned away again, marched to the curb with all the dignity a limping man can muster, then paused and looked back at her. "Nine o'clock. Don't be late." He was already getting into his gleaming white sports utility vehicle before Kirsten could attempt to think of a reply.

# TWENTY-ONE

Kirsten could still hear those words the next morning as she stood in front of the police station, impatiently waiting, not at all soothed by memory of her victory the day before.

*And now he's late,* she thought. *No, I'm early . . . he's still not late for another . . . five minutes. But what if he is late? Do I start without him?*

Kirsten dredged in her purse for the slip of paper on which she'd written the name—Constable Dick Mooney. It was the first thing she'd done after watching Kendall drive away . . . write down the policeman's name before she forgot it again!

Also in her purse was written down every detail she could think of that might now be necessary. Emma's address—which she had found after a three-hour marathon of searching the evening before. That exercise had led her into the long overdue task of cleaning up and rearranging her office. It had taken half the night. Emma's email address, the picture, her phone number, her agent's name and phone number. But no names of any friends, co-workers, neighbors.

*Did Emma even have any friends? Well of course she did. She must have!*

Firm, brave thought . . . but Kirsten wasn't entirely sure she actually believed it. Emma was . . . difficult. Always had been. It was that actress mentality, Kirsten thought, her sister's total, unarguable conviction that the world revolved around her, so that no matter what the circumstances, she saw them only as they affected her, only as they related to her.

*Self-centered . . . thy name is Emma!*

And it was true. Emma could portray any emotion . . . weep at will, switch from anger to tears to stubbornness to sorrow at the drop of the proverbial hat, but Kirsten had become increasingly unsure as they grew older if Emma really felt the emotions, or merely displayed them as a superficial façade.

Kirsten's own flaw—one of many, she was certain—was too great an ability to see things from everyone else's point of view . . . often at the expense of holding to her own. She was a born pacifier . . . had been a natural victim for a control freak like Ed. His death had freed her from being controlled, and their brief marriage had made her determined never, ever, again to put herself at risk of being controlled!

*Which is why I'm standing here waiting for Teague Kendall? Who's late. No, not late yet. But if it wasn't for him I could probably have this interview over and done with.*

Kirsten shook her head ruefully. How typical, to try and blame Kendall for being late because she was early. Because she didn't look forward at all to another interview with a policeman who probably thought she was crazy in the first place. And no points for trying to figure why she'd dressed for the occasion, this time, even applied discreet makeup, worn stockings, high heels. The nail polish was left over from the dinner party, so it didn't count. Her only concession to normalcy was to maintain her usual ponytail.

It wasn't the ponytail that Kendall looked at when he came round the corner. He was limping ever so slightly, which Kirsten couldn't help noticing, but there was nothing wrong with his eyes. Bright, twinkling with . . . amusement? Twinkling with something, anyway, as they first met hers, then his gaze flowed across her like a beam of light, touching her almost tangibly as it ranged from face to bosom, hips to ankles. And back again. By which time—and it seemed to her to take a long time—he was close enough to speak. His voice wasn't injured, either. Still that rich, soft, silken-whisper smoothness.

"All set?" he asked. Kirsten nodded. "And you're still fine with having me there?" She nodded again, then thought she'd better try and speak, lest they get inside and she find herself mute.

"Yes. Please."

Kendall, too, had dressed for the occasion. His dark business suit was no off-the-rack model. It was obviously expensive, tailored. Very classy. His white shirt gleamed almost as brightly as his teeth and highly-polished shoes.

"Well, let's do it, then." All business, now. Polite, charming as usual, but . . . damped down, held in check, cool . . . headed for cold. And the more so when they were escorted into Constable Mooney's office. Kendall held her chair, but seated himself slightly behind her, clearly putting Kirsten in charge.

The policeman sat down behind the desk, and he, too, focused his attention on Kirsten herself, although not—she noticed—before throwing a glance at Kendall that seemed somehow . . . suspicious. Mooney waited, his attention firmly on her now, and Kirsten started searching for words, stumbling over them because her own attention had been jolted, divided, when the two men had shaken hands and she'd noticed Kendall's cufflinks and her mind had snapped back to the dinner party and the jigsaw puzzle incident and her intention to speak to him about it, and . . .

She sighed heavily, took refuge in the exercise of pawing through her handbag for her notes. And was surprised—and pleased—that neither man took the opportunity to rush her, to try and force control. Instead, they both waited quietly, patiently, Mooney looking down at his desk blotter, then up again, then picking up a pen, shifting his notepad closer.

And in twenty minutes that seemed like an hour it was over. Painless, only marginally productive, perhaps, but straightforward enough. Mooney listened with growing interest as Kirsten related her "ring" tale, only glancing at Kendall when Kirsten mentioned having turned up at his dinner party and their joint realization of having encountered each other during her first visit to the police station. Otherwise, his attention stayed solely with her. Kendall said not a word during the entire interview.

Nor did he speak while Kirsten spent time filling out the appropriate forms to list her sister officially as a missing person, while she sifted through and handed over all the information she'd brought with her.

Mooney—this time—seemed impressed. "Good. This will help. I'll get this over to Vancouver, and we'll make a start at that end, try to figure out if she ever got as far as the ferry, if she ever even left for the ferry. It'll take a few days . . . I want you to realize that . . . but I'll get back to you as soon as I know anything."

"What about the ring . . . and the cave?"

Mooney shook his head. "Of itself, the ring isn't evidence of anything but a mystery," he said, throwing a glance toward Kendall as if to suggest mysteries were the writer's business. "And you said yourself the only logical way it could have got into that cave is for somebody to have taken it there. Neither is evidence of . . . foul play, and you cavers didn't find anything else to suggest it, either."

He paused, stared intently at his notes. "But since I expect you'll be going there again to continue your . . . survey, is it? . . . that you take extra care, be perhaps more alert for anything that's out-of-place, that actually might be evidence. In which case . . ."

"In which case there might have to be an investigation, so you'd want us to touch nothing, come straight to you. Yes, I realize that. But . . ." Kirsten took a deep breath, chose her words carefully. ". . . surely you must agree it's too weird, just too strange to simply be a coincidence?"

"I think there's far too much coincidence in all of this," the policeman replied enigmatically, and shot a lightning glance at Teague Kendall, a glance so swift, so fleeting, that Kirsten almost missed it. "But what I need is evidence, so let's go back and start at the beginning, in Vancouver, and see what turns up."

And that was the end of it. Mooney rose, shook hands with both of them, escorted them to the entrance, watched them as they left the building. Teague Kendall remained silent until they were on the sidewalk.

"I'll call you," he said, then, but it was in that tone of voice any woman could recognize, the tone that really said, "But don't hold your breath." His voice, which had been cool earlier, was now cold as the grave. And Kirsten knew why, knew her over-reaction on the front porch had spooked him, her refusal to explain was forcing this sudden distance between them as much as Kendall himself.

She had hoped he would offer coffee, lunch, a walk . . . something! Some opportunity for her to at least try to explain. But she couldn't push the issue. Would not! All she could do was offer her thanks for his time this morning, a thanks he accepted with a silent nod, then just stood there, clearly waiting for her departure.

Kirsten hated the situation, hated herself, hated everything to do with it all, but she was powerless. She endured his silence only a moment before turning away and heading toward her car.

She was nearly there when her eye caught the gleam of Kendall's SUV, parked only a few parking meters further along, and she turned quickly, half-expecting him to be right there behind her. The man was nowhere to be seen, and the vehicle—she realized—could have been one of a thousand . . . ten thousand . . . in that make and model and color. Still, she took her time getting into her own battered vehicle, took more time setting her purse just so, adjusting her seat belt just so, even readjusting the rear-view mirror. No Kendall, no driver for the shiny white machine parked four cars along.

*No sense to this. None at all.*

She was most of the way home before she remembered that she'd forgotten once again to mention the business of the jigsaw puzzle. And that, for reasons she couldn't quite understand, bothered her even more than Teague Kendall's cold politeness.

# TWENTY-TWO

The specialist watched Kirsten as she got into her car near the police station, absently noticed the attention she gave to the white SUV parked several spaces ahead of her. Watched, without seeming to, as she eventually drove away. But his mind was mostly far from Duncan, far from Canada, even. He was visualizing summer in Tasmania—only a month or so away—and toying with the logic of returning there permanently.

Then he shook his head. It was a silly thought, really, and a needless one. It could be done, of course . . . anything could be done, at a price. And certainly he had the money, along with a work situation that allowed him such a choice; no problems on that score. There were, of course, other price factors in the equation, not least the fact he'd be condemning himself to a lifetime as a stranger, a total outsider no matter how seemingly accepted. Splendid as Tasmania might be, it wallowed in that island mentality. If your ancestor didn't come off a convict ship—preferably in chains—you simply couldn't be a proper, fair-dinkum Tasmanian. End of story. Being Canadian by birth added to the problem, of course, but he was more than half convinced that even a Canadian could eventually be recognized as Tasmanian, given the right ancestors.

He would always be a sort of stranger, anyway . . . no matter where he lived. It went with the job, being always on the outside looking in. Listening to people, hearing their sad, bad, mad stories, trying to weave chaos into conformity, normality. He shook his head sadly. It didn't matter. None of it mattered. There was no need even to think along such esoteric lines, not if he was careful. And he was always careful. So careful that he'd even stopped on his way home in the wee hours of dawn just to see for himself that scavengers had properly disposed of the director's innards pile, which they had. Not—of course—with the thoroughness Tassie devils would have shown, but . . . sufficiently.

He had spent most of the night at his aerie, double- and triple-checking every aspect of his usage of the site. He knew that modern forensics were probably unbeatable, but would never be put in place without a serious investigation—and there was no reason for such investigation. Nor would there be, assuming he got together a proper plan for dealing with the delectable Kirsten. Although . . . he would like to somehow see where she'd found that accursed ring, see with his own eyes whether there was other damning evidence there, or the chance of some being found. And time was running out for what he termed the "sister experiment," indeed for any new adventures this Canadian season. With the September 23rd autumn equinox, he must be gone. Perhaps for good? He shook his head, angry at the way this thought kept intruding. There was no need to make the move permanent.

None!

So long as he was careful.

He shrugged aside the thought of any permanent move; this was time to consider Kirsten and his plans for her, not to be worrying about esoteric long-range theorizing.

*A plan . . . that's all I need. A good, solid, workable plan. There is time, and if there isn't . . . then I will make time!*

He could do that . . . and would. He could do anything! And for now, anything meant returning to work. A little bit late was one thing—the reasons were justification enough. But to be much later would be slacking, and slacking was not to be tolerated. It equated with sloppy work.

Through the mercifully short working day, he accomplished a fair amount, by his own standards, and still had time to worry at the Kirsten situation during spare moments. She occupied his attention throughout dinner that evening . . . a conventional dinner of pan-roasted chicken thighs with mashed potatoes, pan gravy, fresh summer vegetables, and the luxury of Okanagan cherries for dessert. Kirsten also occupied his dreams that night, untasted but looking delectable. Indeed, she hovered at the edges of his consciousness for several days in a row, then resolved by herself his problem of somehow uniting her with her sister.

And . . . the mystery of the ring!

# TWENTY-THREE

Kirsten didn't want to ask, and didn't even try to hide the fact he was her last resort.

"I absolutely must go back and look at where I found the ring," she said with no significant preamble, not taking time for conventional telephone manners and not—astonishing even to her—doing her usual thing of running off at the mouth with a litany of triviality.

Teague Kendall was at first astonished, then annoyed, then . . . intrigued. He made no attempt to hide any of his emotions.

"You want me to go with you? Well it can't be to hold your hand, dear lady, because you'd have to be holding mine . . . literally, figuratively, any way there is. I cannot imagine what possible benefit my presence would provide except to reveal claustrophobic tendencies I'm quite happy to admit to without putting them to the test." A small white lie, but it suited his mood.

"Please." Not quite begging, but close. As close as she was prepared to go.

"Why, for goodness' sake?"

"Because I . . . have to. I just . . . do. And there's nobody else can spare the time mid-week to go with me and I can't go alone. It isn't safe and it . . . it isn't done. Although . . ."

"I should bloody well hope it isn't done!"

For just a moment, Kendall felt his confused feelings for this weird woman begin to dominate his thinking. Then he thought about it some more, forced a new hardness into his voice.

"Didn't you say this place was accessible only by four-wheel drive?" He grinned to himself at her silence, then added, "So . . . it isn't just me you want, it's my vehicle. Why am I not surprised? You don't like my books, you persist in smashing hell out of my poor old body, and even *I'm* not that enamored of my mind, some days, so it isn't that, either."

He expected to generate some more typically Kirsten response, but again got only silence. For an instant he was afraid she'd hung up, then was more afraid when he realized just how much that concerned him.

"I suppose you want to go at some ungodly hour of the morning, too," he said, rushing to continue, "because of course I'll have to go with you or I'd waste the day anyway worrying if you'd tried it on your own."

There was a long silence, but he could hear her breathing, could almost visualize her sorting out the words before she opened her mouth.

"I'm ready now," she said.

"Now? It'll be dark in a couple of hours. We'd be lucky just to get there before dark! And besides, I haven't eaten yet."

"It's always dark underground, and I'll buy you dinner on the way."

She said it so logically, so matter-of-factly, he couldn't help reacting. Especially not when his own mind dealt with the logic part.

*It's always dark underground. How bloody profound is that?*

Certainly profound enough to kick-start a chuckle that erupted into a roar of laughter that almost, but not quite, eclipsed her own. Everything got easier after that, and they went through the rest of the arrangements without that earlier tension. Teague didn't even bristle when she told him she couldn't get Sid, but had borrowed his gear for Teague to use. He didn't even—and this surprised him!—suggest she'd been more than a tad sure of herself.

"Sid would have come with me, but he's tied up on a job," she said. "And he's only a bit taller than you, so when I told him I thought I could convince you, he offered his gear. I didn't automatically assume you'd help; I just . . . hoped."

Half an hour later, they were loading what seemed to him an inordinate amount of gear into the back of his SUV. An hour after that, following a quick pub meal, they were headed back into the hills north of Lake Cowichan, with Kendall driving and Kirsten as navigator, a task which took so much of her attention it stifled all but essential conversation. And a task she handled so badly, in her own eyes, that she grew progressively more angry with herself as they traced and retraced their route.

*I've made the trip four times. Four! What on earth was I doing . . . traveling with my eyes shut? He must think I'm an idiot.*

It was no consolation that every time she glanced over at Kendall, he seemed to be deliberately avoiding her gaze. He focused on the road, a necessity at times as they worked their way progressively further into the hills on roads and tracks that demanded his attention and the four-wheel-drive capabilities of his vehicle. Strangely, he showed no concern, no impatience, just went along quietly following her directions, pausing at each intersection, each possible turn, until Kirsten indicated which way he should go. Even when—and if she could see it, surely he could?—they wound up at the same intersection for the third time, Kendall merely slowed to a halt and sat there, silent, while she fussed over the topographical map.

Ed would have been raging by now. Worse than raging. Her mind echoed with memories of her ex-husband's voice deriding her. Soundless echoes of torments endured, survived, but scarring. Once again, she glanced over at the quiet, calm man driving the SUV, found herself making comparisons that were as illogically frightening to her as they were flattering to Kendall. Ed, of course, wouldn't have been here in the first place. Ed had never done anything simply because Kirsten wanted or needed it done . . . unless it could somehow enhance his power over her, his ability to demean and control.

She looked across at Kendall for the tenth or twentieth or perhaps hundredth time, silently willing him to do something . . . anything . . . that would reveal his impatience, his growing frustration. It had to be there; nobody could put up with such incompetent navigation and not get annoyed. Nobody, it seemed, but Teague Kendall, the soul of calm and reason and somehow . . . worrisome because of it. He didn't even reveal himself when they finally reached their destination, except with a weary shake of his head and a typically vague remark.

"Well . . . that was interesting," he said. "We'd best get moving, I guess, or we'll be walking round in the dark trying to find this damn cave." And almost before she could reply, he was shifting the caving gear out of the vehicle.

Kirsten led as they made their way to the cave entrance, and as usual, the going was too rough to allow any sort of communication. Both of them were forced to concentrate on their footing. It wasn't until they'd reached the site and shrugged off the packs that there was much opportunity to discuss anything, and even then, Kendall kept his comments to a minimum as she directed him in the process of getting suited up. When he saw the size of the entry, however . . .

"You're surely not serious." And his eyes said even more, flickering from the small, narrow opening to Kirsten and back again.

"It gets better once you're inside," she replied matter-of-factly.

"Maybe for you. How do I get inside? I'm an author, not a contortionist."

She couldn't help but smile. "You'll be one before this is over. But it does get roomier inside, I promise you. Sid managed all right, and he's taller and wider than you are."

"And younger and fitter, I'd bet."

"No . . . older. But . . . maybe fitter, now that you mention it. He's a tiler, so I guess bending and stretching goes with that sort of work. Are you certain you're all right with this? You did say you'd been in caves before, or was that just to reassure me, or . . ."

". . . or gilding the lily? No, it wasn't. But the caves I visited in Tassie were tourist-type caves. I somehow doubt this one is going to have electric lights and concrete footpaths."

Despite his grousing, he managed to follow her through the small opening, audibly sighed with relief at being able to straighten up once they got down the first passage a bit.

"Stay close, and if you have a problem or need to stop, just reach out and tap me on the shoulder, or whatever part you can reach," she said. "Or shout, if you have to. But really, there shouldn't be any problems . . . it's an easy push, no climbing or nasty crawls." Then she pointed out the ribbon of survey tape on the floor of the passage. "All we have to do, really, is follow this. It couldn't be much easier."

Kendall remained silent, although she could hear his feet moving behind her and the rustle of his jumpsuit, and see the flicker of his headlamp once they'd got past the twilight zone, moving into the Stygian darkness of the inner cave system. She moved swiftly, confidently; she'd made this trip several times, now, knew the route, had the ribbon of tape to follow in any event. They were almost to the well room when she suddenly realized she might be making the push too fast for her companion, and stopped abruptly.

"Sorry," he said as his hands thudded lightly against her shoulders, not sufficient to push her off balance, but certainly enough to tell her he'd been following very, very closely indeed.

"Am I going too fast for you? I'm sorry . . . I sort of forgot . . ."

"That I'm a novice at all this? No need to worry about that, dear lady. I can keep up, and I damned well will keep up, too. I shall stick to you like the proverbial glue, and that's a promise."

There was an unusual tone in Teague's voice, one which Kirsten recognized, remembered from her own first trip into a "wild" cave, where the only light was what you brought with you, the only reality what you could see in that light. The reality now was that they were almost at the well chamber, with that tricky bit of footwork to get down into it, and if he was feeling panicky . . .

And then it was time to find out, because she was on the lip of the perilous descent into the well chamber, and her light revealed it was unchanged from previous visits, with slippery but sound footing once you got down into it, and that dangerous, dominating well in the middle.

"I'm going to send you down first," she told Kendall after tugging him in beside her so he could see what lay below. "I'll steady you going down, and then you can do the same for me. The footing's better than it looks, once you're on the level floor."

She used the strap of her side pack to give him support as he clambered slowly down into the chamber, testing each foothold, each gloved handhold, before letting himself move. He moved well, she thought. Good balance, intelligent choices of what felt right. When he announced himself safe and "as secure as I'm going to get," she warned him first, then turned off her light.

"Are you nuts?"

"I don't want to blind you as I come down," she said, already on the move. She let go the pack strap and slithered downward, trying to keep her footing, but lost her balance just at the bottom and ended up thudding squarely into his outstretched arms. Had he been shorter, they'd have banged safety helmets, but as it was, she only ended up in an impromptu hug, her arms widespread around the bulk of his coverall, her face flat against the front of him.

Where she stayed, for what seemed a very long time indeed. Kendall's arms had automatically closed around her, and even in the hug she could feel him shifting his balance to compensate for her weight against him, steadying them both while trying at the same time not to lose his footing. Then he stilled, and she fancied she could even hear his heart beating against her ear, could perhaps smell the infinitesimal tobacco aura she'd come to associate with him. But he didn't release her. Nor did he say anything until she began to try and wriggle free. Kirsten found it unnerving. All her instincts warmed to the embrace . . . she wanted to be held by this man, and she could feel that he wanted it too, until he spoke.

"I do not like this."

Not panic; she'd have recognized that. This was a blunt

statement of fact, merely an assertion he obviously expected her to heed.

"If you can manage just a bit further," she said, "there's a big, comfy room where we can take a break. We call it the 'coffee shop.' "

"Will it have room to sit down comfortably? I'm taller than you, don't forget, and this stooping is starting to ruin my back, big time. I wouldn't want you having to try and drag me out of here if it gives out entirely."

"You'll be able to move pretty much upright from here on. Until we're on the way out again, at least. Just be glad Sid found an easy way between here and the 'coffee shop' . . . the route I first took meant crawling nose-to-the-ground for about fifty meters."

"Not a pleasant thought, thanks. I am suitably and eternally grateful to Sid," was the gruff reply, and as Kirsten moved free of Kendall's hug, she felt him stretching, could imagine the spasms he was trying to avoid.

"How bad is your back? I'm . . . sorry, but it just didn't occur to me to . . ."

"It was already buggered before that weird woman smashed open the cop-shop door in my face," he replied. "And made infinitely worse by being chucked off her front porch, I might add. But it will survive if I do. And I will. Let's just get going, if you don't mind. The sooner this is all over with, the happier I'm likely to be."

He insisted he didn't need a rest at the "coffee shop," and managed to follow her without problems as she made her way through the remembered maze that led to the small chamber where she'd found the ring. A room, she immediately noticed, where nothing whatsoever had changed. With Kendall right behind her, she slowly and systematically moved her light around the room, inspecting floor, walls, and those parts of the ceiling she could see . . . finding nothing out of the ordinary.

At his request, she showed him exactly what she'd done on the first visit, where she'd stood, what she'd seen. Kendall scrunched down on his heels to stare into the cup formation where the ring had been, then moved his head so his own helmet light moved up the wall, revealing the Romanesque fountain-type formation and the wall above it. Then he straightened and moved the light to try and reveal the ceiling above and behind that wall, only to find that the wall seemed to bend back at the top, disappearing into shadows that neither of their lights could penetrate.

"If we'd brought a ladder, that might be worth a look," he said, "although I can't imagine there'd be much to see except more rock."

"I didn't expect us to find anything," Kirsten replied. "Not . . . really, I guess, although . . . But damn it . . . it makes no sense at all. That's what's so frustrating. The ring had to get here somehow, and all I can think of is that somebody brought it in here and somehow just . . . dropped it. But . . ."

"Probably because they were in a hurry to get out where it was warm," Kendall said. "I would never have believed it could be so cold this far underground, except maybe in winter."

"Winter or summer is pretty much the same. It's really the dampness that's making you feel the cold so much." Kirsten gave the chamber a final look-over, then turned away. "There's no sense suffering any more of this, and we can't do any further exploring . . . it isn't safe with just us two." She had already pussy-footed round the ring chamber, but found no other access, no indication of any.

Each of them took one more turn at shining their light around, but there was nothing to see, nothing to resolve the mystery. "And we can't go wandering further into the system, just on spec," Kirsten said, repeating herself, using the words to reinforce her good sense against the inclination to go further, to explore just a bit more despite the risks. "Bad enough we're here . . . just the two of us. There should be three, by rights."

Kendall didn't bother to reply, merely followed silently as she retraced their steps until they came again to the "coffee shop." But he did exactly as he'd promised, staying close behind her, within touching distance, well within shouting distance. Kirsten was all too aware of him, began to think she could hear him limping, began to worry.

"We'll rest a bit, then do the final push to the outside," she said. And got no argument. She pulled a space blanket from her side pack and spread it on a flat space where their presence could do no damage, and both eased themselves down on the foil surface, legs outstretched but keeping as far apart as the space blanket allowed.

"Might as well save batteries, just in case," she said then, and reached up to turn off her head lamp. Kendall followed suit, and they sat silent in the blackness, absorbed by it, engulfed by it. They could have been two feet apart or twenty or two miles; in the silence of the cave's primeval dark they were each alone with nothing that could be seen, nothing to be heard but their own breathing and heart-beats.

Until both of them began to speak at once.

# TWENTY-FOUR

"We have to talk."

They spoke together, saying the same words at exactly the same instant, and the effect was eerie in the extreme. It was, to Kirsten's ears, as if the cave itself had spoken, as if her impulsive four words had magnified ten times over in some weird subterranean echo that was followed immediately by a return to total, absolute silence in total, absolute darkness. It was startling, but not frightening . . . to her. But she wondered how Kendall might react—she hadn't warned him about just how disorienting the total absence of light might be.

"Are you okay?" she finally asked, keeping her voice soft, half-afraid they would both try to speak at the same time again. Kendall waited until he was absolutely certain she'd finished speaking, and she had this mental picture of two moles using tin-can-and-string telephones and having to say "over" after every speech.

"I'm fine," Kendall replied, then continued almost too quickly, as if afraid of being interrupted. "Do you want to start, or shall I?"

"You go ahead. I know what I want to say but I don't know how to say it, if that makes sense. You're the wordsmith, so I doubt you'll have that problem."

Even speaking softly, the resonance inside the huge, underground space made their words sound strange, their voices disembodied by the total blackness. Kendall's voice, she noticed, still had that silky, velvet texture, but somehow the cave added sibilance, created a sort of hollow, false echo quality. Knowing he was within touching distance, yet sounded so distant, was at first unnerving, then strangely comforting. What he said was even more so. At first . . .

"I don't need fancy words to tell you I'm attracted to you. Or at least I hope not . . . I'm not real sure about anything where you're concerned. But that incident on the porch has me really spooked, because I don't know how to deal with it and I'm not sure I can deal with it at all. Sure as hell I don't understand it. You were terrified, but I couldn't see any reason and I still don't. Not that it matters . . . what matters is just the fact that you *were* terrified." He didn't give her any chance to reply, and Kirsten somehow sensed he didn't want her to . . . not until he was finished.

"We're neither of us children, which means we come at this situation with . . . baggage," he continued. "I'm no angel, never have been, and although I don't claim to know you very well, Kirsten, I doubt if you're an angel either."

Her own name slid out to her from the nothingness of the dark, sounding unusual, sounding strange in Kendall's voice. Was this the first time he'd actually spoken it? She found herself pondering this while listening for his next remark.

"But angel or not, I do know I have never intentionally frightened a woman in my life, or done so unintentionally, either, far as I know. Except you. And I didn't like it. Don't like it. I've been trying to come to terms with it ever since Sunday, and I can't. Now I can't demand an explanation, and I wouldn't even if I could . . . but I sure would like one, because without it I can't see us going anywhere at all except out of here and out of . . . well . . . everything. And I don't want that either . . . I think. What I do know is that I can't go on worrying every time I make a move that I'm going to frighten you. It doesn't work for me, and I can't ever see it doing so. We all have baggage. We all have ghosts and demons and past relationship issues. I can deal with my own ghosts, but I'm not sure I can deal with yours . . . especially not knowing what or why they are."

Followed by that unique, hollow silence of the underground, a silence as deep as the darkness, as all-encompassing. Kirsten could hear her own heartbeat, hear both of their breathing, but she couldn't hear herself speak because she hardly dared to speak, wasn't certain she could.

"Your turn," he prompted after what could have been a minute or an hour. Followed again by the all-encompassing silence as she fought to find the words, find the courage to arrange them, get them out, somehow, into the void between them. Eventually got as far as, "I . . . I don't know where to start."

"Try the beginning. Or the end, if that's easier. Just . . . just start, dammit."

So she did, falteringly at first, then with growing energy, growing confidence, a growing sense of security created in part by being here, in her world as opposed to his, here in the dark, where her voice seemed to come not from herself, but from some other disembodied entity that shared the darkness with them, that knew her, could speak for her. She listened and spoke at the same time, hearing this voice describe her life with Ed . . . the controlling, the domination, the destruction of self, the cocaine, the eventual overdose of cocaine, the accident that freed her and enslaved her at the same time. She went on and on, until eventually, ". . . it wasn't your fault on Sunday. It was just the . . . the suddenness of your movement, something in your stance, I guess. Except it wasn't you I really saw, it was . . ."

"Ghosts . . . bloody ghosts," his silken voice muttered in the black, quavering with a bitterness she could almost taste. "Ah well . . ." Which said everything and nothing, was as much a resignation, a conclusion, as it was a simple verbal sigh. Then he went silent and the black void seemed to expand around them like an echo of itself. Kirsten wanted to reach out and touch him, but didn't . . . couldn't. Instead . . .

"I wanted to talk about something else, too," she ventured, hearing the cautiousness in her own voice, desperate to change the subject, to somehow keep them in communication.

*As if that would change anything! He's right . . . ghosts.* She shivered, and was glad he could not see her do it. And when he didn't reply, she rushed on with it, describing the incident she'd viewed in the puzzle room, describing it in vivid detail and thinking even as she spoke that it was an enigma equal to that involving Emma's ring. Except that she had seen it!

*He's really going to think I'm crazy, now. Seeing things, finding rings that shouldn't be where they are, puzzle pieces being stolen . . . and for what?*

"Well, it'll be a damned long time before we figure out which piece got stolen," he said. "That's a fact. As to why . . . ?" She could almost see him shaking his head, despite the total blackness, the fact she really couldn't see her hand in front of her face. "Almost nothing people do really surprises me anymore," he continued. "I really doubt, though, that there's anything very sinister involved."

Kirsten frowned, shook her head as she thought about it. Then answered. "I didn't say anything about sinister. Not a word."

"Your voice did. Maybe a touch more simple, like *bitter and twisted,* but you said it all right. It was in your voice, and if I could have seen it, I'd bet the farm it was in your face, too." And then again, his enigmatic, all-encompassing, "Ah well . . ." followed by, "sitting here yammering about it won't shed any light on the subject, but speaking of light . . ."

That was all the warning she got before his head lamp ripped open the darkness, spearing into the void of the huge chamber, then wavering unsteadily as he clambered to his feet. "Time we got a move on."

He waited until she turned on her own head lamp, let her take the lead, then followed as he had before. In silence. Helped her negotiate the clamber out of the well chamber, grunted as he heaved himself up and into the passage, aided by the strap of her side pack. In silence. And followed her as they negotiated the rubble-strewn track back to his vehicle, saying nothing the entire way.

Throughout the trip back to Duncan, what little conversation there was stayed with neutral, wholly safe topics. Teague Kendall concentrated on his driving, as well he had to. Kirsten didn't realize until it was done that he didn't once pause for directions, didn't once ask her for any. He turned the SUV around right where it was parked, and drove unerringly through the maze of tracks that eventually brought them to the main road, Lake Cowichan, and—eventually—home. And even then . . .

"Thank your mate for the use of his gear," Kendall said when things had been unloaded, stowed in her garage. Well past midnight, the world almost as quiet as the cave, the two of them shadowy figures in a landscape that was, by contrast, far brighter.

Anything would have been brighter than Kendall's parting remark.

"I'm sorry we didn't . . . find anything," he said. "I know you wanted to, but . . . sometimes that's just the way it goes."

No word, not a single mention, of what he, himself, might have been seeking, also hadn't found. No further mention of his self-confessed inability to deal with her ghosts, her demons. Nor any request or demand that she, herself, deal with them! Just the gleam of his departing tail lights that signified, for Kirsten, a loneliness akin to that of the underground.

She sat in that well of loneliness, huddled on her own front porch until the night sky began to soften, losing its edge of blackness, giving in to the onslaught of day. Kirsten's thoughts were as scattered as the disappearing stars, everywhere and nowhere, unable to help her confusion, let alone ease her troubled mind. She went inside at dawn, drank three too many cups of coffee, then telephoned Pauline.

*This is all her fault anyway. If she hadn't made me go to that stupid dinner party, none of this would have happened.*

Then she chastised herself for such idiotic thinking and thanked the disappearing stars for providing her with such a true and good friend. Venting would probably solve nothing, but it would make her feel better.

# TWENTY-FIVE

"I can get you in to see Dr. Stafford. And I really think you should see him, Kirsten. You're so . . . well . . . I've just never seen you like this. It worries me, really it does. Let me arrange it, please."

Pauline was beginning to sound like a broken record, but she was winning and had the instincts to know it. She had listened before breakfast, then come straight to Kirsten's right after work. She'd been badgering Kirsten for hours, it seemed, having heard chapter and verse about Kirsten's adventures involving Teague Kendall, having offered up her own litany of answers, solutions. Most of them, Kirsten thought, just plain damned foolishness, except . . .

"I'm not sure I'd be comfortable seeing a shrink," she insisted. "And I'd need a referral, which means going to my family doctor first. What am I supposed to tell her—that I'm in . . . lust and making a mess of it?"

"If it was that simple, I wouldn't be worrying about you," her friend replied. "It isn't how you might feel about Kendall that worries me . . . it's this business of you still reacting to that sonofabitch Ed's domination and control. You should be over it . . . really you should. Not letting it mess up a potentially great relationship with a really nice guy."

Pauline prattled on along those lines for an eon or two, then added, “And I wouldn’t be surprised if this business with your sister and that ring aren’t part of it all, too. I mean . . . how are you supposed to react sensibly when totally nonsensical things like that are going on? Please, Kirsten . . . see Dr. Stafford. I can set it up without you having to have a referral, if that’s your worst objection. He really likes you; he’ll bend the rules that far. I know it.”

Kirsten wasn’t sure if she agreed just to shut Pauline up or because she actually believed her friend was making sense for a change, but at four o’clock the following Thursday, she was scrambling to get on something besides stained, crumpled work clothing so she could be on time for the appointment she now half wished didn’t exist.

Pauline’s good doctor—seen professionally—turned out to be surprisingly different from the man who’d recently treated them to dinner, who had so unexpectedly sent flowers in appreciation of their company. In his comfortable if rather Spartan office, Ralph Stafford was so incredibly low-key about it all that Kirsten’s nervousness didn’t stand a chance. He skillfully brought her from self-consciousness to a detailed and frank appraisal of how Ed had treated her and how thoroughly she had apparently been conditioned by his abuse.

She did not, of course, so much as mention Teague Kendall.

But she did, at the doctor’s prompting, go over again her sister’s disappearance and her own feelings about it, because Stafford seemed to think her guilt feelings on that score might be re-opening the feelings of inadequacy so thoroughly imprinted by her brief but volatile marriage. She had no great trouble discussing either situation. Yes, she felt guilty about Emma, but to what extent? “I honestly don’t know. Once I know what happened to her—if anything actually did!—then I'll have to deal with that. But right now . . . there are too many variables. I truly believe Emma always wore the ring, but I haven't seen her in two years. Maybe she sold it, or lost it, or had it stolen. Maybe it has nothing to do with anything."

The good doctor raised an eyebrow, and when he spoke, even that chocolate fudge voice seemed skeptical. "Coincidence? Do you really believe that?"

"What else can I believe? I know the ring was in the cave . . . therefore somebody had to put it there. I know that couldn't have been Emma, because Emma wouldn't set foot in a cave to save her life. So who? No way to find out . . . no way to even guess. It wasn't done as a joke, or at least I have to assume so, since this has all gone well past the joking stage."

The doctor took her round and round, back and forth, guiding her thoughts from the ring and the cave to Ed and her thankfully brief marriage to a man memorable only for being a control freak. A coke-head whose addiction led him to believe himself invulnerable—a belief shattered like his car and head and body when he argued the right-of-way with a moose on the Banff-Jasper highway.

Kirsten had used the insurance money to take jewelry-making and design classes, then to abandon Calgary and—supposedly—her memories, moving to Vancouver Island before Emma's violent marriage had even begun. But of course, she thought, she hadn't abandoned her memories, not even done a credible job of working her way through the problems her brief marriage had caused. All she'd done was bury everything in an emotional compost heap [Stafford's words, which caused her to think maybe he should take up writing, like Kendall] where they slowly rotted without producing anything of future value, and could not, without being properly used.

"What I'd like you to do is write some lists," the doctor told her as their time neared an end. "Write down every instance of your former husband's controlling, mental abuse, everything like that. And then put down your own reactions, because while victims are victims—don't get me wrong on this score—they often contribute to the situation because they can't or don't or won't stand up for themselves, and because they have been manipulated into guilt feelings that are deliberately created by their tormentor to create even more guilt feelings. It is a never-ending cycle. You must understand, Kirsten, that you are not the same person you were then. I watched you at the dinner party, for instance, and you handled yourself brilliantly despite Kendall's attempt to manipulate you."

"But . . . he didn't attempt any such thing," Kirsten insisted. "He left the door open, I admit, but he did it very considerately, I thought. I didn't have to say a word about our encounter, much less anything about the ring, and Emma, and . . ."

Again the raised eyebrow, the hint of skepticism in the wondrously rich voice. "There are many ways to manipulate. Indeed, we all manipulate, quite often without intending to or even being aware of it. You were manipulated . . . trust me!"

And then it was back to Emma, the ring, and the cave, until their session ended. Kirsten drove home with her mind still bouncing from one subject to the other and back again, but with each mental journey her thoughts had to leapfrog over the startling fact that Teague Kendall had possibly been manipulating her right from the start. It was not—given her acknowledged feelings for the man—an auspicious line of thought.

# Twenty-Six

Fred Hollis was in a quandary, not an unusual state of affairs for him, but on this occasion somewhat more worrying. The nagging, ever-present backache did nothing to ease the mental burden, and now his eyes were playing up. Hardly surprising; he'd been hunched in front of his computer screen for nearly twenty-four hours straight, oblivious to everything but the on-screen images he snatched from the web, absorbed, and discarded with unconscious clicks of his mouse.

Like a bloody great human spider, he thought, and chuckled at the analogy. It was truer than it should be, especially since he'd been forced by the back injury and the incidents surrounding it to give up active caving. He'd always been something of a loner; now it was worse. His entire contribution to the caving fraternity had degenerated to surface exploration and what could be done by computer. Here, at least, he was in total control.

The thought of having a police investigation anywhere within miles of "Kirsten's" cave gave him the screaming willies. All his mind could see was squadrons of uniformed cops, backed up by even bigger squads of bulldozers, earthmovers, and the equally destructive media contingent. Probably no chance to maintain the relative secrecy of the cave . . . not if the police got seriously involved. The various caving and environmental groups had managed—through intensive lobbying and a wealth of persuasive argument—to keep great numbers of Vancouver Island caves off the more easily-accessed maps. Most were too dangerous for the inexperienced to explore anyway. Every year or so, BC Cave Rescue got called in response to situations that all too often could have been avoided by a modicum of common sense. Caves can be dangerous places. Caves can kill.

But for Fred, the issue was almost the opposite—people can kill caves. Many on the island had been virtually destroyed by over-logging, poor planning of logging access roads, destruction of the surface that fed and maintained and nourished the cave systems. And—truth be told—because so few people really cared about them.

Fred loved caves. Passionately. And now, unable to venture beyond the twilight zones, unable to ever again see and feel and breathe the unique atmosphere of the underground world, he loved them even more. It was the tormented love of a jilted suitor, and he reveled in it. He missed "real" caving, even missed the excitement and terror and horror that accompanied cave rescue expeditions, journeys into an abyss where all too often the result was a foregone conclusion, the essential equipment including a body bag and the necessary gear to move it through places no body should ever have to travel.

Or so he told himself. And lied, and knew he lied. The truth was he was burnt out, scared, ghost-ridden. His last rescue attempt, the one in which his back was so badly injured, had been that of a friend . . . and a failure. His fault, because his back injury was the result of his carelessness, and his friend's death the result of the delays it caused. His fault.

He shook his head angrily. Stupid to be thinking this. A

waste of time. He was dealing with it, handling it just fine, so long as he didn't venture underground.

So . . . what to do about Kirsten and her cave? His marathon of web-surfing had produced a theory . . . tenuous at best but a theory for all that. Testing that theory without going underground was a different thing entirely. It would involve more walking than he might be capable of; all common sense and logic told him he wasn't fit for what he was considering. True enough, and he knew it, but still . . .

The real problem was whether to take Kirsten with him. It was tempting, but doing so would mean—unless he was extremely careful in his choice of words—explanations he didn't really understand and wasn't even certain he believed.

But he had to know.

A click of the mouse brought up the weather forecasts, and he nodded to see a fine, dry day ahead. There hadn't been much rain in the past week, so vehicle travel was no problem. In the old growth forests, foot travel was never easy at the best of times, but some things had to be endured for the sake of resolving problems.

Fred sat up abruptly, wincing at the spasms of pain the sudden movement caused. Reaching for the telephone added to the pain, waiting for an answer was merely pain of a different sort, and quickly gone.

"How would you like to go walkabout tomorrow . . . early? There are some things about the access to your cave I want to explore, and you might find it interesting to come along."

Kirsten's voice in reply sounded hesitant, but she agreed. He'd known she would.

*Curiosity, thy name is woman! Except . . . what does that make me?*

# TWENTY-SEVEN

There was no sunrise to be seen when Kirsten sat down on her front stoop to await Fred's arrival. It was out there, somewhere, but obscured by a fine, light cloud cover . . . at least here in the valley. She stretched, sipped at her second cup of coffee, wondered if she ought to offer Fred coffee when he arrived. Probably not; he would most likely want to get going, having insisted on this early start.

*Going walkabout at sparrow-fart, he said. No denying his Australian connection. Maybe he should get together with Kendall . . . No! Nonononono . . .*

She was not, she determined, going to exchange one fixation for another. Her session with Dr. Stafford and the resultant lists—*How could I ever have thought such things?*—seemed to have brought her to terms with Ed and his domination tactics. *With me being a classic victim type! But not anymore. Not ever again . . . no how, no way!* Only now that she was free to mentally explore the situation—*possible situation!*—with Teague Kendall, she couldn't get him off her mind.

Even worse, she kept hearing Stafford's chocolate voice repeating that one word, over and over again. *Manipulate . . . manipulate . . . manipulate . . .*

She didn't want to believe Kendall had manipulated her,

but recognized him for a man of exceptional intelligence, obvious cunning. She'd listened to his explanation about letting his dinner guests tell him stories, *about manipulating his dinner guests into telling him stories . . . stop denying it, Kirsten!* But she firmly believed he had given her every chance to refuse, every chance to avoid, every chance . . . period!

And heard the doctor's words chiming like bells . . . *We all manipulate.*

"Well I don't," she muttered aloud, and looked up to see the white SUV round the corner and rumble into her driveway. Fred Hollis eased himself down from the driver's seat and moved round to open her door in an unexpected show of courtesy, but refused coffee as she'd thought he might. He did, however, flash her a Cheshire Cat grin when she hefted a small but well-stocked picnic cooler up beside her in the cab.

Throughout their drive to the cave area, he regaled her with caving stories, telling tales out of school on Les and Jimmy and—surprisingly—Sid, whom Kirsten would have thought immune to the sort of silliness the boys got up to. Fred had also been underground in various other parts of the world, especially in Tasmania, where he tried to spend at least part of every Canadian winter.

"It's much like here, in some ways," he said. "An island . . . different shape but still an island. Islands have a mentality all their own. Great caves! Good people, too, although until you get to know them, they can seem a bit . . . weird."

He did not mention the girlfriend everybody alleged was his real reason for the annual visits, nor did Kirsten ask. Nor would she . . . but the image was there, and that image birthed her own set of mental images, all with Teague Kendall's face. At one point, she shook her head so violently in trying to dispel them that Fred was drawn to ask if she was all right.

Going "walkabout" was a much quieter affair. They moved along the route to the cave in single file, far enough apart so that Fred didn't have to worry about letting branches flick back at Kirsten when he shoved them aside. He didn't have to worry, she noticed, but he did! On every such occasion, he glanced back, took care to hold the offending branch . . . just to be sure.

They reached the cave, but paused only long enough to assure themselves it looked undisturbed. Then Fred led her a meandering traipse that eventually rounded the shoulder of the ridge and took them substantially higher than the cave entrance in the gully.

"Here's the entrance you found." He pointed to the merest scrap of pink survey tape visible amidst the ravenous claws of devil's club. The second entrance was in a moist pocket, perhaps the result of a long-ago land slip, and from the outside, it looked even more imposing than from within. Kirsten related Les' remark about her having to be stripped down to nothing and greased like a pig to ever use the passage, and they both—being all too aware of the nefarious devil's club thorns—had a chuckle.

That pretty much ended the conversation for the next few hours; neither had the inclination or strength to waste on idle conversation as Fred led the way on a convoluted journey that kept moving them further along and around the ridge and further up it as they went. They floundered over deadfalls, tripped, slipped, and slithered on the damp forest floor as they worked their way upward, always seeking the easiest going, only occasionally finding it.

Here, above the valley, there was no mist to obscure the sun, and it became noticeably fierce. Fred had brought himself a hiking staff, and not long after leaving the cave entrance had insisted on cutting one for Kirsten. He wore at his belt an enormous hunting knife, honed to a razor edge. He was an expert with it, too. He whittled her a hiking staff with dexterous skill, using a minimum of quick, skillful, slashing motions.

Walking became much easier, then, and she was suitably grateful for having something to aid her balance, to give her something to brace on, to lessen the shock of the occasional slippery descent as they followed the contour lines around the ridge. Following Fred, however, was a challenging and sometimes curious business.

He was shorter than Kirsten, with a figure her mother would have described as "a tall man's body on a short man's legs," and with his tonsured, shaven scalp and the over-long hiking staff he looked like a diminutive Friar Tuck wending his way through a medieval greenwoods. And he kept looking back, usually flashing her a smile that seemed at times almost apologetic. At first, she took it for an overzealous desire to ensure she didn't get struck by errant branches, but as the trek progressed she began to feel distinctly uncomfortable about it, started seeing the smile more as a grimace—was his back really hurting that much?—or even, eventually, as a leer. She gradually let herself lag further behind, hoping he'd get the message that she'd hiked before, knew better than to follow too close, but it made no difference. Every few minutes, he'd turn swiftly, his eyes flashing to brush past her own, his lips curling to show that curious smile.

It began to get distinctly unnerving, and twice she stumbled at the suddenness of the gesture, the abruptness with which he moved. Then she stumbled again as he turned, only this time he didn't flash her any deprecating smile. He completed the turn and rushed toward her, shouting absolute nonsense at the top of his voice, raving like a lunatic, waving the hiking staff like a quarterstaff as he approached. This was no tonsured pseudo-monk—this was a homicidal maniac!

There was no time to think, hardly time to react. Kirsten threw up her arms in defense, already trying to turn away as he reached her, struck out, knocking her to her knees, her own staff flying off to one side as she fell.

# TWENTY-EIGHT

Kirsten floundered, trying to roll away from the attack, trying to reach her feet, to reach out for her own staff, to do anything defensive, but it was too late. Fred was already past her, still screaming, still raging like a madman, his hiking staff a whirlwind as he spun it in both hands. And as she struggled to get to her feet, she realized he'd struck her not with his staff, but with his shoulder.

And that he wasn't attacking her, but defending her! Kirsten's vision cleared just in time to see the tawny shape of a cougar, all soulless eyes and gleaming fangs, the animal obviously leery of Fred, but not terrified . . . and not retreating.

She leapt up and grabbed her own walking stick, rushed in behind Fred, adding her own screams and letting her terror boost their volume. Just as she caught up, the big cat treated them both to a baleful, sullen stare before loping away down their back trail, moving in great, graceful bounds that quickly took it out of sight.

That didn't stop Fred from glancing regularly over his shoulder as he turned toward her, panting like a marathon runner and limping, leaning heavily on the long hiking staff with every step.

"Sorry about that. I didn't really mean to run right over you."

"Sorry? My God!"

She was trembling now as reaction set in, had to turn away briefly in case she got sick. Fred didn't look any better . . . his face was white and his eyes still held that hint of madness she'd seen. But his panting slowed once he was able to stand still, glancing constantly over his shoulder, eyes flickering from side to side as he looked not only at the trail, but at the forest surrounding them.

"I . . . I . . . I've never seen anything like that! Ohmigod . . . it's just . . . unbelievable. I . . . I don't really know what to say."

"Nothing left to say; it's over now. I hope. Still, we'll have to keep a damned close eye out as we go on, because you just never know with cougars. Usually they're cowards and stay that way once they've been faced down, but . . . well . . . you never know."

Kirsten was still trembling, her own eyes following his as Fred continued to scan the underbrush around them.

"Go on? You want to keep going after . . . after *that?*"

He shrugged. "Long way to walk whichever way we go, and I still haven't seen what I came to find. Besides, the cat's behind us—between us and the vehicle if we go back. If we assume he's been properly scared off, let's leave him there. We're nearly at the top now anyway. We'll get there, have a snack and a rest, and consider our options, but first let's get somewhere that's a bit more exposed so the damned cat can't sneak up on us so easily if he changes his mind."

To Kirsten's surprise, they reached the top of the ridge within a few minutes, and easily found an open, rock-strewn glade where they were able to take a much-needed break, sprawling out comfortably to work their way through the lunch she'd transferred to their rucksacks back at the vehicle. The food had a calming effect, but both of them spent more time looking around than at each other as they lunched.

"Why did you decide to rush the cougar like that?" Kirsten asked. "I always thought you were supposed to just stand still, look away, that sort of thing if you met a wild animal."

"Not if it's a cougar. If they aren't afraid of you in the first place—which they should be and in which case you likely wouldn't see them at all—they're already seeing you as prey, and you don't get a lot of time to convince them otherwise. With most other wild animals, even bears, usually, standing still or at least backing away and appearing non-threatening is supposed to be the best idea, but cougars apparently interpret that as weakness, so it's better to try and scare them off. That's the theory, anyway."

"A proven theory, now. Thank God! And did I remember to say thank you, by the way? Because I do. Ten times over!"

"Once is sufficient." And he bowed his tonsured head almost in embarrassment, leaving Kirsten, for the moment, unsure what else to say. But it was only a moment; then Fred took up the conversation himself.

"I was with a bunch of cavers up island a few years ago," he began, and went on to relate how five of them had emerged from a cave in the middle of the night to find the entrance virtually surrounded by cougars.

"Dozens of them, it seemed like. We stepped outside and their eyes were just everywhere in our headlamps. At first we thought it was a herd of deer, or elk, but then we got a better look."

"Dozens? What on earth did you do? You couldn't launch an assault on dozens of them with only five of you."

"Well, maybe there were only four or five of them," he admitted with a slow grin, not at all ashamed of the earlier exaggeration. "And what we did was drop all our gear and take off down the hill like a bunch of rabbits. Good thing the cats were just as surprised as we were, with hindsight. We had to go back in the morning and get all our gear, and you never saw such a bunch of shame-faced ninnies in your life! It was after that incident I started researching a bit on animal behavior."

"So you were afraid back . . . there? Just like I was?"

"More than you. I knew from the start what was going on. You must have just assumed at first I'd lost my mind."

"I'm ashamed to admit it, but that's the truth. I thought you were attacking me!"

They both had a chuckle at the all-too-recent memory, then Fred continued in his role as storyteller, relating incidents from his Australian visits.

"Put any Australian in the bush here, and he'd be terrified of cougars and bears—especially bears! In most of Canada, we don't worry about either all that much. They're out there, of course, but not all that high on the risk list. Except maybe here on Vancouver Island with the cougars. Did you know we have the world's worst record for cougar attacks? Anyway, in Australia there are no big predators to worry about, but put the average Canadian in the bush there, and it's the snakes that they fear.

"Australian kids run around barefoot in the bush and don't even seem to worry about it. Mostly because they've grown up with the risk, they're aware of it even when they're not thinking about it, and in fact the number of actual snakebite cases is very, very small. Nobody really worries about them, despite the fact almost every damned snake in Australia is highly venomous . . . and they're everywhere! And if it isn't the snakes it's the spiders—about half of them can do serious injury, too."

"But you spend a lot of time in Australia, or so I've heard. Surely you're used to it all by now?"

"Not on your Nelly! Every time I see a snake I go all strange inside, even though I know intellectually that they aren't going to bother me if I don't bother them. Because I grew up where there are no venomous snakes, hardly any snakes at all. You might have seen on television or in a movie the trick of grabbing a snake by its tail and cracking it like a whip? I've actually watched it done—in Tasmania—to a six-foot tiger snake whose bite could have killed him—by a person I would otherwise have thought reasonably sane . . . for a Tasmanian. They're really a weird mob."

Kirsten was left to ponder that image while Fred stepped behind a bush, and he returned with the abrupt suggestion that they get on with their expedition. "Long way to go yet, although at least it'll be mostly downhill. And, if I'm right, maybe mostly by road, too."

"What, exactly, are we trying to find?" she asked. A question she'd been asking herself most of the morning, but one which Fred had yet to discuss.

"The bear went over the mountain . . . to see what he could see," was the enigmatic reply. Fred was already striding out ahead of her, back in Friar Tuck mode, and Kirsten could only follow.

Both of them did a lot of looking back as they moved along the ridge-top.

# TWENTY-NINE

Sergeant Charlie Banes was perhaps the least surprised of anyone at what the forensics team found . . . and where. Except, perhaps, for old Viv and his obnoxious dog, who'd led the small army of police technicians.

Viv, of course, expressed no surprise. Only that sly, smug, rat-bag grin, which became almost as toothy as the dog's when the animal once again proved the intelligence credited to it by its master.

Banes was actually more relieved than surprised. His contemporaries had been giving him quite strange looks ever since the expedition began, not least because of the way he was forced to defer to old Viv's knowledge and bushcraft. The situation had been improved not at all by the contempt the old bushie showed for the forensic team, which he said blundered around in the scrub like a mob of lost sheep. Far worse comments emerged under his breath, which was bad enough to keep everyone well away from him in the first place, but Banes not only heard the old man, he understood the comments and generally agreed with them.

*City cops . . . the lot of them. We'll be lucky to get out of this without losing one of them, never mind finding anything useful.*

But they did find something useful. Or at least the Jack

Russell terrier did, although the small, geriatric, evil animal made them all work for the privilege of sharing the knowledge. He led them a merry dance along the ridge-top of Blue Tier, dashing around like the demented dervish he was, yapping and yodeling and occasionally turning to snarl at some hapless forensics officer who got too close. Banes had been forced to bring both dog and owner to the area in his own vehicle, not daring to let them loose amongst the forensics crew in case Bluey decided to start his day with an early police breakfast.

The vast region at the top of the tier was a maze of old vehicle tracks that wound their way through the scrub. Here and there, aged tailings dumps were visible, if overgrown, and Banes knew there were uncounted open shafts that posed serious threats to the unwary. Old Viv knew it too, and took the greatest of delight in yammering on about bottomless pits, deadly, man-eating tiger snakes, and devils so huge "they'd eat me poor old dog for brekkie if he wasn't so damned tough." At first his repartee was amusing, but by the time they'd spent a fruitless hour wandering with no apparent plan or purpose, even Banes was getting sick of it.

Still, he had faith in the old man. Marginally less in the dog, although . . .

*I'd better have faith. There's a case of rum riding on this, and it'll come out of my pocket if the old bugger doesn't come good. Probably even if he does!*

He followed as close to Viv as he dared, trying to keep an eye on the obnoxious old dog as it bounded hither and yon, yapping and yaffling and sniffing dangerously close to the edges of various abandoned shafts. All to no avail. And just as Banes began to realize what was happening, the old man proved him right.

"I've misjudged. Sorry about that, lads, but we're too far south. We'll have to go back and drive on a bit."

Old Viv whistled up the dog and was hiking his way back toward the vehicles before the already exhausted forensics people realized what he meant, and Banes could only shrug and grant them a sympathetic shrug as he, too, passed them in the turn. Then he put on a burst of speed, which he shouldn't have needed—but did—to catch a man half his size and twice his age.

"You rotten, conniving old bugger! You've been playing games and don't bother to deny it."

Small chance of that. Viv looked him square in the eye and said, "Good for them to have to work for their crust for a change. Healthy. Fresh air. Sunshine." And the look he shot back behind them revealed he was totally unrepentant and—worse—certain of his own power in the current scheme of things.

"Well give it away, dammit," Banes said. "They'll be no bloody use to us if you run them right into the ground, and if you keep this up it's me who'll end up in strife, not that I expect that worries you. Or that mongrel bloody dog."

Which self-same animal waited until they were driving further on a suddenly much-improved track before leaning over to lick Banes on the ear, nearly causing him to drive off the track and into a gigantic stringy-bark tree. Both dog and master favored the Sergeant with their canine grins when he finally got the vehicle straightened out, just as both ignored his vehement curses.

"He likes yez, Bluey does. Told you he would . . . given time."

There was no suitable reply.

They rounded a curve and found themselves right back on the rim of the escarpment, where a collection of buildings huddled beneath the trees. They were in far better condition than the usual run of abandoned shacks in old mining country, and Banes found himself sharing a wondering look with his aging companion, who merely shrugged and waved a gnarled hand to direct their course. Everyone parked well away, so as to disturb nothing significant, and Banes wasn't surprised to see a similar look of interest on the faces of the forensics team as they emerged from their vehicles.

There was nothing obvious about the place, except for the slightly unnatural good order of the buildings, and yet . . . There was . . . something. An atmosphere, an aura, maybe just a feeling. It reached out and touched his policeman's instinct just as it did those of his companions . . . city cops or no! Even old Viv's attitude had changed subtly. He moved slowly, looked around a lot more than usual before making any step.

Not so, of course, the damned Jack Russell. Bluey flew out of the police vehicle and into a dervish dance of maniacal delight, fairly bouncing from tree to building corner to the next building, cheerfully cocking his leg at every stop, letting his piercing yap precede him.

*Bloody oath! There's been a bitch in season here. That'd be right, and about my luck, too. We'll get nought from the mongrel bastard now.*

Banes looked to Viv for confirmation, but the old man was a statue, standing motionless and staring . . . not at his dog but at the shacks, the rain water tanks, the unusual sense of . . . orderliness that emanated from it all. When he did deign to turn and look at Banes, his earlier attitude of let's-play-games-with-the-coppers was gone, replaced by an obvious expression of deep concern.

"Not right, this. You know it."

Banes could only nod. The aura of wrongness was so intense he half expected the forensics people to demand the dog be pulled back out of it before he contaminated everything in sight, but nobody moved, nobody spoke.

After a moment, they stepped forward, approaching the buildings cautiously, all spread out and keeping an eye out ahead, behind, and to all sides. Banes, the only member of the entire party carrying a weapon, found himself reaching to it, touching it as if for reassurance, until old Viv touched his arm, halting the gesture.

"Nobody here. Dog 'd say if there was."

"You didn't know about this." It was neither statement nor question, really. Banes knew the answer anyway from the look in the old man's eyes. This wasn't anything old Viv would have known about, much less been involved in. Then the old man's head lifted sharply, his eyes turned to where the dog had gone out of sight behind the buildings. Banes could sense no change in the terrier's incessant yaffling, but obviously Viv did.

"He's onto something," came back over the old man's shoulder as he scampered off in that curious bushman's gait that looked so slow and was so difficult to keep up with.

Banes followed after him, the rest of the party well behind him. He had no idea what to expect, and what they found was hardly anything to raise expectations, except maybe that Viv's demented Jack Russell would make a mistake and find himself spiraling down into the abandoned shaft he was dancing around in a grotesque, somehow macabre frenzy, his geriatric fangs fairly clattering with excitement in between yodels of triumph.

"There'll be your bones," muttered the old man, with none of his expectable smugness.

Nobody doubted it for a moment.

# THIRTY

Kirsten was surprised when they rounded an outcropping and saw the cluster of abandoned buildings. Fred was less surprised, as his self-satisfied grunt revealed. They halted, stood silent then, and just looked at them.

Grey, moss-covered, rundown, yet quite obviously still sound and in surprisingly good condition, up close, the buildings looked far better than the surrounding area, which was strewn with rusting, discarded bits and pieces of machinery, lengths of steel cable writhing like rusty snakes, various other junk Kirsten couldn't possibly identify. Nor could Fred, but his sense of self-satisfaction was obvious now even to his companion.

"You expected this. You knew it would be here."

"Hoped. I didn't know, although the old maps suggested it. These hills are covered with old mines, mostly for molybdenum, I think. Shafts, collapsed shafts, we find them occasionally when we're looking for new caves. I didn't know about this one, specifically."

"But even if it was on a map, I don't see how you could have found it the way we came . . . we didn't follow any trail. I don't even know where we are, exactly."

But he wasn't listening. Instead, he was moving away from

her, prowling like the cougar they'd frightened off back down the ridge. All he said was, "Just be careful where you step," and about all Kirsten could do was follow his meandering path, which began at the nearest, most solid of the buildings, and moved in ever-widening circles. Fred moved lightly, carefully, occasionally probing with his staff before trusting his weight in areas he apparently thought unstable. To Kirsten it all looked alike, what could be seen through the jumbled piles of rubbish.

Eventually, she tired of the game and found a place in the shade to sit and watch his progress, but there was nothing happening that made any sense to her, and Fred seemed lost in thought, his entire concentration on the ground in front of him.

She was half asleep, her mind far from the timbered ridge country, when she became aware of being watched, and thought he'd returned. She could hear his breathing, a sort of huffing sound. Only when she opened her eyes he was nowhere in sight, and when she got up and went looking, he was on the far side of the building cluster, staring at the doorway into the soundest of the structures. Puzzled, suddenly apprehensive, Kirsten looked quickly behind her, but saw nothing, except in her mind, where a great tawny cat lurked, only partially visible and the more threatening just for that vagueness. She shivered at the thought.

Fred waved at her approach, then slipped off his rucksack and took out some sort of instrument, which he consulted as she approached, and by the time she got there he was writing down what looked to be a series of numbers.

"GPS—global positioning system," he explained. "Good one, too . . . I borrowed it from a friend in the mining game. Assuming I'm using it right, it will pinpoint exactly where we are . . . this very spot."

Kirsten didn't understand, and said so.

"I used it to locate the entrances to your cave . . . both of them," he explained. "And I've got a really large-scale topographical map at home that might help me locate them in relation to here, and to the road and the ridge line. Ultimately, it might make a difference in trying to figure out just how extensive the cave actually is, even if there are parts you can't reach, or nobody gets to for a long time."

He put away the instrument and shouldered his pack again before continuing, "I had been hoping, actually, to find evidence up here that might reveal an entrance from the top, but I haven't had any luck. One thing, though . . . we'll have an easier hike back to the vehicle. Somebody's been using this place, perhaps as a base camp for mineral exploration or something, and there's a halfway decent track that I'd bet my boots will take us out to the same road we're parked on, although probably way further up."

They took only a cursory look at the old buildings, two of which had rusty but solid locks and what might have been evidence of recent use. Fred pointed out a trace of what appeared to be fresh oil on the flattest portion of the site, where one might expect a vehicle to park, but overall there was just so much rubbish strewn about it was impossible to make any proper assessment.

"Best not to mess about too much," he said. "I expect there are still valid claims, maybe, and prospectors take a dim view of intruders. We'll make our way back by using his track, though. No law against that."

Which is exactly what they did, making the overall journey in half the time it had taken them to climb through the forest. Going downhill helped speed their trek, of course, as did being able to walk on a primitive but recognizable roadway, albeit one that was almost closed in places by fallen timber and brush. When they struck the main road, they had to jump a deep gully that suggested to Kirsten nobody could have used this track in a long time.

She had a moment's hesitation too, about which way to go when they did get to the road. Fred had no concerns; he turned left and marched off purposefully, humming under his breath as he went. It was easy going, now, and within a half hour they rounded a bend to find his SUV waiting for them and just enough time to get home for dinner.

The drive back to Duncan was made in relative silence. Both were tired, if still exhilarated by the events of the day. Mostly they talked about the cougar. Kirsten thought about mentioning the business of feeling watched, then forgot about it. Maybe it was the great cat, she thought. Or just her imagination.

One thing for sure, it would make a fantastic tale to dine out on, she found herself thinking. Which led her to thinking about the last such experience, and then to Teague Kendall, and . . .

*That's all I need . . . more thinking along those lines. Keep this up, my girl, and you'll be a regular patient of Pauline's good doctor.*

That was something she had no intention of becoming. She had gained some insights from that first visit, was already half-regretting her promise to return next week, but was thoroughly determined not to make a habit of it. Dr. Stafford was leaving for Australia soon anyway, for his regular job switch with a colleague who operated a similar clinic there. He'd mentioned it only briefly, as a prelude to turning her files over to his friend, but Kirsten had hardly been listening. She was far more intrigued by his reason for making the annual winter visit in the first place.

Surely there were better ways to deal with . . . whatever

they call it when not enough light causes depression? He'd explained it to her, told her the name she'd immediately forgotten, too. She remembered reading somewhere about new therapy using strong light to defeat it, but—thinking about it—maybe a complete change of scene for half the year made just as much sense. And one thing Pauline's doctor did have was plenty of sense. Given the way she'd been reacting, anybody else would have been trying to force her onto some kind of tablets.

# THIRTY-ONE

Sid Drew was on hands and knees, meticulously measuring one of the most intricate pieces for the complicated tiling project he'd been working on non-stop for nine days. When his pager and cell-phone both began screaming at him, and over the din, he could hear his chief assistant screaming, "No . . . no . . . no . . . ," he briefly considered taking time out to chuck all three into the Cowichan River so he could get on with his work uninterrupted. He had a headache, his eyes felt like they were going to cross any moment, but he . . . was . . . al . . . most . . . done! Then he heard a voice that was familiar, but shouldn't have been there.

"There's no sense having a cell-phone *and* a pager if you never answer either one!" said Fred Hollis from too close behind him. "And will you tell that fool to stop shouting at me. Bloody oath! You'd think I was interrupting Michelangelo at work on the Sistine Chapel."

"Worse than that, but I wouldn't expect you to recognize genius at work," Sid replied, struggling to straighten up. "Is this important?"

"I think it might be. Can't you turn this over to the hired help or something?"

Sid's only reply to that was a fierce scowl, but five minutes later, the two men were sipping coffee—at least Fred had shown the sense to come prepared!—and Sid was listening with astonishment to his friend's theory. It was long and rambling and complicated and occasionally outright incoherent, and so ludicrous he kept wanting to laugh, but as unbelievable as it seemed . . .

"You really believe this?" he finally asked, already half believing it himself and wondering if both of them were suddenly going senile. Fred merely nodded, which prompted Sid to continue.

"I just hope you haven't mentioned this to Kirsten."

"I'm not stupid. I probably shouldn't have taken her with me in the first place, but . . ."

"Taken her with you?" Sid interrupted. "What the hell are you using for brains these days? And have I mentioned, by the way, that you look like hell?"

"Just tired. I've been working pretty steady on the computer, trying to see if this theory will fly. Which is your fault! If you guys had done your survey properly as you went along, I'd probably have enough information already to be sure. Maybe."

"If you'd stop being . . ." Sid caught himself just in time. There was no good time to twit Fred about his fear of the underground, and he sensed this was probably a worse time than most. "You know Les and Jimmy," he finally said, knowing it was a lame recovery. "They're good boys, but they're not real reliable."

"Not the point." Fred clearly wasn't mollified. He then launched into another overly detailed account of his research, the logic of his theory, and—after some prodding by Sid—the epic tale of Kirsten and the cougar. *That* got Sid's full attention.

"I'd love to have seen it, but . . . you guys were lucky as

hell. And probably crazy as hell going out there alone in the first place."

"Two people is not alone. Anyway, it's done now. What I want is your take on this business of how that damned ring got into the cave. Assuming somebody didn't put it there, which is the obvious answer, couldn't it have . . ."

"Been dropped into an old mine shaft and got washed into the cave by water? Down through God knows what system of . . . rock fissures and . . . whatever? I think you spend too much time playing with that damned computer. You want to get out in the real world more often."

"It's possible. And probably no more improbable than assuming somebody took the damned thing into the cave," Fred insisted. "Nobody's been in the cave but you and Kirsten and the boys."

"Nobody we know of."

"But . . . still . . . the buildings I told you about are left over from some old mine. Just because I couldn't find the shaft doesn't mean it isn't there."

"So what do you want to do, call in the horsemen and tell them your amazing theory? *That* I want to be there to hear."

Both men laughed, if bitterly, at the thought of going to the RCMP with such a hare-brained concept. Sid related Kirsten's last attempt at such a thing, when she'd gone to the police with Teague Kendall.

"I want you guys to get in there and finish a proper survey, so I can see if it really makes any sense, just for starters," Fred finally said. "And we could go have a serious look around up on top, although that might be tricky if somebody's got an active claim on the go. I suppose I could check . . . there must be records." He was already away in his head, trying to think of Web sites and links, when Sid's words interrupted the process.

"Maybe going to the cops isn't so silly, if the right person did it," he said. "Kirsten mentioned that writer guy who went with her before. Said the cops seemed to like him, and he's famous, after all."

"You've met him?"

"No, but I'm planning to. Kirsten borrowed my gear so she could take him into the cave with her, and I sort of got the impression there's . . . something shaping up between them. If we're going to have our girl mixing with the rich and famous, might be worth finding out a bit more about the guy. She's a good girl and I'd hate to see her . . . well . . ."

"She's more than just good. She's tough as old boots. You should have seen how quick she recovered after that cougar thing." Fred paused, shaking his head. "And you say she took this guy into the cave . . . just the two of them? She ought to know better than that."

"She does know better, but I've been tied up here and will be for the next month, the way things are going. All they did was go straight in to where she found the ring and then straight back out again. Not a lot of risk in that."

Fred listened, but again his attention had gone elsewhere. He knew only too well about risks underground. Sid, seeing his friend's eyes lose focus, waited patiently for it to pass.

"She said he knows a lot about cops and the way they operate," Sid said then. "What say we pay him a visit and run this up his flag pole to see who salutes? Can't hurt, and like I said, I'm sort of curious about him anyway. If he's going to start getting all . . . involved with our girl, we have a right to at least talk to him."

"What are friends for, after all?" Fred agreed. "We'll take him for a beer, maybe. Pick his brains, demand that he state his intentions, maybe work him over with a rubber hose if he gets difficult. Do you think we ought to take Les and Jimmy along?"

Sid's expression mingled laughter with apprehension. "We only want to talk to him, not scare him off. Unless he deserves it, of course."

# Thirty-Two

Teague Kendall couldn't manage to seduce Kirsten even in his dreams, but he was nearly there when a thunderous knocking at the front door woke him from an after-dinner nap.

Dressed in his usual working gear of well-worn jeans and t-shirt, he sat bolt upright on the extra-long leather Chesterfield he'd been sleeping on, then fumbled his way to the door, rubbing sleep from his eyes as he went. Not bothering with the peephole, he simply flung open the door, half-expecting it to be somebody selling something he didn't want . . . somebody who was about to learn some new and interesting words!

What he got was the sight of four men standing there, men all roughly his own age—one somewhat older, two a bit younger—dressed in flannel shirts, jeans, ball caps, work boots. All looking at him with an expression that suggested he might have forgotten to zip his fly.

"Sid Drew." The tallest of the men thrust out the largest hand Teague had ever seen on a human. Instinctively, he met the proffered handshake, half expecting to lose his hand in the process. It was strangely comforting to find the big man's grip firm, but . . . normal, as Kendall introduced himself.

"This is Fred Hollis. Les Green. Jimmy Norris," the tall stranger continued, punctuating his introduction with blunt finger-pointing. "We're friends of Kirsten. We want to talk."

"Okay," Kendall replied, not knowing what else to say, his mind still half-befuddled from the intimacies of his dream. He stepped aside, ushering them into the house, then stood and watched as they all removed their boots before passing the doormat. It was a somehow comforting gesture, though he wasn't at all sure why. Then concern struck him.

"Is Kirsten okay?" he asked, not wanting to show alarm, but able to feel it. He recognized the big man now from Kirsten's description, and his first thought was that there might have been a caving accident.

"She's fine," was the reply. All four men were looking past him, now, their eyes taking in every detail of the mansion's admittedly impressive entry hall. The two younger men were visibly awed, the other two aware, but obviously harder to impress. Kendall decided this was no time to offer a guided tour.

*When in doubt . . . keep it simple.*

"You guys want a beer?" he asked.

"Have you got Hermann's?" Unified thinking voiced by the two younger men gained them a scowl from Sid Drew, and they visibly retreated, like boisterous but usually obedient young Labradors.

"I have," Teague said, noticing the assertion gained him immediate Brownie points, but lost them again immediately when he added, "but not cold." Fair enough too, he thought. The English might drink their beer warm, but the finest dark lager on Vancouver Island deserved better.

The two looked to their leader, who maintained his scowl

although Teague couldn't tell if it was aimed at them or at himself for not having icy Hermann's on tap. The reply came directed at him.

"You want to go to the pub?"

"I'll just go find some shoes," he said after a microsecond of thought. He was ready to leave before the others had their boots laced, and they were halfway to the pub, all jammed together in Sid's vehicle, before he realized he still hadn't the faintest idea what this was all about.

They arrived. Hermann's—on tap, no less—was duly ordered for all, and they were into their second glass before any of it made any sense at all. It began as a simple-enough-seeming exercise . . . these were Kirsten's caving friends, and he was a stranger apparently interested in her, and they'd decided to find out who he was and why and what and whatever. Simple enough; even flattering. He was inwardly delighted she'd obviously evinced enough interest in him to warrant such action. Also smart enough, he hoped, to keep his head, hold his grog, mind his mouth. And not make too much of it all.

He managed that, even when the subject of Tasmania came up, and Fred proceeded to lead him on a merry dance of *Who do you know who knows who I know?* That exercise proved fruitless; they made not a single match, which seemed to surprise Fred as much as it did him. Then they touched briefly on what he wrote, although it seemed *why* he wrote it was more important than what.

Teague was fascinated. None of these men showed the remotest interest in Kirsten romantically, somewhat surprising considering the way Les and Jimmy kept ogling the buxom barmaid. But Kirsten, they obviously just . . . liked. And, he quickly realized, they respected her, as a woman, a friend, and as a fellow caver. That pleased him immeasurably. These were good men, and he found himself wanting them to think well of him, in return.

They were into the fourth beer, except for Sid, the driver, before the conversation infinitesimally changed, and he began to sniff out the pattern. That made it all the more interesting; all four pricked up their ears like dogs as he related his own involvement in the strange tale of Kirsten's ring, especially when he verbally took them into the police station and the discussions there.

Then Fred began his convoluted explanation of his theory and the logic—logic?—behind it, which had Les, Jimmy, and especially Teague himself almost spellbound as Fred spun the tale with enviable skill. They spent one beer talking the thing to death, but reached no satisfactory conclusion or course of action.

By the sixth beer, Fred was to the *eyes closed—arms waving* stage as he wove the expansive tale of Kirsten and the cougar, and Teague was beginning to feel competition as a wordsmith.

He was also feeling the urge to punch Fred in the mouth, despite knowing the cougar attack was the sort of thing that could happen to anyone, at any time, and certainly nothing the man should be blamed for.

They had another beer, recounting and recapping the entire evening's discussion, then decided enough was enough. They weren't getting anywhere with it and weren't likely to. Sid was getting cranky with Les and Jimmy, who'd hit their limit, and Teague was feeling marginally smug at their effrontery in assuming they could out-drink an old journalist who'd refined his skills in Tasmania, where beer drinking is serious business. Fred's experiences there held up, though. He'd matched Teague glass for glass despite holding the floor half the night, and looked ready to last the distance if needed.

When they poured him out on his front lawn—all friends, now, with business cards, phone numbers, cell-phone numbers all exchanged and promises to talk about this once anybody had anything new to report, Teague was a happy camper indeed. He knew he'd be less so, come the morning, but that was hours away.

*Good friends means a good woman . . . I like her friends . . . I like her. Too much, maybe. And they knew it, too. Know it. Cunning buggers. Damn, but that Fred tells a good story. Not sure about his theory, though. He should be writing fantasy or something. Maybe a good plot element for my book, though. Serial killer knocking off fair young maids, disposing of the remains down an abandoned mine shaft . . . No . . . too ridiculous. Nobody'd believe a theory like that . . . not even me.*

But the theory nagged him into sleep and the hangover that followed.

# THIRTY-THREE

Kirsten was apprehensive about her second therapy session. More so than the first, which made no sense at all. Still, it had been scheduled and she'd promised.

*But I don't need it. Not really. I know what the problem was, now.*

What the problem was—now—was that she didn't want or need to talk about Ed, or her shortcomings in dealing with his controlling and abuse. The subject of most interest—now—was Teague Kendall, and she certainly didn't want to talk to the good Dr. Stafford about that! She wasn't even talking to Pauline about that!

Much as she liked Dr. Stafford, she didn't really want to be his last appointment today . . . or any other day. But she was committed; he'd been so gracious in rearranging his schedule to give her the time that she didn't think it fair to cancel. But there wouldn't even be the prospect of a chat later with Pauline, who had taken the day off and gone to Vancouver without even asking Kirsten if she wanted to keep her company.

*Which I couldn't, of course, because of this appointment. But still . . .*

Kirsten laughed at herself. Imagine complaining about

not being invited to do something you couldn't do in the first place.

*Get a grip, girl! Just go along and be a good little nut case and get it over with. You can deal with Pauline later.*

As it turned out, she needn't have worried, because the good Dr. Stafford didn't want to talk all that much about her problems with Ed, nor indeed was Teague Kendall's name so much as raised, except by her. He did, however, seem fascinated when she told him about her trek with Fred, and their cougar adventure. And he was most focused on the finding of Emma's ring and Kirsten's reactions inside the cave, both the first time and with Kendall.

"It is just such an amazing saga, and I haven't been able to get if off my mind," he said. "There is something about it that . . . bothers me. I'm ashamed to admit I can't quite put my finger on it, but I do sincerely believe there is some connection between the ring, the cave, and the problems you seem to have been having with your conscience. Logical enough, of course, what with your sister still missing . . . you haven't heard from her, I assume?"

He didn't wait for an answer, didn't even seem to expect one. Instead, he voiced a proposal that at first seemed crazier than Kirsten felt, then described it in professional terms she didn't understand but assumed made perfect sense. Enough sense, anyway, that she found herself agreeing to go home, change, collect her gear and Sid's—thank goodness she hadn't returned it yet—and be picked up by Dr. Stafford for another visit to "her" cave.

"Are you sure? I mean . . . it's not that easy a thing to be doing. It's easy enough by caving standards, of course, but . . ."

"You mentioned you still had that other man's gear, and if it fit Kendall it would certainly fit me. Please . . . I really do think this is important. Everything you've told me suggests you're at your strongest when you're underground," he said. "It's like there's a quite different person there, and I am compelled to explore that. This is exactly the sort of thing we must look at. It's my job, after all."

Kirsten was both tempted and . . . not. The problem was she couldn't think of any viable excuse not to go. Except . . .

"We need four-wheel-drive to get there," she said. "My car wouldn't make it in a fit."

"Not a problem. Mine can handle anything, and I've hardly had a chance to put it to any serious test."

So much for that excuse, but she wasn't overly bothered. If he wanted to see where she'd found the ring, baffle her with psycho-babble about what it all meant . . . fine. Maybe in the dark it would actually make some sense.

Kirsten drove home wondering if the entire "ring" situation wasn't driving everybody mad. Here she was, arranging to take yet another man—another non-caver, which was something Sid would be less than impressed by; he'd raised an eyebrow about her taking Kendall—into a cave where there was nothing at all to be seen, or at least nothing all that unusual. Still, they weren't going exploring . . . just following an already known path, really.

Anyway, she'd agreed, and there wasn't much time. She had changed her clothes and was throwing some energy bars into her side pack when she noticed the blinking light of her answering machine, so she poked at it and kept on rummaging through the fridge to see what else might be useful. Probably Pauline, she thought, and only half listened until she realized it definitely was not!

*Kendall here. I was going to invite you to a late dinner. Or a drink. I'll be out for awhile, but back about . . . eight, if you're home by then and . . . interested. I'm at . . .*

Kirsten looked at her watch. She'd be gone before then, which might be just as well because she was far too interested and not that sure she wanted Teague Kendall to know it. Saved by the ubiquitous previous engagement, she thought as she dialed the number he'd left and got his machine.

"Hi, it's me. Sorry, but I can't tonight. Going caving. Well . . . sort of. Our good doctor Stafford wants a look at where I found Emma's ring. I'll call you . . . later."

She heard the doctor's vehicle arriving as she hung up the phone, and was on the porch with all the gear before he'd turned off the engine. Five minutes later they were loaded and on their way.

# THIRTY-FOUR

Kendall listened to Kirsten's message not three minutes after she hung up and debated briefly if he should call her back or not. Decided not. Even though he dearly wanted to hear the sound of her real voice, it was clear she had other plans and he didn't want to appear any sort of nuisance.

He didn't feel like going out to dinner alone, and he felt less like cooking, so he searched the fridge for an overlooked breakfast bar and then settled down at his computer to run his emails and see what the world had to say. Five minutes later, he was transfixed, scrolling slowly through the long, long message from his old police friend, Sgt. Charlie Banes.

The tale of his friend's adventures with the old bushie and his Jack Russell Terrier [*hereinafter referred to as "THAT DAMNED DOG"*] had him laughing so hard he could hardly see for the tears, and took him mentally back to some of his own experiences in Tasmania. He'd never met Viv Purcell, but had encountered his type and lauded Charlie's ability to describe it. And the old man's dog—in one incarnation or another—was all too familiar. Teague became totally lost in the story, although occasionally paused between bouts of laughter to wonder if Charlie's official reports had this same, unique flavor.

Then he got to Charlie's description of the second visit, and felt that inner tingle, that never-to-be-trusted-but-never-ignored *ping* of his mental wake-up call. Part of it all was the way Charlie's story could be woven into his own novel, which had stalled—all too explicably—upon the entrance of Kirsten into his life, but there was more than that, only he couldn't figure out what it was.

*You never saw such a bun-fight in your life! Old Viv went all feral and cranky, and* THAT DAMNED DOG *was bound and determined to take a chunk out of anybody he could reach. And here we are trying to organize equipment to be brought in . . . with cell phones that won't work out this far, and radios that kept breaking up, and nobody knowing what sort of equipment they wanted, exactly, in the first place. And* THAT DAMNED DOG*! And nobody knew where the hell we were, and even when they did know, they couldn't reckon where they were by then, and Viv was cranky and wouldn't give me fair dinkum directions. And nobody believed him anyway, except they did, only they daren't admit it in case he was wrong, or right. Took us until the next bloody morning even to get* STARTED*! And then they had to find somebody small enough to be lowered into the shaft, and that wasn't easy because the only one really small enough was Viv, and they wouldn't do that, would they? A geriatric old bushie and not even a copper!*

*And then there were the buildings.* [*This is that first night I'm talking about, case you got lost.*] *Locked up tight and no easy way to even see inside, and nothing to justify a warrant or anything proper legal like that, so anyway, I go off to check on* THAT DAMNED DOG *who's tied to me truck so he doesn't bite anybody important, and of course he's chewed through the bloody rope, hasn't he, and he's on his way back to take a chunk out of ME . . . or at least he was thinking about it. And I daren't drop-kick the mongrel bastard or Viv'd get even more cranky, and we didn't know but what we'd still need him, and anyway I get back to find the old bugger's found an iron bar somewhere and pried the bloody padlocks off and he's standing there directing the activities of the bloody forensics people, who are NOT happy.*

Kendall continued, mentally translating the abysmal account into something comprehensible, learning how, once inside the buildings, discoveries had been made which made redundant any thought of a warrant!

*Like a cross between a hospital emergency room and a wrecking yard, it was. Bloody great stainless steel table, boxes of bloody rubber gloves, bits and pieces of all sorts of medical type equipment. And an oxy torch with all the fixings, and welding gear. And the knives! You never saw such knives in your life. Skinning knives and boning knives and bloody little scalpel things and half a dozen I couldn't even describe. Old Viv went proper spare with envy, he did. I had to keep a right proper eye on him or he'd have nicked the lot. And THAT DAMNED DOG kept running around like a pork chop, yaffling and barking and growling and snarling at people and pissing on everything he couldn't eat. God save us from all Jack Russells. I finally threatened to shoot the bugger, which was a mistake because it made Viv even crankier. Good thing I had the only gun round the place, or he'd have shot ME. As it was, that iron bar had me worried. So there we are, a dozen forensic types with no camping gear and bugger-all food, and Viv and THAT DAMNED DOG, and only the two of us who could direct them how to get back to town, and bloody sure Viv wasn't going to help much that way except he wanted to get back too because we didn't have any grog, and somebody had to stay and keep an eye on things and nobody wanted to be the one left behind. And it's rising dark and half this city mob is getting spooked as hell. But I had to go because nobody else could have found their way and I daren't leave Viv behind lest* THAT DAMNED DOG *eat somebody and by this time everybody's hungry and tired and cranky and I daren't tell them we've got to make a bloody great detour just to drop off Viv and* THAT DAMNED DOG *until I'd done it and then didn't they go spare! It was the funniest stuff-up you've ever seen.*

It went on and on and on, a blow-by-blow description of their travel back to St. Helens—leaving three of the forensics team to keep each other safe, which amused Charlie no end—and of their return *at sparrow-fart* with climbing gear and half a dozen winches of varying types.

And the first descent into the abandoned mine shaft.

And the white, panicked, terrified, haunted face of the investigator who'd been first into the shaft, who'd been first to see what THAT DAMNED DOG had been telling them from the start.

And the bones. And the purses and back-packs and wallets and personal trinkets and bicycle parts. And the smell, the ghastly, ghoulish, foul smell of what came first from the pit.

And the skulls, some still distinctly long-haired, female. The first ones. Later, they found that insects and rodents and scavengers—probably going in from the bottom like *that damned dog,* had picked the earliest deposits clean.

Kendall kept reading, couldn't stop. But inside his head that warning *ping* was getting louder and more insistent, disrupting his concentration. He started thinking about Fred's theory, about coincidences—which he hated and loathed and despised unless they happened to suit his purposes—and then he scrolled back to be sure he'd read it correctly. And he had . . . there were the words: *bits and pieces of push-bikes*. He scrolled forward, picked up where he'd left off, having unconsciously translated the Australian term for bicycle.

He found his vision getting blurred; no surprise since he'd been staring fruitlessly all day at his work-in-progress that had been going nowhere on the computer screen while he tried to write thrilling words and think lustful thoughts at the same time.

He thrust himself from the chair, dashed to the fridge and cracked a beer, then rushed back to the computer as if that brief lapse might cause him to miss something. And continued reading . . .

*Funny thing is, they reckon even the oldest stuff is only a year or so old. Something about the climate or the humidity or some damn thing. The bones* THAT DAMNED DOG *found at the bottom must have been from the first, I reckon, although it'll probably be months before we know and you can be damned sure the forensics mob won't be telling me because the only ones less popular with them right now are Viv and* THAT DAMNED DOG *and just maybe the media when that mob of vultures gets hold of all this, which won't be too long now. I give it two days at the most, maybe less, which is all I need because I'm out of it now anyway because they've got* THE BRASS *in there now, haven't they? I mean think about it mate, it looks like they've solved the missing bicycle tourist caper, so of course the first thing they'll want is to capitalize on the publicity and get everybody out of it who might actually know anything. Country coppers, especially. Not that they know who did it or any-*

*thing important like that of course but at least they know what's been done, or at least they think they know. I expect THAT DAMNED DOG knows more than the mob of them together, but they're not going to ask him. The case of rum for old Viv will come out my pocket and not the expense account here, and you mark my bloody words. It'll come out of somewhere, anyway, because he's onto the case with a vengeance, now and he's not going to give up until he gets it. Maybe two cases. Maybe a new driving license if the old bugger thought he'd get away with it. Which he might. I actually can't wait until the press gets hold of this, just to see them trying to deal with old Viv and THAT DAMNED DOG. You're well out of it, just be glad you're not a journo anymore and you're there, although you'd be missing the story of the century if anybody ever reckons who actually DID IT. But don't hold your breath on that score, because it's a puzzle and no two ways about it. A PUZZLE, mate, with most of the pieces missing. They'll probably never find out WHO DID IT, but at least now they know who had it done to them. The ID they found cleared that up pretty smartly, although of course now it'll be DNA tests for all and sundry, up to and including THAT DAMNED DOG, I shouldn't wonder. I'd love to be there when some tech tries to get a saliva swab from HIM. Fair dinkum, they're running around like blue-arsed flies on this one. All THE BRASS are trying to cut poor old Viv out of the loop because he can't help but be an embarrassment to them. Careers will be won and lost on this one, and a cantankerous old bushie like him . . . well . . . My oath! They should make the old bugger Commissioner, and THAT DAMNED DOG ought to be Premier, since knowing where the bones are buried is important in politics. And the forensics mob are cranky, having to spend their time down that bloody great pit with all that gore and not even a hot shower until they get back to town. Course if this happened in the Big Smoke, there'd be nothing much to do but consult the surveillance cameras, like on the telly, and dozens of pretty secretary birds to do all the real work, but there you go. It's a puzzle—that's what it is, and going to be more of a bloody puzzle before all's said and done.*

The litany went on and on and on, and Teague was compelled to read it because he couldn't "not." But his *ping* was also going on and on and on, and finally he realized why.

And surged from his chair with an almighty curse, almost tipping over the computer in his haste but not caring as two unconnected words in Charlie's email suddenly did connect, which was what his inner alarm had been trying to tell him if he'd only had the sense to listen. The chair landed with a crash, but was ignored, or unnoticed. Teague was already out of the room, taking the stairs two at a time as he rushed to the top.

# THIRTY-FIVE

The specialist had indigestion. The bad kind, the sort that comes with spurts of burning acid and wannabe burps that never quite make it. He was not surprised, even knew the cause. Anticipation!

It was just sooo close, now. Only a few more threads to be gathered in, carefully interwoven, knotted. He had the steaks from the first sister. Indeed, they were with him now, carefully packaged and iced in the camp cooler along with choice, new potatoes, crisp vegetables, even a small tub of that ever-so-decadent ice cream. He had the time, the place, and now, the plan. All he needed was Kirsten.

*Soooon* . . . The word was a sigh against the lava bubbling up from his stomach, but it did little good. Only time would cure the heartburn, and he was—unfortunately—running out of that. There would be enough, of course. He was sure of that, now. But overall, things were going quite, quite out of control. Which was terrifying, but exhilarating at the same time. A rush similar, he assumed, to heroin, or perhaps cocaine . . . not that he'd tried either. Nor would he. The specialist had his own drug of choice, and it came with knives, not needles or plastic straws.

Still, the going out of control bothered him. It was atypical, not like him at all, really. And it was that damned director's fault!

*If he'd only had the sense to put the play on properly and just . . . do . . . it . . . right . . .*

But he hadn't, of course, so the specialist had been once too often tempted, and had succumbed. And the coincidences must also share the blame. Who could imagine, even in an hallucinogenic dream, this business with the ring? The incredibility of it being Kirsten who found it? Although, of course, the juxtaposition of the two sisters now presented such a wonderful, unique opportunity . . .

*Once is chance, twice is coincidence, and three times is conspiracy.*

Too many coincidences, really. But such interesting coincidences, so many twists and turns in the warp and weave of it all . . .

*Soooon* . . . It didn't ease the indigestion, but it sounded right in his head, felt good. The sibilance, perhaps.

All falling into place. Soooon, he would tempt the lovely Kirsten with a morsel of perfectly cooked [medium-rare tending to rare] steak, would be treated to her reaction when she was told the source. And then the privilege—it could only described thus—of helping her to share her sister's experiences, to share *his* tastes, to understand them, and ultimately to contribute her own experience to his magnificent experiment. Would she appreciate the wonder of it? What flavor might it impart to the finality of her situation?

Soooon . . . he would know!

After which, he feared, there might be repercussions. He might be found out, perhaps even caught. That was a worry, but the inevitability soothed the concern. He'd always known of that risk, had—to some extent, anyway—prepared for it. Once he had finished with Kirsten, had—so to speak—tasted the fruits of his labors . . . He grinned inwardly, savoring the word-play.

Then returned to the problems: too many coincidences, too many disposal problems, too much evidence that might return to bite him in the bum. That thought brought another slow grin. Tasmania, he thought, was a better venue for him. Tasmania, with its devils, the epitome of world-class scavengers . . . noisy, cantankerous, flea-and-tick-infested creatures with a television cartoon reputation not half so interesting as their reality. Ugly, loathsome, and absolutely superb at their job! No worries about disposal in Tasmania; he'd seen a mob of devils reduce a 'roo carcass to no more than bone shards—and those widely dispersed—in less than a day. The efforts of Canadian scavengers were paltry by comparison.

*Soooon* . . . The thought brought his tongue across perfect teeth, which brought to mind dentists, and then that old stand-by, nitrous oxide . . . laughing gas. Wonderful stuff . . . a few whiffs and you felt the drill, knew the pain, but simply didn't give a damn! And no saggy lips afterwards. Better than drugs. He hated drugs. Always the concerns about side-effects, always the risk of after-taste.

# THIRTY-SIX

Kirsten found Dr. Stafford's rich voice hypnotic. She loved the sound of it, enjoyed immensely the way he rolled the words around, coating them with a sort of rich, verbal chocolate syrup.

*It must be difficult for him, really . . . trying to get his patients to talk when they'd probably rather listen to him talk. I know I would. I do.*

Although, to be fair, she half wished he'd talk about something other than the circumstances of finding Emma's ring in the cave. She wished everybody would talk about something else . . . or at least let *her* talk about something else. She'd almost developed a rote recital of the incident, having told Sid and Pauline and the dinner party guests and Kendall and the police. It wasn't solving anything!

On the good side, Pauline's good doctor was proving an interesting caving companion, if a bit too talkative for Kirsten's taste. Maybe it was just the difference, seeing him in rough, obviously well-worn outdoors gear instead of the tailored office clothing of a professional man. Taller than Kendall, only a bit shorter than Sid, so Sid's coveralls fit him admirably. He moved well, seemed totally undeterred by the underground, the darkness, the occasional need to stoop and twist his way through the passages.

She had sensed the strength in him when they negotiated the tricky entrance to the well chamber; he'd been able to make the descent easily, had then turned and reached up to lift her bodily from the ledge above, rather than let her slither down the greasy slope and be caught. Now, in the chamber where she'd found the ring, he used his great height to advantage, peering about in the light from his head lamp, carefully studying the walls of the chamber and the parts of the ceiling that were visible.

"It is quite amazing," he said. "There is simply no logical way that ring could have got here without human intervention. And yet you say nobody's been here who could possibly have brought it." He seemed to be talking as much to himself as to her, and all the while moving, taking mincing, tippy-toe little strides across the floor, careful to damage nothing, putting his feet only where the floor contained no visible cave formations. Even as Kirsten watched, he negotiated his way to the far edge of the chamber, something she and Kendall hadn't bothered to do, and now was shining his lamp back toward the section of wall with the Romanesque fountain formation.

The light went up, down, across, forcing her to duck her head when it passed across her own face; she didn't want her low-light vision affected. Then, as she looked, he focused the light high on the wall above the fountain, back in where it should roughly meet the wall. Too far for her to see anything, given the difference in their heights; even Kendall hadn't been able to really see anything there.

Then the doctor returned to join her near the entrance, sighing with what could have been satisfaction or frustration, and renewed his gentle, probing queries about Kirsten, about Emma, about their relationship. Right from childhood, as if that had anything to do with all this. Kirsten could see no logic in discussing whether she and Emma had been sibling rivals for boys [they hadn't] or fought over clothing or fashions or records or parental attention. But she humored him; this was his field of expertise, after all.

But it wasn't pleasant, and she did her best to cut the interview short by suggesting they ought to be moving. *Batteries don't last forever.* Especially, for reasons nobody could determine and perhaps it was only a myth, underground.

"It's probably just a superstition," she found herself explaining, hoping perhaps to divert his attention to a dissertation on that subject. Anything but Emma and their childhood and sibling rivalry that had never existed.

*Well, almost anything. I don't want to talk about Ed, either. And won't. And definitely not about Kendall, not that there's anything to be said. Not really. His invitation tonight was interesting, though. The way he acted last time we saw each other, I'd have expected not to hear from him until he had to pay off the bet. If then!*

Kirsten wasn't tired, and Dr. Stafford didn't seem to be, so they didn't stop to rest at the coffee shop, but continued back to the well room before taking a break. The doctor had no trouble keeping up, though he didn't crowd her as Kendall had—nor had she asked him to!—but stayed well back. He stopped talking, too, on the return journey, although she could hear a sort of toneless, tuneless humming sound from behind her, and assumed it must come from him.

She had warned him about the dangers of the well on the way into the cave, so was totally unprepared when they reentered the chamber and he strode—almost briskly—over to inspect it.

"Careful!" she warned, keeping her voice low so as not to startle him, but loud enough to get the message across. She'd been in the process of sitting down beside where they'd come in, didn't notice him moving until he'd already done so.

"I'm very sure-footed," was the bland reply, and true enough, too. He kept his strides short in that curious mincing gait, but was able to walk right to the edge of the pit without a single slip.

"How deep did you say it is? The water, I mean."

"We thought about three feet, if the water's the same height as then," Kirsten replied. She was too far away to check the water level, and caution forbade her from moving too much closer. Sure-footed he might be, but it only took one slip, and best she was on secure footing herself if it happened.

"You mightn't drown if you slipped in, but look how slick those walls are. There's no way known a person could climb back out without help. I wish you'd move further away from the edge."

"I'm fine. What happens to the water level when it rains? We saw signs that there has to be some flooding through parts of the cave."

"There's likely a siphon effect, or a drainage of some sort in the sides. We've seen it several times, now, and it seems to remain at almost the same height no matter what happens. That's not uncommon in cave systems."

"Fascinating." He was staring down into the black, bleak water as he spoke, and Kirsten wasn't sure if it was a reply or just a random thought. What she was sure of was wishing he'd move the hell away from there!

"The problem wouldn't be drowning," she repeated. "But that water is just above freezing, I expect. A person forced to stand in it for any length of time would give way to hypothermia awfully quick. Once you're wet, in these temperatures . . ."

"It would take a few hours, actually. It would depend how much of the person was actually in the water, of course. But yes, it wouldn't take long."

Kirsten could hardly believe it. The doctor was standing inches from a known peril and studiously discussing the technicalities of it all.

*Will you please just come away from there! Damn it, damn it, damn it . . . I do not like this.*

"You don't like me being here because it changes the dynamics of the situation," Dr. Stafford said, almost as if he'd read her mind or heard her thoughts. "One of the reasons you love caving so much is that you are totally in control, but having me here, out of range, so to speak, and possibly at risk, reduces that control, because of course it affects you even though you're removed from it." His voice was low, barely audible, in fact. And still the same, chocolate fudge brownie richness. But his timing, she decided, was lousy.

Worse, he was right. Even as they spoke, she could feel the tendrils of Ed's manipulation tactics, the subtle creation of possible future guilt, the directing of it for maximum benefit to himself.

*This is not the time or the place. There is no time and place for any of this, damn it. If you want to psycho-babble, fine . . . but not here. Not now. Not like this.*

"I'm not worried about trying to control you. I'm concerned about having to try and get you out if something goes wrong," she said. And resorted to tactics she loathed and hated and despised, but—like any sensible woman—would use as a last resort. "You're a big man. I'd have trouble dragging you across level ground, much less up out of that well. And . . ." for good measure, ". . . you'd weigh even more, wet."

"That is not going to be a problem because I am not going

to fall in. I am perfectly well balanced and quite comfortable." Then he changed topics so abruptly she had to mentally run to keep up. "You showed no hesitation in trying the . . . unusual specialty at Kendall's dinner. Why was that?"

It took her an instant to catch up, another to figure out what he was talking about. "I was raised in cattle country. I've eaten prairie oysters before."

Stafford had been staring down the well, but now turned abruptly to look at her. "Of course." Then he paused. Then, "Do you remember the first time? How you felt about it then?"

"I was a teenager. I was drunk, I think. I don't remember. Will you please come away from there? Please? You're making me very, very nervous."

"Nothing to be nervous about." But he took one pace away from the lip of the well, although not without looking back at it, sort of swiveling his head so that the beam of the headlamp made little circles.

*Like a little boy peeing in a snow bank. Please, please, please just come away from there. I don't know what this game is about, I don't know the rules, but I . . . do . . . not . . . like . . . it!*

Then he made another abrupt subject change, actually a reversal. "It really bothers you, losing control, now that you've realized how seriously your former husband damaged you."

"Is that a question? If it is, I don't think I want to answer. What I want to do, if it's quite all right with you, is get out of here. Soon. I'm starting to feel the cold, being still like this." A lie, but an easy one. What she was feeling wasn't physical cold, but the chill factor of seeing herself being manipulated, however subtly and for however a good and professional reason.

"Was your sister by any chance a vegetarian? I understand

a lot of theatrical people are." Another abrupt change of conversational direction, and this one truly confused her.

*What the hell are you on about?*

Now Kirsten was starting to lose all patience. She struggled to her feet, was about to speak her thoughts when she heard the noise coming from the passage to the entrance. Obviously they both heard it, both turned in time to see the flickering of the light inside the passage, the grotesque figure created by their light beams crossing, saw the figure materialize to become a recognizable Teague Kendall, waving a long, fat flashlight like some sort of conductor's baton. The light wavered, and the silence was so total Kirsten could hear Kendall's hoarse panting, could see his chest heaving from the exertion.

Kendall? Running through the cave? It made no sense, but then neither did the fact he wasn't wearing proper caving gear, only jeans, hiking boots, what appeared to be an eiderdown ski jacket, winter gloves. The light from his flashlight—dim by comparison to their head lamps—was unsteady as it wavered from Kirsten to the doctor and back again.

She watched as the doctor moved quickly over to help Kendall make the slippery descent into the chamber, saw how clumsy it would be for Kendall with one hand full of flashlight, began to move forward herself.

"Noooooo!" The roar echoed through the chamber like a gunshot, and she paused involuntarily, saw the doctor's hands grasp at Kendall's clothing, saw the strength and ease with which he pulled him down the slippery descent, then used the momentum to keep Kendall moving, to literally skid him across the slick floor of the chamber and land—feet first—into the well!

Kendall had no chance to resist, no chance to do anything but flail his arms as he slid like a body-checked hockey player, the flashlight soaring from his fingers to land with a clang and a tinkle, then go out. It was too quick, too unexpected, for any defense. But he could still shout, and he did.

"Run . . . Kirsten. Run!"

# THIRTY-SEVEN

Kendall didn't even notice the coldness of the water, at first. His mind was still trying to figure how he could let Stafford trick him so easily. His entire rescue attempt, defeated in a single gesture of apparent aid . . . the security video should have warned him, he thought.

Once he'd made the connection between security camera and puzzle, Kendall had hit the top of the stairs running. Then he flung himself down the hall, into the former closet where all the gear for his security camera system was controlled. He had watched when they installed the security cameras, watched as he was instructed in their use. It had seemed a logical step to protect his valuables, given that strangers would be in the house for his dinner parties and . . . you never know. Better safe than sorry. He had faithfully turned the system on for each such occasion, trying to form a proper habit.

But he'd only once bothered to try and watch one of the tapes, found the exercise tedious, and now—now when he needed to watch, and needed to watch carefully, but quickly, dammit, he was all thumbs, had to consciously think of every step in sequence. Then he had to get the right tape, the right room, the right moment in what seemed like weeks, months, of time.

*If you're going to panic, dammit, then organize it!*

Which he did, eventually, and eventually found that crucial instant, the moment Kirsten had seen half upside down as she was bent over in the hall, the moment when Dr. Ralph Stafford reached out to pilfer that single jigsaw puzzle piece, his action obscured to Kirsten but frighteningly clear on the tape.

*Jesus Christ on a crutch!*

Kendall ran the bit of tape back and forth, not wanting to believe it, unable not to believe it. Ridiculous. It made no sense. Except that it did, or at least might. And if it did . . .

He went down the stairs even more quickly than he'd gone up, his mind racing as he tried to juggle several things at once, tried to formulate something approaching a plan. If he was wrong, there might be embarrassment. He'd look like a complete idiot and feel like it too. But if he was right . . . the implications didn't bear thinking about.

Too many coincidences. The good doctor, spending half of each year in Tasmania . . . in the Tasmanian summer. *Where the hell are my hiking boots?* Female bicycle tourists in Tasmania—Kirsten's missing sister. *Gloves. I'll have to have gloves.* The ring, the cave, the Tasmanian mine-shafts, Fred's bloody stupid, ridiculous—but what if it's right?—theory. *Ski jacket, long-johns, goddam wool socks. Flashlight!*

He chased his mind from room to room, gathering the gear as he went, trying to change clothes even while on the move, finally having to stop, sit down, do it right. But he couldn't stop his mind, couldn't stop the horrors of his imagination. Was halfway out the door, keys in hand, when he remembered Kirsten's friends, the logical source of help. Found the numbers, grabbed up the phone, dialed.

Sid: voice mail. A stammered, probably incoherent blurting of his suspicions, the only simple part the words, "Go to the cave. Go now. Go quickly."

Fred: voice mail. This time the message somewhat more coherent. The salient points screamed into the telephone as Kendall inwardly raged and cursed against voice mail, against people who didn't live beside their telephones, didn't carry cell phones, like . . .

Pause . . . rush all over the damned house trying to find the bloody cell phone, trying to remember when he'd last carried it, what he'd worn, where it might be, should be, must be! "Gotcha!" Then the frighteningly long time it took to write down all the numbers so he'd have them, to try unsuccessfully to reach Les and Jimmy by phone. No voice mail, at least, but no answers, either.

"Damn it all to hell!" Screamed at the darkening sky as he rushed outside for the second time, flung everything into the SUV, screeched out of his driveway, and headed west toward Lake Cowichan and the hills, pushing the speed limit as far as he dared while in the town, trying to think of what he'd forgotten, knowing it would be some damned thing and praying it wouldn't be anything too important.

He was already out of town when he thought of the police. Glanced at the cell phone, tried to bat down the horrors in his mind sufficiently to achieve rational thought.

*Call the cops. And say what? And even if they did believe you, how long would it take? They'd never find that place in a fit, not without you waiting to lead them. Can YOU even find it, running in the dark?*

He could, and he would, Kendall decided. He was good at bush navigation, usually had fantastic recall of roads once traveled, unconsciously noticed landmarks that came back as clues when needed. And never more needed than now. But wait for police, even assuming he could convince them to come at all? Not a hope in hell and not worth further thought.

Slowing for Lake Cowichan community, sudden confusion, totally unexpected. South Shore Road or North Shore . . . or did it matter? One would be faster, but which?

*Stupid . . . stupid . . . stupid!* Wheeling the SUV onto the route they'd used on their return journey. No time to be experimenting. And then, into the darkening night, trying to balance speed with the risks of accident. One foolish driver could be the difference. Or a deer. Or, worse, an elk, or somebody's loose cow or horse or pig. Or a bear . . . hadn't he heard somewhere that hitting a bear was like hitting a pig? Take the undercarriage of a vehicle slick as anything.

Memory coming back, if erratically. Straight stretch, here, grab the cell phone, the list, try to drive and dial and read at the same time. Yank the wheel just in time to stay out of the ditch. *Idiot!* Try it all again, going slower this time, but no more effective.

*Oh, bugger-bugger! You're a fool, Kendall! Find a wide spot, pull over, do it right.*

Five hours later, it seemed, a safe place to do that. Sid: voice mail. Fred: misdialed. *Bugger it!*

Onto the gravel, now, forget phoning, forget everything but concentrating on the road, the twists and turns and ten thousand bloody possible turnoffs that all looked the same only different . . . *Was it this one . . . or that one I just passed?*

*Neither. This is where she got us to three different times. Can't forget that intersection. Now, right, then left, then right again. And now the fun starts.*

Slowed by the worsening condition of the track, having to slow far too much, begrudging the need for care but getting better control, now, calmed by three right decisions in a row, terrain that looked familiar, a dangerous curve, a place where rock had slid into the roadway, a place where a fallen tree had been cleared away in a hurry, the road still halfway blocked.

*Right, here. Now slow . . . easy through that damned ditch; harder to get through going uphill.* Hearing the rocks and fallen branches being spit out from all four wheels, giving silent thanks for all-wheel-drive, cursing the condition of the track, the lack of time. And then—finally—rounding the final bend to slew in beside a clone of his own SUV.

And then he was running, stumbling, falling, getting up again. At first following the flashlight beam, then realizing he'd make better progress with the light off and a slightly slower pace; it was dark, but not that dark, the route from the vehicles to the cave entrance was clear enough, once the eyes were adjusted to the dim light.

Not so, of course, once he'd squeezed through the entry, having to take off his bulky eiderdown jacket to do so and cursing the cavers for not making the entry big enough in the first place. Once inside, he quickly put the jacket back on, added the ski gloves, fumbled for the switch on the flashlight. He could already feel the temperature dropping. Could also feel his incipient claustrophobia returning, but knew he could ignore that!

The flashlight beam picked up the well-trodden survey ribbon on the floor, but Kendall hardly needed the guide. Memory guided him as he surged his way through the passages, almost running in places, going painstakingly, agonizingly slowly in others.

In his mind, the horror generated by his imagination, the stream-of-consciousness email from Charlie. The coincidences! He could hear Kirsten voicing the feelings she'd gotten from the jigsaw puzzle incident, could remember himself poo-pooing them as irrelevant, unimportant. Until he saw the security tape, until he made the connection.

He nearly got stuck in that last squeeze before the well chamber, thought for a minute he'd have to shuck the jacket again, then popped free, hearing the jacket shell rip as he did so but ignoring it. Not important. What was important was . . .

He rushed to the lip of the descent, saw Kirsten and the doctor there, saw that Kirsten was apparently unhurt, apparently unafraid, that the doctor was over near the well, but the horrors remained, magnified by the darkness, the closeness of the cave, the shadowy figures. His first instinct was to get to Kirsten, to get himself between her and the doctor, worry later about what else to do, what to say. He put one foot onto the slope, hesitated, feeling the clumsiness of having to hold onto the flashlight, having only one hand to assist him in the descent, was consciously aware of Stafford moving to help him, of the doctor's hands reaching up, grasping at his clothing in a gesture so perfectly natural, so perfectly logical, he didn't think to question it . . . instinct guided him into the waiting hands, a different instinct forcing his scream of denial. "Noooooo!"

And then he was aware, could feel the power in the grip, could even—intellectually—realize what was going to happen and did happen as the doctor slid him across the greasy floor like a greased pig, straight for the well. The flashlight flew as he scrambled for any sort of grip to slow the journey, anything to keep him from hitting the target. But it was too late; he hadn't a chance. Could do no more than scream in denial, then slide, then land with a splash into water so cold it took his breath away.

"Run . . . Kirsten. Run!" He got the words out as he felt his boots thud into the floor of the pool, but now he could see nothing but the eerie play of light from their head lamps, hear nothing but faint, indecipherable noises as they moved.

Kendall clawed at the slickness of the well's inside walls, knowing from the first that it was useless. The water was only to his knees, although he could feel the coldness climbing his legs as it saturated jeans and socks and long-johns. He couldn't reach high enough to even try and grasp the rim of the well, knew it would be futile anyway. Knew he could do nothing . . . except shout.

"Get out, Kirsten. Get out . . . get out . . . get out. The puzzle piece . . . it was him!" He screamed into the void, mentally cursing his inability to see anything, then stopped screaming, too, because he couldn't see anything at all!

Whatever had happened, both Kirsten and the doctor had left the well chamber, or turned off their head lamps, which seemed unlikely, ridiculous. Kendall forced himself to stillness, trying to see with his ears, to somehow penetrate the primeval blackness and silence of the cave.

It didn't take long to realize he could see nothing, hear nothing, do nothing. Nothing . . . except set himself to battle the union of his claustrophobia and the horror of his fears for Kirsten. And the other horror he could feel, if not see . . . the fierce, unrelenting iciness of the water that could kill him.

# THIRTY-EIGHT

Kirsten froze, for an instant, unable to take in what she was seeing and hearing. Unable to make any sense of it as she watched Dr. Stafford reach out to assist Kendall down into the chamber, then—almost casually, it was so quick, so slick—skid him across the floor and into the well.

She heard Kendall's warning, understood the words, but could make no sense of them, no sense of anything, except a sudden flare of inner caution, the total feeling of wrongness that sent her adrenalin racing, her every sense suddenly alert.

It was when the doctor, hardly breaking stride, moved to block the exit from the cave, that it began to come together, but she didn't consciously make the decision that followed. Or didn't think she did . . . wasn't aware of conscious thought because it all happened so quickly. Stafford was moving to block the exit . . . Stafford was some sort of threat . . . Stafford had just chucked Teague Kendall into the well! Kirsten didn't bother trying to cross the chamber, didn't try to somehow elude the doctor and escape. It would have been fruitless and her instincts knew it without her having to think.

She turned and fled back into the cave system, quick as a rat up a drainpipe . . . her only hesitation being to grab up her side pack as she did it. All sense of tiredness was forgotten, all thought of everything—except flight—was forgotten. She just turned and ran, moving through the passage as quickly as she could, achieving a full-on, proper run in some places. Until she reached the first intersection, where the demand for some sort of decision brought her mind back into some semblance of working order.

Snatching off her helmet, she turned quickly to peer behind her. No sign of the doctor's light, no sound of pursuit. Yet.

*Why should he chase me? He's blocking the exit and he knows it. Why should he chase me anyway? What's so terribly bad about stealing a jigsaw puzzle piece? Well it must be something bad—something terribly, horribly bad—for him to do that to Kendall. Kendall! Omigod, he'll die in that well if he's there too long.*

Then she saw the first flickering of light in the tunnel behind her, and all thoughts of Kendall's predicament had to be set aside as she floundered for a decision, a choice, a course of action. She didn't dare allow Stafford to catch her; he was too big, too strong. If he got those hands on her, she stood no chance. But in the cave, here in her own element . . .

*He's good, and he moves too damned well to suit me, but he's no caver. And he doesn't know this cave; I do.*

She had time, if not much of it, so Kirsten thrust her mind out, trying to visualize the cave system as she knew it, searching for places she would have the advantage. Crawls, tight spots, any place that would grant her speed while slowing down her much larger pursuer. She remembered Sid mentioning one totally circular passage . . . that would allow her to get behind him, to make a dash for the exit, give her a chance to try and haul Kendall out of the well so they could both run. Except . . . she'd never seen that section of cave, wouldn't recognize it, couldn't negotiate it from description alone. She had to stay with passages she knew, had to get ahead, stay ahead, but . . .

*The other exit. He doesn't know about that!*

Her spirits sang, until she remembered the tightness of the crawl to get there, the devil's club with its fierce, unrelenting spines. But at least it was a chance, and a good one . . . if she was lucky, if she was fast enough, tricky enough!

Then she heard the voice . . . that beautifully-modulated, rich, chocolate-fudge voice, amplified by the underground, the more beautiful for that . . . and all the more frightening, too.

"This is silly, Kirsten. You have nowhere to go and you know it. I have only to sit and guard the entrance; you'll have to come out sooner or later."

She didn't answer, kept her attention on the tiny flicker of light, knowing it wasn't as far back in the passage as it looked, knowing she would have to move, soon, and move quickly. Knowing, too, that once the doctor got close enough, he had only to follow her own light, and if he could maintain her speed it would be impossible to lose him. She would have to pause, look back, if she wanted to know where he was, how close he was. He would be advantaged by not having to pause in his pursuit.

Her light! He was already too close . . . she couldn't duck into any of the side passages here because he'd see, he'd know. He'd see her light. And she couldn't move without light, despite knowing there were no really dangerous parts of the passages ahead. She knew only too well the way total absence of light blurs the senses, removes all sense of perspective. Light . . . both a necessity and a curse, unless . . .

Fumbling in her pack, she quickly found her emergency flashlight, a small, compact, extremely powerful instrument with—thank God!—fresh batteries installed immediately after her last trip. Then she reached up and turned off the head lamp . . . at least she could shield the flashlight against her body, given the right situation, maybe yet lure Stafford into passing her, into giving her a chance to make a break for it. Then another thought surfaced. The survey tape. If she could remove that, she would block him, might trap him. They'd made several twists and turns already, several choices of route dictated by that damned tape.

*Now you're thinking, my girl. Get rid of the tape. Make him work for his rabbit.*

It was easy to squat down, grasp the tape, less easy to gather it as she went, hoping he wouldn't notice. Apparently he didn't, and at the next intersection she discarded the mass she'd gathered up, throwing it into a side passage. Then started on another bundle, was inordinately pleased when her fingers found a knot where two lengths of tape had been joined. She knew exactly where she was, now, could find her way out from here with no problem . . . tape or no tape. But could he?

"I might just do that, Kirsten . . . go back at least to the well. I can wait for you there and watch your boyfriend die. Because he will, you know. Much sooner than later. Mind you, it won't hurt, terribly . . . hypothermia is quite gentle."

Damn it! While she'd been doing things, he'd moved closer, was now dangerously close, although she doubted he could realize that. Kirsten scurried forward, now using the flashlight to illuminate her way. It was fairly easy going; she couldn't run, but she could trot, in places. Stafford would have to move more slowly because he was taller, had to be watching the ceiling, be aware of where his head was. Then, that ceiling dipped so that she, too, had to stoop, to move carefully, especially since she was used to following a head lamp, used to the angle of it, the way it revealed ceiling heights and high obstacles. The flashlight showed things differently. Collecting the tape was a nuisance, but a vital one. She kept doing it, throwing bundles of it aside whenever she spotted a good place to do so, a place he wouldn't notice it.

"It will be your fault, you realize, if Kendall dies. If you'd just stop all this nonsense, we could get back to him, get him out of that awful, frigid well."

*Why don't I believe you? It isn't my fault and won't be. It's your fault . . . you shoved him in there and you did it deliberately. As for getting him out . . .*

She stopped that thought abruptly, realizing that by herself, she'd have a nearly impossible task hauling Kendall out of the well. Nearly impossible, but . . . she did have rope, ten yards of proper static line and also a waist-length piece of one-inch, tubular nylon webbing. But to use any of it, she must first get back past the doctor, and do it in a way he couldn't quickly follow.

Kirsten pushed ahead, pausing every so often to glance back, inevitably to curse because while Stafford wasn't catching up, she wasn't gaining any ground, either. She stopped trying to gather tape as she moved, just let it flow along behind her. He would be past noticing, now . . . he was well past the spot she'd begun removing it.

"Surely you don't want him to die, Kirsten. You don't want that on our conscience, don't want to live with that guilt. It isn't necessary, you see. Just stop this foolishness and we'll have him out of there in moments."

*Or me in there with him! Was that the idea, I wonder . . . to lure me close enough to shove me into the well so he could stand there and quote psycho-babble at me as I froze to death? But why?*

It made no sense, but then none of this did. Except the flight part. Whatever was wrong—and she had no doubts about that much, now—was very wrong indeed. Deadly.

Kirsten moved ahead, trying but failing to make serious progress in lengthening the gap between them.

"Will it make any difference if I tell you about your sister, Kirsten? Would you like to know about Emma, about what . . . happened to her? It's a very . . . tasty story, I can assure you."

She almost screamed at that. Felt her breath surge in, bit back to keep it there, forced herself to exhale gently, to be calm.

*Calm? My heart's going a mile-a-minute. Any less calm and I'll explode, fly out of this cave like a flock of bats, all in pieces.*

The thought was irreverent, and ridiculous. There were no bats in this cave, never had been, from the evidence. Or lack of it . . . no guano, no mummified corpses.

"She had a flat tire, Kirsten. That's all it took. That, and coming across on the latest ferry, then trying to make it from Nanaimo to your place in the dark."

Kirsten felt real fear, now. Could hear the evil in that rich, beautiful voice, could sense the madness there even if she didn't understand it. Got confused, then, when he abruptly changed the subject.

"I didn't realize you'd seen me take the piece of jigsaw puzzle. But then I guess you didn't see *me* take it, did you . . . only *someone* take it. Did you run to Kendall then and tell him, or did you save it for pillow talk?"

He always paused to speak, she noticed, then realized with alarm that she always stopped to listen, too. Dangerous! She moved ahead again, trying for speed, worried because nothing seemed to look quite right. Her memory of these passages was formed by the light of a head lamp, and this was subtly different. Perhaps dangerously so, but . . . maybe not.

"Such a pretentious project for a grown man! Did he give you that little story about it helping him with writer's block?

It wouldn't, you realize. Merely smoke-and-mirrors, a placebo."

This time she didn't pause. She let his words follow as she scampered through a low-ceilinged section, moving almost on hands and knees in a waddling gait, like a chimpanzee. It was exhausting; she could feel it in her back before she'd gone twenty feet, but there was satisfaction in knowing it would be even more exhausting for the tall man behind her.

"If we rescue Kendall before he freezes, I could probably find a place for him in our little experiment," came the voice. Was she right in thinking she'd gained some ground? It sounded further away than usual. She jammed the muzzle of the flashlight into her stomach and turned to check.

"Not your part of the experiment, of course, but I could perhaps . . . assess his quality against that of the director. Totally different types, of course, but still . . ."

*What the hell are you talking about? Experiment? Director of what?*

It took only a tiny part of her conscious mind to question this muddle of useless information. The rest was suddenly faced with the fact she'd gone too far, now, to even think of sneaking into a side passage, of trying to lure the doctor past her so she could make a dash for the cave mouth. A familiar calcite formation flowed into her light, and she realized she was now beyond intersections, beyond side passages. All that lay ahead was the steadily-narrowing route to the long crawl and the greased pig entrance blocked by devil's club.

"Kendall's time is running out, you realize? He's been in the water . . . what? . . . just over an hour? You're killing him with this silliness, Kirsten. Please consider that. You have only to turn around, come back here to me, and we can have him out of there with hardly any damage at all."

*Too little . . . too late. I couldn't turn around here if I wanted to. Only one spot left I might manage it, and if I can get that far without you catching me—and I will!—then I might as well go all the way. If I can squeeze myself out, it'd be ten times faster to run back to the entrance than go back the way we've just come.*

She was crawling, now, but crawling quickly, scrabbling along on elbows and knees, the flashlight replaced by the head lamp because she needed both hands free. Crawling, then squirming, then wriggling like a snake, thrusting forward first with one shoulder, then the other, pushing the helmet ahead of her, dragging her pack behind, clipped to her waist but dangling beyond her feet. And she was tiring, but not concerned with that. The concern was when she reached the end and had to find a way to wriggle out of the cave . . . assuming there was room to get through the narrow slot in the rock, assuming she didn't leave more of her behind on the devil's club thorns than she took through.

"Really, Kirsten, this has gone on long enough. Do you not realize you're risking our entire experiment with all this? The effect of all that adrenalin, surging through your system for an extended period. It is not good, my dear. Not good at all."

The voice was taking on a slightly frantic quality, she thought. Was he feeling the constriction? He was much taller than Les, far broader across the shoulders. She tried to remember how much trouble Les had in getting this far, but couldn't. It hadn't mattered at the time; there was that small pocket right near the end where they'd both been able to get turned around.

*Maybe he'll get stuck!* The thought was comforting for only an instant. Then she had to consider what might happen if *she* got stuck, if she couldn't fit through the final exit, couldn't push through the devil's club, couldn't . . .

The passage eased. She was able to transform wriggle to

scramble. Then it closed in again, and once again she was a subterranean worm, not blind but forced to wriggle, to push with her toes and claw with her fingers for every inch she traveled. Worst of all, she couldn't look back, couldn't determine if she was making up ground or losing it. Stafford was incredibly strong; she'd seen the way he'd almost effortlessly tossed Kendall across the well chamber floor. The thought made her wriggle harder, faster, pushing the light ahead, dragging the pack behind and half expecting to feel Stafford's hand grabbing it, dragging her back.

"Your husband was right to chastise you, Kirsten. You're nothing but a recalcitrant, obstinate child. You think only of yourself and then wonder why you feel guilty later. Emma told me how self-centered you are, but I didn't believe her. I should have."

The voice sounded closer. Was it? Or was it the constriction of the passage that made it seem so? She couldn't pause to wonder, could only keep wriggling, keep scrambling whenever there was room, finally reached the pocket she and Les had used to turn around. Passed it, could see that faint change in the light, could already imagine the torture, the torment, to come.

*My God! We were here just the other day and didn't think to grub out the damned devil's club and be done with it.*

They hadn't, of course, because they'd wanted to keep the entrance properly disguised, but now, this instant, that decision thundered in her head like the guilt trips Stafford was trying so hard to create.

*I'll give you guilt, you crazy bastard!*

And then she was there, could see the thorns of the evil plant in the dimness of her head lamp, could finally reach out and touch the nearest with a finger just as quickly withdrawn.

The exit was as constrictive as she remembered. Worse,

even! Her first instinct was to recognize the futility of even trying, but desperation quickly knocked that aside. She shoved ahead with her helmet, trying to push it through the shrub, trying to make herself a passage—assuming she could actually get that far!

If she could do it, she ought to be safe. Stafford was far bigger, broader, and he hadn't the caving experience to teach him how to twist and contort and position to best advantage when in a tight spot like this. Which was what she began to do, stretching one hand out before her, trying to shrug her opposite shoulder back, pushing with her feet wherever she could find purchase, but with her body stretched out like a reaching swimmer.

She moved an inch. A centimeter. A millimeter. Another inch. The devil's club began to chew on her forward-reaching arm and hand despite the helmet's protection. What would happen when/if she got her head that far, Kirsten didn't dare think about. All she could do was concentrate, keep pushing, control her breathing so her lungs were empty when she pushed hardest.

*Thank God for small breasts and non child-bearing hips, although I might have less of both before this is over. Push, dammit!*

# THIRTY-NINE

Fred was inclined at first to ignore his answering machine. He hated interruptions when he was working, so he kept the machine in the kitchen, out of sight and sound of the room he used as an office, and only dealt with messages when he was taking a break anyway. Often—especially when his back was playing up and he felt like death warmed over—he managed to ignore the infernal machine entirely.

And he had been working. He'd been on the computer for hours straight, networking with friends in Tasmania, networking with friends of friends, and friends of friends of friends. Checking out Teague Kendall, which had turned out to be easy enough, if slow. When he and Kendall had played the "Who do you know that I know?" game without a match, he'd been half surprised but not overly concerned. He knew Tasmania, knew how incestuous the place was, knew that if he put in the time, he would eventually get his answers. Now he had them.

Kendall's reputation—once past the "famous writer" bits, was sound. He was highly regarded as a journalist, had only a few friends, but good ones! There'd been a marriage to a psych nurse which had apparently ended very badly for him, emotionally, and while he was considered popular with the opposite sex, he was notoriously gun shy.

*Work to do there, Kirsten. Probably worth the effort, though.*

Fred had instinctively liked Kirsten from the start, and their shared experiences with the cougar had only intensified that. Not romantically . . . she wasn't his type, but she'd shown herself to be a solid companion, a good, strong, sensible woman. He was also strongly sensitive to the way Sid and the boys felt about her. They weren't fools. He'd instinctively liked Kendall, too, was glad to have his feelings vindicated by the long-distance checking.

He was mentally playing matchmaker when he walked into the kitchen with the intention of making a coffee, didn't even notice the blinking light on the answering machine until he'd set the jug to boil, spooned instant into a cup and was reaching for the sugar.

Will I or won't I and should I bother? He almost didn't push the message button, then reasoned it might be somebody from Tassie wanting to "talk" instead of playing email ping-pong.

Kendall's garbled message made total, complete, and logical good sense to him right from the beginning, but he ran the tape back and listened a second time, just to be sure. Good sense and . . . nonsense, but clear enough, especially the urgency part. Coffee forgotten, he grabbed up a jacket and headed for the door.

He had the engine of his truck going, was actually shifting into first gear before his mind caught up, and he turned it off again just as quickly. Out of the truck, rushing to open the garage door, make a hasty but specific selection of gear, itemizing in his mind as he did so. Coveralls, helmet, side-pack, proper boots, gloves, finally an array of climbing gear . . . just in case.

*I won't need this, but somebody might. Better to have it than not.*

He threw open the back of the truck, tossed in the gear, spun up clouds of his own driveway gravel as he hurried away. Was five miles down the road before he thought of the GPS unit, decided he'd been stupid not to have thought of it earlier, but would have to live with that.

Fred knew the back roads far better than Kendall did. He took short cuts, shattered the speed limit when he knew it was safe. His geriatric pickup truck had four-wheel-drive, and while it looked a bit rough, the vehicle was soundly maintained and totally reliable. But not fast. Still, that didn't matter once he was off the sealed roads and heading up the same maze of tracks Kendall had negotiated less than an hour ahead of him.

When he rounded the final turn to find Kendall's SUV jammed in against another that looked pretty much identical, all Fred could do was back and fill until he'd made space for his own truck, then get out, unload, and get moving. He was experienced, organized, but it took time he begrudged.

The jolting during the last part of the journey had been hell on his back; the first thing he reached for was the all-important hiking stick. He thought about changing his boots, then thrust away such thoughts. He'd be going *to* the cave . . . not inside! It wasn't a contradiction, of course, to be shouldering his caving gear, though the load would slow him in the long hike to the entrance. Somebody might need something he carried, and better to have it than not. He would not need to go inside the cave, could not go inside the cave . . . would not go inside the cave. He fortified himself with those thoughts all the way through the dry ravine, every time he stumbled over loose rock, every time he gingerly made his way past a clump of devil's club.

And it worked, until he actually reached the cave entrance to find nobody there, no sign of anybody anywhere around, nothing but the night and the silence and the entrance that stared blankly at him . . . terrifying and seductive at the same time.

*I can't do this. I will not do this. Please . . . God!*

He poked his head in, tried to listen, was granted only the sensation of the cave blowing in his ear. They had to be in there someplace. No logic to them being anywhere else. But what was going on? Fred withdrew his head, began to pace around in nervous little circles, trying to make a plan—any plan!—that didn't involve actually going into the cave. Wished he still smoked . . . an excuse to waste another five minutes. Wished he had a drink; there was a container of water in the pack, but he wanted a *drink!*

Besides, I can't go in alone. It isn't safe. It isn't done. Bloody Kendall said he'd phoned Sid. Sid will come. He's probably already on the road. He never even turns on his cell phone, won't answer his pager. Does he ever check his damn messages?

He lasted another five minutes.

Once through the narrowness of the entrance . . . a minuscule problem . . . the first thing he noticed was the trodden survey tape on the passage floor. That made it all somewhat easier; at least somebody had done something right. But he moved slowly, and only partly because of his back. There was room, thank goodness, for his walking stick . . . and he needed it, too.

*Carelessness kills. Can't be careless. Can't hurry . . . mustn't hurry. Double-check everything. Oh, hell . . . did I bring enough extra batteries? When did I last check the ones in this helmet?*

All the while moving steadily, if far more slowly than he used to before the accident, before he got careless, before . . . And all the while straining his eyes, his ears, for any sign, any sound. He got the sound first, a rhythmic sort of sloshing sound that made absolutely no sense at all, that caused him to halt in his tracks once he became aware of it, only to move on after a moment because he couldn't figure it out, was totally confused by it.

But as he passed the final constriction before reaching the well chamber, almost inclined to congratulate himself for so well remembering everything his friends had told him about their exploration, the routes they'd taken, the identifiable signposts within the cave, the strange sound became increasingly loud. It wasn't until he paused at the actual descent to the chamber that the sound suddenly stopped. Fred stopped too, slowly moving his head as he scanned the chamber, mentally noting the other exits, the all-too-familiar patterns of cave formation.

His eyes moved past the well itself, then he looked back, down, could see the distinctive skid marks on the cave floor. They weren't that obvious, except to his experienced eye, which traced them from almost at his feet to the well itself. He looked, thought he saw movement, decided he hadn't—not really; it wasn't logical, after all—then saw it again.

*Hair? It can't be. Surely not . . .*

"Who's there?" His voice, kept deliberately soft, nonetheless echoed in the chamber. And again he saw movement, this time obvious as a gloved hand raised into sight, weakly waved about, then disappeared again.

"Hang on. I'm coming."

"He . . . l . . . p me . . ." The voice so weak he almost didn't hear it, focused as he was on getting down into the chamber without slipping, without putting out his back entirely, without being . . . careless. It was no easy task, but the nuisance value of the hiking staff paid off, big-time, in helping him get down to level, if slippery footing.

He was inching his way across the slickness of the floor,

each step an agony for his back, a worse agony for a mind obsessed with carelessness, when he heard the sloshing sound resume, realized what it had to be. Whoever was in the well was rhythmically stomping their feet, probably desperate to try and maintain circulation, keep from freezing from the bottom up. Fred kept moving, finally was close enough to see that whoever was in the well was . . .

"Kendall? How the hell . . . ?"

"Got to get me out of here. Can't feel my feet . . . my legs. So cold . . ." The words were understandable, but emerged from the first truly chattering teeth Fred had ever seen. Kendall's face was too white, his eyes wild with suppressed panic and exhaustion.

"Hang on." Fred fumbled in the pack, dragged out his waist-length of nylon webbing, the neat, tidy coil of rope. "Are your hands okay? Can you move them, can you tie a knot"

"I don't . . . know. Maybe . . . So cccccold . . ."

"Well you're going to have to manage somehow. Look at me. Lift your arms up . . . both of them."

"Kkkkirsten? Have you seen her? And the ddddoctor?"

"No. Nobody but you. If I get close enough, can you hand me your gloves? You won't be able to tie this up without bare hands." Fred was thinking, now, feeling the focus in his thinking. What to be done, in which order. What might work, what couldn't possibly work. He thrust away the obvious problem—a man with a bad back trying to haul two hundred pounds of dead weight out this damned well!

"Ttttry . . ."

"Don't try. Do it. Look at me! I'm reaching out, now. Give me your gloves." Fred was as close to the edge as he dared get, was concerned Kendall might try to grab him, which would be a disaster. Having both of them in the well didn't bear thinking about. But the man was nearly panicked, too cold to think straight.

*So you do the thinking. You're supposed to be good at it.*

One glove, then the other. Now . . .

"Take this, wrap it around you below your arms. Tie it tight as you can. Try not to get it wet, Kendall . . . you're wet enough already."

"Not water . . . ice. I'm sssstanding in a block of goddam ice."

"Stop standing. Keep moving your feet. Now, can you tie this rope around that webbing? Don't answer me, damn it . . . just do it. And do it right, because you have to get it right."

Fred directed his light squarely at Kendall's mid-section, trying to give him light to see by, but light also for Fred to see the sorts of knots that were tied, to be sure they'd hold. He knew about knots, could even describe how to tie them, but Kendall was in no condition for lessons.

"Okay . . . here, take your gloves back. Put them on . . . one at a time . . . carefully . . . that's right . . . Good! Now I've got to try and find someplace I can get braced so I can try and haul you out of there. Do you think you'll be any help?"

"Ddddon't . . . knnnow."

Fred doubted it, but didn't say so. "You'll just have to try. Hang in there. I'll shout when I'm set." He started backing away, dragging the pack, dragging the rope's free end, wishing his back was better, wishing he could see anything in the chamber but greasy, slippery, rock floor that would give him no purchase at all.

# FORTY

Kirsten was stuck. She had her head out, and one arm, but the point of her opposite shoulder was caught, or else the coverall was. Either way, she was stuck, lying half on her side, her feet scrabbling to find enough purchase for one more push, the push she needed to free that shoulder . . . free herself.

It was like trying to force the earth into giving birth, she thought, and would have laughed at such irreverence, except it wasn't funny. It was serious! Damned serious!

*And what would I know about giving birth? I've never tried it. Sure as hell there's nobody to do a C-section, except maybe the devil's club . . . assuming I can get that far.*

She was getting light-headed, probably from forcing herself to exhale, to try and shrink herself enough to fit through the narrow hole in the rock before the devil caught up and dragged her back into . . . into what? She didn't know, couldn't even imagine . . . all she did know was that she didn't want to go. And there was little satisfaction being almost positive the doctor couldn't fit through this niche in the rock if she couldn't get herself out of it. And quickly, too. He must be almost up to her, unless he was already stuck, himself, further back.

"Push, dammit!"

She twisted a bit more, dug in with her boot toes, felt the thorns of the devil's club right through her gloves as she grabbed near the root and tugged, and tugged, and tugged.

And suddenly was free, if that was the definition when you yanked yourself face-first into a thicket of devil's club. The thorns were razors, claws, talons . . . slashing at her face, ripping at her hair, snagging at her coveralls. She yanked the helmet back on to try and protect her head, then tugged and pushed and squirmed and shoved until she was finally, gloriously, bloodily FREE!

She rose to her feet, shaky, out of balance, nearly fell when she yanked to free the side pack from the thorns, nearly fell again when she felt her face wet, wiped off the tears and saw—in the soft light of the head lamp—the blood all over her hands.

"He was blood from hip to shoulder from the spur," she whispered, quoting from "The Man From Snowy River." Aware she was doing it, fascinated by the concept, appalled by the timing.

*Get a grip, girl! This is not the time for poetry, much less Australian poetry! This is the time for . . .*

For blocking that exit, somehow, only she could see no logical, quick, simple way to do it, had to settle for sitting down again and using her feet to try and jam as much devil's club into the entry hole as she could. She kicked and smashed at the tough, wiry shrub, wishing she had even more of it, wishing she could jam the passageway with it fifty feet in, wishing she could somehow kick it square in the face of Dr. psycho-babble bloody Stafford. But she couldn't. What she could do was get herself the hell out of here, get herself back to the real entry to the cave, to where she could find Kendall, somehow get him out of that well.

The thought spurred her. She stopped kicking at the

devil's club and clambered to her feet, grabbing up the pack as she rose. Swept the scene with one swiveling turn to get her bearings in the head lamp, then began to run. Even if Stafford did get through, he couldn't know exactly where he was, couldn't know the fastest route back to the entrance was actually uphill—at least for the first few hundred yards—couldn't know that going downhill, the logical route assuming he knew where he was at all, would only run him into a veritable thicket of devil's club.

Her running didn't last. She quickly found the footing too uncertain for such speed, had to drop back to a jog-trot, occasionally being forced to a walk. That's what she was doing, trying to catch her breath, when she stepped around a fallen, trail-blocking dead fir tree and found herself face-to-face with a cougar.

Her first reaction was that it had to be an hallucination. She'd been light-headed ever since being birthed from the cave, knew she wasn't thinking quite straight. Then the animal moved, she saw those cold predator's eyes in the gleam of her head lamp, saw the paw lifted as it sort of squatted back on its haunches.

Saw it, recognized it, then refused to accept it, refused to be deterred by this . . . not after all she'd been through. Compared to the threat behind her, the need ahead, this—she thought in her insanity—was nothing!

"No," she said in a voice strangely quiet in her own ears. "No." And she turned, grabbed at a stout limb on the fallen tree beside her, yanked it free with what seemed an Herculean gesture. And charged!

"Get out! Go . . . run, you mangy, moth-eaten thing! Get . . . out . . . of . . . my . . . way!"

The cougar was happy to oblige. Probably the same one they'd encountered earlier, she found herself thinking. That would make sense. She didn't halt her charge as the animal turned and bounded off to her left, moving downhill and away from her light. She didn't bother to worry about it, either, merely slowed her charge to a trot and continued on her way, totally, illogically certain it wouldn't be tracking her, was nothing to worry about. She did hang onto the stick, though.

She reached the cave entrance in what seemed like a very short time. Once there, she took a moment to inspect herself, and was appalled. The coverall was ripped, slashed as if somebody had been at her with a razor. There was blood everywhere; she could feel the wounds from the thorns on her face, her chest, her arms, even her scalp. Her right hand, especially, was a mess.

*If Kendall hasn't already died, the sight of me might be enough to finish the job. Oh . . . stop it, Kirsten. Just . . . stop it!*

With which thoughts she readjusted her gear, wriggled through the wonderfully huge—gigantic, even—entrance to the cave, and began to hurry toward the well chamber as quickly as she could move. There'd been no sign of the doctor behind her outside . . . she would have time. Or she would make time! When she reached that final little squeeze, she began shouting, screaming Kendall's name, praying he could hear her, praying he could answer, not daring to even think about the difficulties she'd face in getting him out of the well.

"Kirsten?"

Not Kendall's voice, but she recognized it, then saw Fred across the chamber from her, staring in horror . . . or what certainly looked like horror. He was crouched, hanging onto a length of rope that led . . .

"Kendall? Is he . . . ?"

"He won't be anything if you can't give me a hand. Can you get down from there all right? I don't want you sliding in there with him . . . I need you to help me drag him out. Slow down, dammit! You know better."

Fred's voice . . . steady, reassuring, calm—but what was he doing here?—got her down the descent, was like a lifeline, guiding her across the chamber to where he knelt. She heard Kendall's voice stammering her name, tried to force calm into her reply. "I'm here. Just wait . . . we're going to get you out of there." Gingerly made her way across to Fred, then listened carefully, did exactly as he directed, forced herself to pay attention, forced herself not to keep glancing back at the entry, not to keep expecting the demon doctor to suddenly appear.

It turned out to be easier than they could have hoped for. Kendall was exhausted, his legs and feet chilled to useless numbness. But he still had some strength in his hands, could still provide at least some help. Once they were properly braced, both able to put maximum heft on the rope, he surged up out of the well in a single motion, and they dragged him along the slick floor of the chamber like a harpooned seal, not stopping until all three of them were safe, all three of them there at the exit from the chamber.

"We have to get out. We have to get out of here now!" Kirsten was trying to explain things to Fred and at the same time massage some feeling into Kendall's legs, praying he wasn't permanently damaged. Her attention was divided, her eyes constantly lifting to see what she feared most—the doctor's figure cutting them off.

She and Kendall both talked at once, trying to impress upon Fred the great danger they might all be in, both of them babbling like children, trying to make sense of it all, trying to be sure Fred could make sense of it.

"There are three of us. Unless he's got a gun or something, I think we're fairly safe," he finally said, forcing them into silence by the command of his voice, then demanding that they pay attention, realize what had to come next, prepare themselves.

He boosted Kirsten up the descent; together they hoisted Kendall up. Kirsten managed to drag Kendall out of the way far enough so she could help Fred get up, then past them and into the passage. Together, they physically dragged Kendall through the narrow corner, ignoring his demands that he could walk, dammit. It turned out that he actually could walk, or at least do something that passed for walking. Between them, they managed to get him through to the entrance, but not without a lot of rest stops. It was like trying to walk a hopeless drunk up a "down" escalator.

Once outside, it was even worse. The footing in the cave had been variable, but consistent in at least some places. And they'd had the walls to bounce off of, to reach for when balance failed. Outside, in the fading night, the vision seemed worse and the footing definitely was. But they managed. They reached the vehicles just in time for Kendall to slump into unconsciousness, both of them too tired to do more than help him slide to the ground without visibly hurting himself any more than he already was.

"Get his pants off while he's horizontal," Fred gasped, reaching around to prod at his obviously aching back. "Boots, too, and socks. Everything that's wet. There's a space blanket in my pack and you should have one too." He shot her a scathing look that told Kirsten she'd damned well better have one, or face Fred's fury at some time in the future. He gentled the impression by asking then, "How about you . . . are you all right?"

"Bloody but unbowed," she chirped, wishing she believed it. By comparison to Kendall, she was in splendid shape despite all the cuts and bleeding. His feet and lower legs were like ice, the flesh unhealthily white.

It took both of them and all their strength to shift Kendall up and onto the back seat of Fred's truck, a poor fit but the best they could do. He was six inches too long for the seat, and starting to come out of it . . . mumbling drunkenly about being able to walk.

"Let us pray, buddy," Fred said in absent reply, but his face showed his concerns and Kirsten shared them. She also had concerns, and they couldn't wait until after a trip to the hospital.

"What do we do about the . . . ?" She had to pause, stumbled over the word "doctor." "I'm almost positive he can't get out where I did, unless he's Houdini, but . . ."

"Tell me what happened, but make it quick," Fred said. "We've got to get this man into proper care."

So she did, touching only on the highlights, pausing whenever he had a question, grateful when he enlightened her with his own impressions, with what Kendall had said.

"It's . . . insane," she finally said. "But . . . he did know something about Emma. He said so. And he's crazy as a loon . . . I don't doubt that for a minute."

"Good place for him, then, up here. So we'll just make sure he stays here, at least for the moment," said Fred, reaching into his toolbox and withdrawing a folding knife with a short but wickedly sharp blade. "You get to explain this to your boyfriend, by the way. Not that he should begrudge us a few tires for such a good cause."

Whereupon he calmly walked around both the doctor's SUV and Kendall's, apparently taking childish delight in thoroughly slashing each and every tire.

"That ought to hold him until we can get the cops up here," he said. "Now let's go! You can sit in back with his legs across your lap. Keep him wrapped up and try to warm him up, but don't overdo it, please . . . my truck's a virgin."

On the drive back to town, they discussed the situation further, not wanting to believe the implications of Emma's disappearance, Fred's suspicions about the old mine site high above the cave, and . . . the rest. Kendall roused about halfway along and insisted on slurring out his own garbled version of events and theories, and by the time they reached town, there was no argument about the need to go straight to the police—right after they went straight to the hospital.

"I'm really proud of the way you handled things back there," Fred told Kirsten. "From what you've said, there isn't a thing you did that was anything but the best choice at the time. Especially ripping out the survey tape; even if the good doctor does manage to get turned around, I can't see him finding his way out without help . . . the place is a maze."

"I hope he rots in there. No . . . I take that back. It would ruin my cave. Let him get turned around, let him wander around until he's crazier than he already is—if that's possible."

She thought for a moment, then added, "Which might just happen before anybody can find him and get him out. He's only got the batteries in his head lamp . . . Sid's head lamp. I changed them after Kendall and I were there together, and I'm certain I forgot to replace the spares in his pack.

"And batteries," she said with grim satisfaction, "do not last forever."

# FORTY-ONE

The cougar was edgy, totally flummoxed by the strange creature's unexpected, screaming, raging attack. He was a young male, forced out to seek his own home range with the onset of maturity, not the best of hunters, less confident than ever after being bashed across the face and head with a stick. What strange creature could this be, he wondered? It should have run, but it didn't. Made all manner of weird noises. He'd never heard such noises, had never seen such a creature before . . . ever.

He prowled after it for a short distance, but couldn't summon the nerve for another confrontation. Everything that had happened was simply too far outside his limited experience; he was—quite simply—spooked.

And yet . . . there was that enticing scent of blood, and that alone was enough to spark his feline curiosity. So he returned along the creature's back trail, moving like a shadow within shadows, drinking in the available light with his great cat eyes, using his nose to follow the fresh blood trail, occasionally dipping his head to lick at it.

He came up over the shoulder of the hill, began to follow the trail down again, then suddenly stopped, alert but cautious. A clump of devil's club had been disturbed, there in a small, moist depression in the hillside. He could smell the odor of the plant's bruising along with the blood scent, and now his great, luminous eyes noticed something else that was strange. Something white sticking out of the clump of thorny devil's club, something with things on the end that wriggled, something . . . alive.

He moved closer, but cautiously. It had been a very strange night already and he wasn't at all sure of himself. Except . . . there was an increase in the blood scent, now . . . fresher blood. He could see it dripping from the white, wriggling things, from whatever it was they were attached to.

Closer yet. Now he could hear noises—strange noises—coming from further inside the tangle of devil's club. For an instant, he thought it might be a grunting porcupine there, and half resolved to just walk away. He knew about porcupines! But then the noises changed, became almost like those of the earlier creature, the dangerous one. Shrieks and moans and guttural sounds like he'd never heard before.

The cat lay down. Still as the moonlight, still as the night itself. Except for the tip of his tail. That twitched. He lay there a long time. Just watching.

At one point, the white things all disappeared, pulled back into the thicket. Strange . . . but the blood scent remained. He waited. Watched. Listened.

More strange sounds, high-pitched, screaming. Then the white thing appeared again as if by magic, thrusting through the tangle of devil's club. Wriggling, bleeding. The blood scent was stronger, now. So was the cat's curiosity.

He flowed to his feet the way only cats can, paced over, patted at the white, wriggling, bleeding things. Leaped back in alarm at the screams from within the tangled devil's club, at the way the white thing whipped back inside.

"Kirsten?"

He cocked one ear at the strange sound. Sat up, for all the world like a domestic cat watching dinner being prepared.

"Kirsten? Is it you?"

The cougar didn't reply, but when the white thing emerged from the thicket he was ready, slashed at it with one lightning paw. The white thing immediately withdrew, a piercing sound emerged from the thicket. But the blood scent was stronger now. The cat licked at his claws. Waited.

The next time the white thing with the wriggling things on the end emerged, he was ready. One paw slashed with rapier swiftness; he lunged, strong neck muscles giving him impetus, strong jaw muscles helping his teeth drive into the thickest part.

He ignored the screams from within the thicket, concentrated on using his weight to drag the bleeding thing out where he could get a better grip. Locking his jaws, he lunged backward and sideways at the same time, rocking his powerful body, waving his long tail for balance as he lurched back and forth, pulling.

The blood taste was strong in his mouth, now. He dug his claws into the ground, thrust with all the weight of his body, felt the resistance lessen. Loosened his jaws momentarily, then locked them again and threw all his weight into the effort.

And succeeded. With astonishing abruptness, the resistance ceased. The cat was flung onto his back, startled, loosening his grip as the tangle of devil's club gave way and the thing he'd been yanking at emerged in a screaming, thrashing, bleeding . . . something.

The cat scrambled to his feet, ready to fight or flee . . . or pounce. Whatever this was, it didn't run at him waving a stick, didn't scream and rage and charge. And there was all that fresh blood.

# ABOUT THE AUTHOR

Gordon Aalborg has been a journalist, broadcaster, novelist, scriptwriter and playwright for more than 40 years—mostly in Australia. His works include the romantic suspense *Finding Bess* [as Victoria Gordon] (Five Star Publishing; 2004), the feline survival epic *Cat Tracks* (Delphi Books; 2002), the stage plays *Stumped* and *Pushing Buttons*, and twenty Mills & Boon (Harlequin) contemporary romances [also as Victoria Gordon]. He is married to mystery author Denise [Deni] Dietz, and lives on Vancouver Island.